Robert Creekmore
Prophet's Debt

Published by: Cinnabar Moth Publishing LLC
Santa Fe, New Mexico

Cover Design by: Ira Geneve

ISBN-13: 978-1-953971-41-8
Library of Congress Control Number: 2022936944

Prophet's Debt

ROBERT CREEKMORE

To Ed Aymar

Dedication:

This book is dedicated to the memory of Mia Zapata.

Do not wait for the last judgment.

It comes every day.

- Albert Camus

1

More than one hundred folded pieces of notebook paper line the bottom of the desk drawer in my small bedroom. Each holds poetry that was written for me by my best friend, Tiffany Bullock. The calendar posted over the desk has a giant red circle around today's date: Thursday, August twelfth, nineteen-ninety-three. Encompassed by that red circle are the words, "Perseid Meteor Shower!" It peaks tonight.

Tiffany isn't just my best friend, she is my only friend. My name is Naomi Pace. At fourteen, I'm already five-foot-ten. This fact is something my classmates will not let me forget. They're also not too keen on me being what my mom calls a "Tom Boy." I cut my blond hair as short as my mother will allow, which is roughly chin length. I have no interest in wearing makeup or dresses. I like wearing oversized overalls. They let me hide my body from the world.

What I am interested in is nature. I spend a lot of time after school and on the weekends, catching any critter that moves and will fit in my half-gallon Mason jar. Usually, Tiffany is somewhere nearby while I turn over rocks, or run a net through Stoney Creek. I think I want to be a biologist.

Tiffany says she wants to be a writer. And that she does in earnest. I have received an average of one poem a day for the last six months. Even when she follows me into the woods, Tiffany has a book, notepad, and pen. She's even gotten pretty good at drawing some of the creatures that fall prey to my curiosity. These temporary prisoners are eventually set free, back to whatever life they were leading before their harrowing abduction.

We live in a small town named Rocky Mount. Despite the name, there are no mountains to be found. Rather, it's nestled in the northern Coastal Plains of North Carolina. Essentially, we live in a swamp, which suits me fine. I'm still looking for my first alligator.

Tiffany and I have few places of refuge. One of them is the old Braswell Library downtown. It smells of old paper and ink. If I had synesthesia, I'd pair the olfactory sensation to intrigue and rare knowledge. Tiffany dedicates her time to literary fiction, and I to whatever biology texts I rummage up. I spend countless hours looking through scientific illustrations, attempting to identify my most recent hostage from the animal kingdom. The head librarian said she doesn't care as long as the jar stays closed.

Tiffany sleeps over most weekends. I assume it's to escape her mother for a while. Her mom isn't a bad person, but she's a lousy parent.

This summer, though, she has slept over almost every night. During the day, she walks the half-mile trek through our neighborhood to check in with her mom. Tiffany doesn't know her father. He abandoned his family directly after she was born. Perhaps that's lucky? My father isn't someone I'd choose to spend time around if I had the choice.

I'm an only child. Tiffany has an older sister named Lesley. Lesley is sixteen and just purchased her first car: a white, four-door, nineteen eighty-six Toyota Corolla. Tiffany is at home right now making sure Lesley will come through and give us a ride to the City Lake later tonight, which is where we intend to view the meteor shower. We wanted to go further out of town, but Lesley only agreed to take us to the lake because she's going the same way. The City Lake is circled by a small road. It's one end of a strip teenagers cruise. The other end is a shopping center about two miles away. They drive in loops for hours, rarely doing more than just looking at each other. Luckily, there's a small, dimly lit island on the lake that is accessible by a bridge and is mostly well-maintained grass.

I hear the backdoor open. Tiffany doesn't knock or use a key. The door isn't locked anyway. I can tell it's her by the light footsteps. My father's resound of heavy boots, and my mom's shoes almost always make a clicking sound on the parquet kitchen floor. Tiffany is only about five-two and usually wears a pair of black Chuck Taylors, thus the slight footfall. But if we're talking about looks, the most striking thing about Tiffany is her bright red hair and pale freckled skin. Her eyes are a light blue. Mine are green.

"What did she say?" I ask.

"She wasn't nice about it, but yeah, she'll pick us up at eight."

"At least we don't have to be stuck with her in the car for long."

Tiffany looks at her feet, as though she feels embarrassed about how her sister yells and berates her. I don't make mention of it now because it would make Tiff upset. Instead, I deflect to a pleasant idea.

"How about we go to the creek?"

"Okay," Tiffany says softly.

Stoney Creek is only about half a block from my house and through a neighbor's yard.

Tiffany and I have a usual spot. It's an outcrop of large rocks leftover from a long-ago eroded mountain range. She always sits on the big one, closest to shore, while I traipse out, tiptoeing over the smaller boulders with a fishing pole.

I fish the next three hours away using a light spin caster baited with a white beetle spin. I catch eleven bream and two largemouth bass. I examine each closely, lower them gently into the water to allow their gills to aerate, then release them. Tiffany reads quietly. I can tell whatever Lesley said to her was being digested by her mind, in the way chewed up glass is by intestines.

Around seven-thirty, Tiffany looks up from her book and says, "We need to get back to the house, Lesley will be here in thirty minutes."

Her tone is still sad.

"I'd like to slap your sister sometimes," I say.

"Don't."

"If she talks to you like that in front of me, I will."

"Lesley never does. She's afraid of you, I think."

"She should be," I respond angrily.

I've known Tiff since the first grade. She's always been smaller, and I've always been protective.

Lesley somehow blames Tiffany for their father's disappearance. Tiffany, in her typical fashion, doesn't talk about it. But I can almost see the shards of self-hatred piercing out of her skull.

We put together a backpack with two blankets, a canteen of water, a bag of chips, a star map, and a flashlight.

We hear a horn honk outside.

A flash of anguish goes across Tiffany's face.

"Yep. That's her," she says.

I sling the backpack over my left shoulder as we make our way to the backdoor. I don't bother to lock it.

I sit in the front passenger seat because I'm the tallest, and Tiffany sits behind Lesley so she can have the legroom not taken up by her equally short sister. Without a word, Lesley backs quickly down the short gravel driveway. She cranks the radio up. It's *Runaway Train* by Soul Asylum. The volume makes it impossible to talk, which is the point. My house is right off of Sunset Road, the cruising drag. The neighborhood is mostly made up of small brick ranch houses with yards shaded by dense pines. It takes less than ten minutes to get to the lake. As our destination comes into view, *Why Go* by Pearl Jam blasts forth at an unbearable volume. Lesley turns onto the drive encircling the lake. She stops in the road, directly across from the bridge, and we get out.

"At least she gave us a ride," I say, as the music from Lesley's car fades into the distance.

"Sorry."

"Stop apologizing for her."

"She hates me, that's all. I don't even understand why," Tiffany says.

"It's like Lesley hates the idea of you because she doesn't truly know you. I do."

Tiffany goes quiet again. I see a tear slowly trickle across her freckled cheek.

"Has she hit you?" I ask.

"Not in a couple of years. Mostly, she ignores me. I suppose I should be satisfied with that."

Tiff feigns a heart-wrenching smile.

I know not to push the subject further. Though, I wish she'd talk about it more instead of keeping the pain locked away in her heart.

We walk across the short arched bridge to the round manmade

island. It's made of treated wood and has white handrails. There's a white gazebo off to the left and, luckily, not another soul. Hopefully, it will remain our private island tonight. Most of the older teenagers are two hundred yards away in a dimly lit parking lot showing off their large pickups and IROC Cameros. They don't even realize how special tonight is, astronomically.

I plop my bag down near the edge of the island, furthest from the bridge. I pull out one blanket and lay it on the ground. I sit on the blanket and pull out the other blanket. Tiff sits on my right. We unfurl the second blanket and lay it atop ourselves. The ground is soft, the air still, and the sky clear. Perfect. The only hitch is the light emanating from distant parking lots.

As we lay there, I ask, "How many stars do you think there are?"

"There are as many or as few as you wish."

"How?"

"The universe is infinite. It's up to your discretion how you want to handle such a staggering concept. The manner in which you perceive it won't change its unknowable nature."

We go quiet as the first white streaks burn through our atmosphere. We watch as they come in in all directions. The larger ones burn green.

"The green color is due to the copper content," Tiff tells me.

I already knew, but I don't tell her.

"Do you think each one of those stars has a planet with life?" Tiff asks.

"I don't know."

She turns her head toward me and says, "Of course there's life beyond Earth."

"How can you be so sure?"

"Existence is so big. It can't just be us."

I lie quiet in thought for a moment before replying, "It doesn't matter. We are so small."

"That's how you choose to see it, Naomi. Just because I love you doesn't mean we always have to agree."

"But if there's not an ultimate answer, what's the point?"

"This," Tiff replies while slipping her trembling left hand into my right. She hesitates. I reach my free hand over and gently pull her face toward mine. As our lips touched, I am transported, no longer aware of anything but her.

I kissed a neighbor boy the summer before. He was sweet, but it felt odd and fake. Later that year, when my mind turned to kissing him, I felt repulsed. As I gave thought to how much physical affection would be expected of me by boys, I became terrified. I don't want their physical advances. I would never be in love with a boy, nor do I want to try. Tiffany and I often express our love. I always assumed I loved her as my best friend, but now there is a new, exciting dimension that I never expected. I am in love, and it has manifested itself into a physical desire I was previously unaware existed.

We continue to hold hands and kiss. We wrap our arms around each other and pull ourselves as closely as physics will allow. I want to disintegrate together, combine our atoms, drift into oblivion, and experience the infinite joy of our togetherness.

We stay intertwined longer than either of us realize.

"Tiffany!" I hear a shriek across the placid water.

It is Lesley.

"What are you, some kind of lesbos!?"

I can feel Tiff's hands begin to shake, but not like before. This time it is pure terror. We both pop up and whip our heads and torsos around simultaneously to see her no more than five yards behind us.

Lesley looks like a portrait of her mother if it were painted by an unaccomplished artist. Both are short, have blond hair, blue eyes. Lesley has bangs cut into her blond hair that she felt the need to poof up with hairspray and a blow dryer.

Despite how ridiculous she looks, her sudden materialization creates a slow, heavy feeling in my bowels. My brain, charged up on adrenaline, makes everything appear slower. To me, she is no different than encountering a large bear at the same distance. My frontal lobe then tells me a story in pictures of what will happen. It involves my father, Amos Pace, who is a giant of a man: six-foot-four, with broad shoulders, brown hair, brown eyes, a thick furrowed brow, and rough meaty hands. I've felt the low thud of either of those hands across my face and body more than I can remember.

Next, comes to mind my mother, who is a secretary for our church, First Baptist. I can see the lines coming out on her forehead when she confronts me. She's not much shorter than me, so I notice them when she's angry because they're at eye level. She has dirty blond hair and green eyes. She usually dresses conservatively, but sharply. The church is her life. If it got out that her daughter went around town kissing other girls, she'd be ruined. This would be handled discreetly and internally. She isn't much for striking me but never gets in the way of my father when he does.

Lesley starts walking toward us, fast and with intent. She doesn't speak, just breathes heavily, frowning, with her nose pointed upward. She almost looks like someone who has smelt something putrid.

"Get up right now!" she screams while grabbing Tiffany by her left arm. As her arm is pulled out from under her, Tiffany's face slams into the ground. Lesley begins to drag Tiffany facedown, toward the bridge.

Tiffany screams, "You're hurting me!" in response.

Hearing her scream in pain ignites something primal inside me. It is the instinct to protect one's mate at all costs. I hop to my feet and grab ahold of Lesley's left wrist with both hands. Lesley looks up at me in disbelief. Before she can yell at me, I twist as hard as I can. Lesley grunts from pain but won't let go. I keep my left hand on her wrist and slide right underneath Lesley's elbow and extend her arm straight. Lesley stops pulling due to the pain caused as I turn her wrist one way and elbow the other. As she looks up, her eyes meet mine. I see the doubt she has in her physical abilities take hold as she realizes just how much larger than her I am, despite my younger age.

"If you don't let her go, I will break your arm," I growl in her face. She immediately releases Tiffany's left wrist, leaving her face down in the grass. Tiff looks up just in time to see me break Lesley's arm anyway.

2

When I release Lesley, there's a shallow v-shaped crook in her upper forearm where the bones broke. Lesley's shrieking pain turns into nausea. She vomits up what looks like swirled pepperoni pizza mixed with bile, all the while clutching the wounded arm against her body.

Moving away, Lesley says in verbal self-defense, "Wait until your father finds out."

That lands like a tranquilizer dart on a bear. I shift from rage to fear. I've done something wholly unforgivable, broken another girl's arm because she called out my sin. That's how it will be seen regardless of how I feel about what they call "sin." Until just now, I was having the most exciting night of my young life. I didn't feel sin, I felt bonding. I felt the comfort of having someone I love more than anyone else physically close. For those few hours, I thought my life could be like this, but as I watch Lesley stumble away sobbing, it becomes apparent that I was wrong.

Lesley's car makes a buzzing noise as she zooms away. Tiffany's eyes are wide when we meet gazes.

"I'll get the bag," I say.

I stuff the blankets, canteen, chips, and flashlight back in, leaving the star map behind on the same spot where we had just laid.

"You broke her arm. I can't believe you actually broke her arm," Tiffany says, stuttering from fear.

"She was hurting you."

"But you didn't have to break her arm."

"No, I didn't. I wanted to."

Tiffany doesn't seem as offput by this as I expected.

"I love you," she says.

"Same," I reply.

I throw the backpack on and reach down to give Tiffany a hand up.

"We have to go somewhere else," I say, as she rises to her feet.

"Where?"

"Just not here is all I know."

Tiffany follows behind me. Instincts tell me not to turn right, toward the parking lot full of teenagers, rather, left to the main drag. We stop when we reach the four lanes of Sunset Avenue. We see headlights in the distance to our left, so we scurry to the island and wait. Then, three cars full of teenagers roar by from the other direction, shrouded by a cacophony of indistinguishable music. We quickly pass over the next two lanes, which delivers us onto River Drive. There's a small power substation on the corner of River and Sunset. Behind it is Tar River. Sunset Avenue has a bridge to cross the river. I am desperate. My brain is racing for a solution.

"We can hide under the bridge," I say.

But, at that moment, I saw the headlights of my mother's white Chevrolet Caprice passing over that same bridge. The high-intensity lighting of the power station illuminates us. There is no doubt in my mind we were seen when I watch the smoke stream from under the car's tires as the brakes are engaged. I almost expect to hear a crash but none comes. We're the accident they're looking for. Tires scream as the large sedan does a 180 around the median. Now it's heading right at us.

"Run!" I shout at Tiffany.

I grab Tiffany's right hand in my left. I'm much faster, and I don't want to run so fast that I leave her behind or risk getting separated. We head down River Drive toward Sunset Park. We only get fifty yards or so when our backs are lit up by the car's headlights.

"We can swim across the river!"

"Are you sure?" Tiff asks.

"No."

"The river is up high and running fast. We'll drown."

"I'd rather drown than never see you again."

"You'll see me again, someday. If we're dead, you won't. Swim across if you want. I won't run any further."

With that, I stop. We turn around still holding hands. My father is driving. In the passenger's seat is my mother. Their faces are still ashen with shock, but it's beginning to turn into fury. My father's imposing frame rises from the driver's side. The idea to fight flashes suddenly. There's no way. I might be able to take Lesley, but I couldn't take Amos. Very few people could.

Another car pulls up, illuminating him. It's a seventies-model Jeep Wagoneer Woody. I recognize it as the vehicle Tiffany's mom drives. I just remembered, Lesley has a bag phone. She must have called her mom on the way to the hospital.

My mother doesn't even bother getting out; she leaves that to my father. The driver's side door on the Caprice opens and out steps Amos's imposing backlit figure.

Even as my father's long strides get closer, Tiffany won't release my hand. As I catch a whiff of my father's endemic cigarette odor, I see knuckles, then feel sharp pain, finally, the details fade into an indistinguishable quantity of numbed thuds.

I think, "I can't believe my father is punching me." I feel like I'm floating next to what was going on, disengaged. I am helpless.

As I go unconscious, I know this: Tiffany held my hand until I flew backward onto the ground and she could no longer keep her grasp.

I hear Tiffany screaming. Then nothing.

When I awake, my face is swollen and my head throbs with each heartbeat. I hear the muffled sounds of a woman singing hymns. It is the voice of Shelby Howell, the pastor's wife. I hear the clank of dishes and the water running. Shelby is the kind of person who likes to occupy herself with chores during a crisis.

I sit up and attempt to swing my legs off the right side of the bed. My arms are snatched back with a clink and rattle. Both of my wrists have been secured to the bed with medium gauge chains, no more than a yard in length. The links have already left marks on my skin. The padlocks holding the loops of chain around my wrists clatter when I moved. I hear the water in the kitchen stop running, followed by the high-pitched snap and clap of cheap flip flops. Mrs. Howell is a woman in her late sixties, short, round, and pale. She has a shitty perm, which gave her hair the appearance of a puffy white helmet.

As Mrs. Howell enters the room, she comments, "I thought I heard you wrestlin'-bout."

"Where are my parents?" I ask.

"They've gone out of town with Pastor Howell."

"Why?"

"They've gone to get help for you."

"I don't need help."

"This help will get you through this sinful lust. Christ's love can heal any malady, physical or mental. You have to be vigilant and ask for his forgiveness. He will erase those abominable urges from your mind."

I begin to feel imminent pressure in my bladder.

"I have to pee, Mrs. Howell."

In saccharine-sweet passive tones, Mrs. Howell says, "I can't unchain you, but I can help you go pee. Last year Pastor Howell's mother passed away. This was her bedside toilet."

She rolls it next to the head of the bed.

"I'll unhook your left hand so you can get on the toilet. Your right arm will have to lie across your lap while you sit to pee because I'm not unchaining that one. Okay, sweetie?"

I teeter over the edge of the bed, with just enough length of chain to get myself in front of the bedside toilet. Now Mrs. Howell undoes my coveralls, pulls them to the floor, then proceeds to pull my panties to my ankles.

"I need to wipe myself."

"Don't you worry about that."

Mrs. Howell picks up a roll of toilet paper from my side table and proceeds to loop it around her right-hand several times. She sticks the same hand between my legs and wipes me.

I realize now my life will never be normal again.

We repeat the humiliating procedure in reverse. She pulls up my underwear and overalls, affixing them just as they were before.

She then chains my left arm back to the bedpost.

"Mommy, Daddy, and Pastor Howell are driving up to the mountains to talk to Doctor Vernon Proffit."

"Who?"

"He's a teacher and pastor at a special school. Doctor Proffit prepares students to be tomorrow's Christian soldiers. He's offered to take you into his own home. There you'll get the one-on-one spiritual therapy you need, honey. He and his wife, Patty, are true warriors for Christ. When you're cured and your spirit is whole again, you'll be enrolled as a regular student and will be welcomed back into the church family with open arms. All are healed by the glory of God. But, because of your temptation for that girl, you will not be allowed to return home. You don't have many years before you'll be needin' to find a good husband. A woman can't make it alone. She needs a man to guide, protect, and discipline her. You don't want to miss out on the wonderful life Jesus has planned for you."

The world peels away, and the sound of Mrs. Howell's trite voice becomes fainter. A blankness washes over me. I feel as though I'm walking the plank into a black hole.

"Hey, you awake?" Mrs. Howell says loudly, clapping in my face as she peers closely at me.

She continues, "I'm afraid you've got the demons in you. A righteous person can tell by looking into the eyes. Yours are empty. The true Naomi is down there, somewhere, fighting for control but losing. The power of Christ will heal you. I promise."

Mrs. Howell begins to sob. She stops talking and leaves the room while whipping her eyes under thin wire-rim glasses.

I lie there, awake staring at the ceiling, trapped in a place of imminent danger. At three-in-the-morning, I see headlights slow and turn down our short driveway. My mom and dad whisper as they enter the front door, obviously continuing a long, long talk that hasn't ceased for over twenty-four hours. The bedroom door opens behind me. Soft ambient light from the hallway is shown on my wall. I close my eyes and pretend to sleep soundly. The door shuts on the room and my old life. It will open onto a divergent road in the morning.

3

At seven in the morning, Shelby Howell gracelessly shook me awake. I kind of thought it would be my mom who'd wake me up, perhaps even come to her senses. But I'm still chained up, a victim of kidnapping by my own parents and pastor.

"It's time for your mornin' pee, Darlyn," Shelby Howell says.

We repeat the urination choreography again. After the lock clinks the chain back to my wrist, she turns around and walks out without saying a word. She returns carrying a bed tray with a plate resting on it. I haven't eaten since lunch yesterday. There are cheese grits, two sausage links, and two pancakes.

I eat indiscriminately. As I get about halfway through breakfast, my eyes begin to shut uncontrollably.

When I wake up, it's night again. My head hurts, likely from dehydration, or whatever was in the food. My mouth feels like it's made of sandpaper.

The dark bedroom becomes brighter as the door opens. It's Pastor Howell. He pulls up the chair Mrs. Howell had occupied off and on.

Pastor Howell begins slowly and softly. "Young lady, I hear we have a crisis in you. Do you know what you are?"

"A person," I reply meekly, my head still throbbing.

"No, you are not! According to Lesley Bullock, both you and her sister Tiffany are practicing homosexuals. Not only are your desires an abomination, but you also assaulted Lesley when she discovered y'all's sins. She's going to need surgery. They say her arm may never completely heal right."

"Good."

"See what choosing homosexuality has done to your character. You revel in hurting the righteous. These are the actions of a debased animal. You and Tiffany are both less than human now. But, you can heal."

He pulls his wife's copy of the King James Bible off of my nightstand.

"Who were the first two people on Earth?" he asks rhetorically. "Of course you know, it was Adam and Eve. Mark ten-six, says, 'But from the beginning of creation God made them male and female.' It's God's will that we are to be born as a boy or a girl. The male and female have complementary parts. It just can't work the other way. It says in Leviticus twenty-thirteen, 'If a man also lie with mankind, as he lieth with a woman, both of them have committed an abomination: they shall surely be put to death: their blood shall be upon them.'

"Your eternal soul is a prize the devil will fight long and hard for. He desires the chance to steal it from The Lord God. In you, he is winning on every front. Naomi, do you understand that if you died right now you would spend eternity in hell, cast away from the love of God? We are here to save you, sweetie. There is a perfect place called Heaven. Inside its gates, the faithful will stand alongside Jesus worshiping endlessly. The centuries will pass like minutes. His love will beam down on all in his presence, and no one will be sad or cry again. If you go to hell, God will erase you from your parents' memories. It will be as though you never existed. You will spend forever in utter anguish. You will be excruciatingly aware of every moment you're away from His Majesty. You will know, with heartache, that your mom and dad, and many friends, will have never known you! Do you want that pain? Do you understand the suffering you're putting your parents through? You're their only child. They want to keep you forever, but for now, they'll have to do that by letting go. You're going away with Doctor Proffit to Solid Rock preparatory school, far away from Tiffany. He and his wife, Patty, have years of experience helping confused boys and girls. If anyone can help you expel the demons inside you, they can. Your mom and dad have decided to sign your custody over to Doctor and Mrs. Proffit. They will love and provide for you as though you were their own. You'll learn responsibility, discipline, and all about your future as a wife and helpmate of a good Christian man. Doctor and Mrs. Proffit are at my house right now. They'll be over in thirty minutes. We don't feel it's healthy for you to see your mom and dad before you leave. A clean break is needed for you to begin your new life. Get ready. Mrs. Howell will be in momentarily. I hope when I see you again you'll be on your way to getting better."

Pastor Howell walks out of my bedroom and Mrs. Howell walks in directly after.

"We have to get you cleaned up," she squawks.

"She unfastens both chains from the bedposts but keeps them affixed to my wrists. She then leads me by my chains across the hallway to the bathroom. She closes the door behind us.

"You got to undress now," Mrs. Howell says.

"No."

"If you don't, I will have Pastor Howell hold you down while I strip you. You don't want that? It would be such an ugly thing."

I believe her.

I have to pull the chains through the armholes of the t-shirt I was wearing under my overalls. After the water heats up, I open the sliding glass door. My chains clink on the enamel-covered iron tub. Everything jingles when I move. 'I hope these are stainless steel. Or they're going to rust.' I think.

I'm forced to put on my hated Sunday dresses. My dirty Overalls, t-shirt, and underwear are left on the bathroom floor.

"I need to pack," I say to Mrs. Howell

"So few of your clothes are feminine enough to bother with."

"The Proffits are generous people. They will provide you with a closet full of dresses."

I hear a voice I don't recognize from the living room.

"Mrs. Howell, is the young lady clean and ready for her travels?" the voice demands from behind the door.

"Yes, sir. She responds loud enough to be heard."

"Well, let's see her, then."

Mrs. Howell opens the door, and I step into my parent's living room. The chains jingle every time I step forward.

There in front of me is a man, about my height, in his mid-fifties. He's dressed in a faded blue tracksuit and exudes the energy of a man used to getting his way. He has thinning salt-and-pepper hair and round facial features. His eyes are magnified, rather unpleasantly, through extremely thick glasses.

I recognize the look of his spurious smile. I see it on every bully from school. It says 'I'm your friend. There's nothing to worry about here' a bit too well. It is usually after they draw you in closer that you see their true smile accompanied by a punch to the stomach.

"Hello child," the man says to me. "My name is Doctor Proffit. And this is my wife, Patty." He motions his arm in her direction.

She was as tall as Dr. Proffit, and noticeably thin and sinewy. Patty has dark curly hair, brown eyes, and a freckled face. She doesn't speak.

Dr. Proffit commands the Pastor and his wife as though he is a drill sergeant.

"Do you have the paperwork, Pastor Howell?" he barks.

"Yes sir, Doctor Proffit," Pastor Howell responds.

"We have our ward here," he says referring to me. "Let's have the papers then."

He snaps the fingers of his right hand and extends it.

"You'll have to excuse me while I retrieve them. Her parents are signing in the other room. Shelby is notarizing the documents."

"Good. It's a six-hour drive from Rocky Mount to Burnsville. I'm tired, and the girl's soul is in eternal peril. What if the rapture happens before we can right this? Expeditiousness is required for the Lord's work. Right now, all I have is a confused girl in a doorway."

A notepad with stacks of paper is placed in Doctor Proffit's right hand. He signs each and initials in places. I'm not sure if what's going on is legal, but I doubt it matters. White men with the authority of a church behind them are rarely questioned. Legal or not, I can't talk my way out of this, and I am physically unable to stop it from happening. Even if my father weren't in the next room, Doctor Proffit has the thick build of a lumberjack.

Patty grabs my chains and leads me out the door. Once outside, I'm placed in the back of a large maroon Buick.

"Move to the center," she says.

Patty reaches into the front seat and pulls out two more padlocks. She loops the chain attached to my left arm around the left chest seat belt and locks it. She does the same on the right. My arms can rest at my sides, but if I try to flee, the chains won't let me. I wished for a knife, as a fleeting thought of cutting the belts crosses my mind. Patty walks back into the house. I wait.

A few minutes later both Doctor and Mrs. Proffit come back. He gets in the driver's seat and she the passenger's. Unlike me, they put on their seatbelts. If we have a head-on collision, my arms would be ripped from my body as the rest of me careens through the windshield.

We drive in silence. It's mostly a straight, flat highway driving for five hours. At one point, we go off the highway, down a country road for a few miles. There, Doctor Proffit stops at a small country gas station with poor lighting and no one around to hear me scream. Perhaps they wouldn't have cared? He fills the tank. We then make our way back to the highway. 'He knew exactly where to stop,' I think to myself.

The silence continues. Each bump of the road lulls my exhausted body into a thin veil of sleep. I'm half-aware and half-asleep. It was twilight as the mountains came into view. We drive through a small town. The streets are empty. It must be Sunday morning. We turn left onto another country road, then right. There are dozens of run-down single-wide trailers on either side of the road. Then there's a sharp round turn, then several more. We begin to gain altitude as each hairpin turn leads us to another leg up the side of the mountain. The movement seems like it will never end. That's when nausea sets in.

"I'm going to be sick! Please, pull over!" I shout.

I try to think of happy thoughts and rub the back of my neck as a distraction. The sounds of uncontrolled retching materialize. It's too late. A hot stream of yellow exits my mouth, blanketing the rear of the driver's seat. It begins to run down to the floor. I feel the vomit's warmth on my chest and legs as well. I inhale the acidic fluid. It burns my throat as I begin to choke. Each time I try to breathe, there's a gurgle but no air. There is no response from either of them. I see daylight break through the trees to my left as I heave back and forth in panic. The light goes dim as we pass under an old bridge. We pull over to the right into a small parking lot meant for tourists to take in the view. It's empty. My vision begins to fade from the periphery first. It closes in until I can scarcely make out the backseat. Then darkness.

I wake up outside the car. Doctor Proffit is behind me with his arms wrapped around me. He has successfully performed the Heimlich. I feel the vomit lodged in my throat running down my chin. Some of it drips onto Doctor Proffit's still clenched fists. I catch my breath in a wheeze and cough. He unleashes me to stand on my own feet. Immediately after I get upright, I feel a boot in my back. I go facedown into the asphalt. My elbows and hands are scraped bloody from catching my body. I'm momentarily glad I didn't feel anything break or hit my face. I feel an arm wrap around my head and hot breath in my left ear. The chokehold is tightened.

As my breathing is restricted again, I hear Doctor Proffit scream into my ear, "when we get home, you're cleaning the sick out of my car even if it takes all day! Until then, you can ride in the back."

The chokehold is released, and I fall to my knees.

"I've been riding in the back," I gasp.

"No. The back."

With a click of a key remote, the Buick's trunk opens.

"Climb in."

Without a chance to react, my chains are grabbed and I'm thrown into the trunk and onto a small bunk mattress covered in dark brown stains. I'm not the first person to be back here. I'm not even the second or third. 'Is the brown stain I'm laying on blood?' I wonder. It occurs to me that they will really let me die. Maybe not now, but eventually. They want me alive for a while it seems. Instead of bracing myself for death, I prepare for captivity. But for how long? If I play along and do what they say, will they let me go eventually? Or am I like a cat's prey they use to entertain themselves with before killing it slowly? At thirteen, the thought of my own death once seemed impossible. I realize in terror that it is not. I hear the driver's door slam and the engine roar to life. The manner of driving seems far hastier than before. The turns are taken faster. The mattress and I slide to the opposite side with every turn. Murmured voices come from the cabin.

As the car slows, I can hear the crushing sound of gravel beneath the tires. The Buick comes to a full stop with the resonate squeal of old brakes. I hear both car doors open, then shut. The trunk latch is released, and light is reintroduced to my eyes. I see my captor backlit by a fluorescent halo. I realize we're inside. Warm sunlight beams through the dusty windows of a garage door.

"Get up on your feet, girly, church is in three hours and you have work to do."

Doctor Proffit wheels a large shop-vac from the corner of the garage toward me.

"Patty, go inside and get the upholstery cleaner," he says.

Patty climbs the interior stairs then opens the storm door and wooden door without a key. She disappears into the house. The woosh of the storm door signals her return. Patty walks up to us and places a bottle of Resolve and a soft brush into my hands. She doesn't bother talking to me.

"Clean up. When you're done, throw all of your clothes into the garbage can. Knock on the door and Patty will see you to your new room."

It takes me an hour to vacuum up the puke and scrub the back of the seat to a presentable state. The spot where I was sitting still has a faint V-shaped outline where the vomit settled between my legs.

Now that I'm done, I approach the storm door, open it, and knock on the interior door. When Patty gets to the door she is furious to find me still clothed.

"Why you still dressed, girl? Take them clothes off now and put 'em in the garbage."

"Why can't I keep my clothes?"

"Those are remnants of your old life. You're starting fresh as of this moment. Walk down them steps and strip you'ins to yer birthday suit."

Patty crosses her arms as she stares at me. I slink backward down the stairs, while firmly holding the rail with my left hand. I make sure not to take my eyes off of her. I stand next to the trash can and remove my shoes and socks first. The concrete is cold and my bare right foot is resting in an old oil stain. I remove my dress. I put it all in the garbage can.

I'm standing in my bra and panties staring at Patty, who is still at the door. I do not want to take the rest of my clothes off in front of her.

Patty reaches for a long cane of dried bamboo that is leaning in the corner next to the door. I'd seen that look in my father's eyes right before he'd whip me with whatever object was convenient. I know to be afraid. I realize that the cane is her weapon of choice. She doesn't have the strength of her husband, but a four-foot-long bamboo rod gives anyone a significant advantage.

With it in her hand, she begins to slowly step down the stairs. I am nude before Patty reaches the bottom step. She motions for me. I walk up the stairs, then lean down and scoot under Patty's right arm, which is holding open the storm door. When the door is released, the tight action of the hydraulics slamming behind me sends me fearfully leaping forward into the house.

4

The only things I'm still wearing are the chains around my wrists. I take a quick note of my surroundings. It's a modest house. There's a living room in front of me and an eat-in kitchen to my right. There's a door past the kitchen that I assume goes to a laundry room. The front door is located in the living room area. To the left of the living room is a hallway.

Patty points to the hallway and says, "Head straight to your bedroom, gather the clothes on your bed and take a shower."

I walk toward the hallway, still clinking with each step. There are four doorways, one at the end of the hallway, two to my left, and one on the right.

"Yer room is the first on the left," Patty squawks.

The doors have been removed from their hinges on all rooms but the one at the end of the hall.

"There's no door," I remark.

"There are five doors in this house: the outside garage door, the inside garage door, the back and front doors, and the one to our bedroom. You are never to go in there. Do you understand?"

"Yes ma'am," I reply, contritely.

"There will be no secrets. Anything you feel must be private is probably sinful, and you're afraid to have the eyes of the righteous see."

The bedroom is stark and poorly lit. Inside is a single bed with an old foam mattress and a dresser that looks like it was repurposed from a cheap motel. A wooden school desk sits, flush, facing the back wall. My new outfit consists of stockings, a blue ankle-length dress with long straight sleeves. My new shoes are simple black flat-bottom slip-ons. I gather up everything and step back into the hallway. I hesitate.

"Couldn't you put up a shower curtain? The liner is see-through."

"What? Do you'ins need a private place where you can thinks about girls and touch yourself?"

"No, I…"

Patty abruptly heads back to the garage door with purpose. She reaches out to grab something. It's that fucking bamboo cane!

Patty came at me quick, with the cane in her right hand. She swung downward. I felt the strike on the outside of my bare right thigh. I drop all my new clothes as I lean over in anguish. My leg below where the cane hit starts to become numb. I'm barely standing. I notice the hardwood floor against my face before I even realize my legs have given out.

Patty's shoe is so close to my right eye that I can't focus on it. I hear her voice overhead.

"That there was just one little smack. Imagine if I'd hit you'ins with it over and over. What if I hand mind to hit you with it until I had to quit because my arms gets tired? No one will care. No one will help you, because they hate you."

I lie there in the hallway of this stranger's house, naked, dazed by pain, and clutching my right thigh. But no matter how much my leg hurts, all I can think is "why would my parents do this to me? Was their love this conditional?"

I feel words leave me. There is only the internal dialogue of shredding pain, bouncing off the interior of my skull until my eyesight turns to static.

I wake up, what I assume is moments later, still face down, but now on the bathroom tile. She must have dragged me. I feel the threshold of the door with my left foot. My right foot remains numb.

My hands are still chained, but the chains are now somehow bound together behind my back. I realize the weight I feel between my palms is one of the padlocks they used to restrain me in the car.

Patty is above me now.

"Stuck, ain't you'ins? I was fixin' to whoop on ya but don't know how well that will work. Your daddy whooped you all the time. I don't see that it's been productive. I will teach you submission. You will never question, and punishments will not end if you resist. We're on God's rules here. I think you'ins got a lot of fight, so I'm gonna' to need to be creative with my methods. Oh, I know! We'll get a witch's confession. In olden times, when a woman was accused of being a follower of Satan, they was tied to a chair, then lowered into the water for a few minutes. If she was still alive when she was lifted out, she was certainly a witch. That meant a burnin'. If she was dead, she went to her just reward at Abraham's bosom. Sometimes we have to trust the Lord to sort the evil with the chaff."

I see the twill of a burlap bag, as it gets placed over my head. Light shows through a little, but mostly it's dark. I feel the string of the bag tighten around my throat.

"Turn over," she commands.

Sobbing into the burlap, I do what Patty asks.

I hear her step into the tub. Now that I'm on my back, she slips her hands under my armpits and pulls me up into the tub. I sense her step out of the tub. She then pushes my legs the rest of the way in. I begin to feel water drip onto the bag right where my nose is. I move my face to the side.

"Ya gonna' need to be restrained more. If you move from where you is, I will break your leg with this cane like you did that poor girl's arm."

I lie still, crying, and trying to imagine what my parents are doing. I worry about what happened to Tiffany. Is something like this happening to her somewhere and I can't stop it?

I hear Patty walk back in after a few minutes. She slips a rope around my neck, then pulls it tight. I begin to choke, then she quickly lets it go.

"The knot is tied so it'll loosen when there's no pressure on it. I'm trying the other end to the faucet."

I feel the rope cinch around my neck again. And just as quickly the slack loosens, but not quite as much. The back of my head can just reach the bottom of the tub. I can feel that the plunger is in the drain hole with the back of my head. Patty turns the cold water on partway. I feel a small, steady stream hitting the bag. I begin to feel as though I'm breathing in water. I'm drowning. I move my head to the side, but then the noose tightens.

"Don't mind me, I have things to do," Patty says.

"Would my parents leave me in the care of someone who would kill me?" I question myself.

I hear her footsteps fade in the direction of the kitchen. "Is she actually leaving me here to drown?"

Soon, I feel the water collecting underneath me. I move my head back and forth between drowning and choking. And every minute or so, I notice how much higher the water feels on my back. I begin to scream and flail uncontrollably.

"Please help me!" I shout through gargled breaths.

I hear slower, heavier footsteps. The faucet turns off and I'm no longer being bombarded by a stream of cold water. A hand reaches under my back and unstops the drain. The rope slackens and the bag is removed. Above me, I see the face of a boy.

He is pale, rotund, and has a round face. His light brown hair is buzzed to the scalp, almost like he's in basic training. The boy is dressed in slacks, a white shirt, and a black tie, all of which look as though they are slightly too large. It's a uniform that has been chosen for him. They're probably hand-me-downs.

The boy throws a towel over my nude body, in a gesture to protect my privacy. He then pulls me up to a seated position.

In the tone of a feminine, southern gentleman he says, "are you okay?"

I shake my head to indicate no.

I see the cane coming down, but too late to warn him. When it strikes his right shoulder, I hear the audible crack of breaking bone. His screams fill the bathroom. Thc next hit is to his right temple. There is a thud, then silence. The boy crumples to the floor.

"Aren't you two a pair?" Patty said. "Arrogant rebellion comes with consequences. Can you see?"

I nod my head in agreeance.

"Now that you know what happens to the disobedient, do you'ins plan on causing more trouble?"

I shake my head, no.

She stares at me momentarily. I await the cane.

"It ain't practical to keep you'ins chained up forever. You'll have to do for yourself. What better time than now to unchain ya since you have his pain fresh in you'ins memory. Once I do, if you try escapin', just know it's thick wilderness, and near 'bout everyone 'round here goes to Solid Rock. They's been told to keep a lookout."

Patty leaves the room and comes back with a key moments later.

"Turn you'ins around."

I turn my back toward Patty. My hands came apart first, and then I feel relief when each wrist is finally unshackled. I can still feel where the metal has dug into my skin for days. I pull my arms forward and hold onto the towel the boy put over me.

"You may take your shower now," Patty says, then abruptly leaves the room.

The boy remains on the floor unconscious. I can't do anything to help. I don't know what to do. I just do what Patty tells me. I shower. There's a single bar of Ivory soap, and a bottle of Head and Shoulders. I turn on the hot water and wait, but it never comes. The hot water must have been cut off to this bathroom. I get clean the best I can, all the while, peeping down on the boy, or perhaps, the boy's body as I dodge in and out of the cold mountain water coming from the showerhead.

I hear heavier footsteps. It's Doctor Proffit. He strides into the bathroom as I shut the water off. Through the clear shower liner, I see him reach down, pull the boy up to his knees, and then onto his back. He begins to pull him out of the room by his arms, leaving his backside to slide across the floor. As he reaches the doorway, Doctor Proffit pauses and noticeably surveys my exposed body, then is quickly out of sight with the boy in tow. I wait for a few seconds, then sprint across the hallway with the towel around me. I snag up all my clothes off the floor on the way. I hastily dress, then sit on the bed and quietly wait.

Patty enters the bedroom doorway, snaps her fingers, and points left, as to indicate to follow her. I get up as quickly as I can and go stand in the hallway. She looks over my clothing and says, "I guess that'll do."

5

My hair is still wet when I climb into the backseat of the Buick, for the first time not in chains. Doctor Proffit again drives, and Patty rides in the front passenger seat. The Proffit's house sits on the corner of an unmarked paved road that meets a dirt road that runs along the back of the house. We drive down that dirt road. I assume it belongs to the church. It winds up a ridge. On our left is a rocky outcrop. On the right is a river. I see two large buildings made from cinderblocks, painted pale green with metal roofs. Then there are four buildings, each about half the size of the previous two. They are of similar construction but painted a hideous jaundice yellow. The land opens up to the left, revealing long rows of vegetables. Near the fields is an ancient log barn. I catch a glimpse of chickens and several goats. When the fields cease, a rock wall hems us tight to the river. On the left there is a small granite draw that looks as though it was being used as a small gun range, with about a dozen shooting alleys. We finally come to a grassy parking area. There sits a small white church with a red door, gracefully built next to a deep bend in the river. If I didn't know better, I would describe it as placid.

We are the first to arrive. There are two small concrete steps up to the red door. The door is not locked. Doctor Proffit opens it and enters, Patty follows, then myself. The chapel has short, dark pews framing the aisle. There are twelve on either side. Patty and I sit down in the center of the front left row. Doctor Proffit takes a seat on the slightly raised stage and silently reads a Bible. Over the next few minutes, I watch the devout slowly fill the pews.

What I assume are three deacons sit to Doctor Proffit's left. The closest is a short, doughy man in his thirties, cursed with dull features. He has short black hair cut in a fashion equally at home in 1903 as it is in 1993. In the middle seat sits a slight man in his fifties, of about six feet. He has a bald head, a long pointy nose, and small brown eyes. Furthest away from Doctor Proffit is a man also in his fifties and even larger than my father, at least six-foot-six. He is hulking and wide. Peculiarly, he is dressed in a police uniform. I believe he's the Sheriff.

Doctor Proffit takes the pulpit and slams his fist down. The wood reverberates in a deep thud that cuts into the silence. The devoted sit with eyes to the front, waiting for wisdom.

"Urgency must be among us! The signs have manifested in the multitudes. I believe that we will be called home soon, probably in less than twenty years. The faithful must be ever vigilant. I have concerns. I'm concerned that some of you may not be ready. Oh, you think you might know. Only the Lord knows your hearts. You may say, 'Lord, take me in your time.' Death is always out there in the distance. It's an imaginary phantom ship on the horizon. You must know that time will sincerely end and we will be sorted. That day might be today. Are you ready? Is your family ready? Have you offered the salvation of Christ to everyone you know? Could you unintentionally find yourself forever apart from loved ones by a gulf of eternal damnation? For whom will he come?

It says in First Thessalonians four verse seventeen, 'Then we which are alive remain shall be caught up together with them in the clouds, to meet the Lord in the air: and so shall we ever be with the Lord.'

We? Who is the 'we' that is spoken of? That's the church. Only his church. Are you a part of it? You may be here, but is your heart? Are you thinking about what you'll have for lunch or who will win the big game? Your mind should be here now. When?

It says in first Corinthians fifteen-two, 'In a moment, in the twinkling of an eye, at the last trump: for the trumpet shall sound, and the dead shall be raised incorruptible, and we shall be changed.'

In Revelation twenty-two twelve, 'And, behold, I come quickly; and my reward with me, to give every man according as his work shall be.' In the twinkling of an eye, quickly, faster than vision, he will have come and been gone with his children.

Your reward will be based on work. Work only toward the holy. Raise ye' holy children. If you don't you must hate them for it says in Revelation thirteen-eight, "And all that dwell upon the earth shall worship him, whose names are not written in the book of life of the Lamb slain from the foundation of the world."

"You will be slain from the world." Doctor Proffit chuckles purposefully, "That sounds very serious, doesn't it? How will we know?

Finally, it says in Matthew twenty-four, thirty-one., 'And he shall send his angels with a great sound of a trumpet, and they shall gather together his elect from the four winds, from one end of heaven to the other.' The holy, triumphant announcement from a chorus of angels led by Gabriel. The sound will engulf all. Even the deaf will hear his proclamation. Then you will be swept up, instantly. The trumpets will fall silent on earth. Those that remain have tribulation to pay."

Doctor Proffit falls into silent contemplation. Then a trumpet rings forth, ceasing seconds later. All tremble in fear. No one is raptured. Horror sets in. Many begin to cry and fall to their knees behind the pews.

"Calm, my children, it's just a test."

From behind the door to the baptismal pool walks one of the choir members holding the offending instrument.

"I wanted to see your reaction. Was it fear? I know now who the true Christians are by the fearful reactions on individual faces. What prompted your fear? Jonathan Edwards talked of slipping at any moment into hell. You could be sitting at a stop sign when you're crashed into. Your head hits the glass, and you go through the windshield. Your earthly existence is extinguished. The soul is then seamlessly engulfed in searing agony and the breath of sulfur. It begins to sink in; you're in hell. You will never leave or die. You will experience ceaseless torment. Jonathan Edward's parishioners were so afraid when he preached his sermon, *Sinners in the Hands of an Angry God,* of literal and immediate hell that they grasped to the pew in front of them as not to be pulled down into it. Let us pray."

Doctor Proffit begins a prayer, then makes a call for salvation and rededication. The choir softly sings *What a friend we have in Jesus.* One by one, those who doubt that they're good enough come forward to be forgiven. I'm not sure, though, who they're groveling to. Was it God or Doctor Proffit? The singing goes through all four verses, then begins again. The singing goes on for another hour.

At the end of the service, Doctor Proffit stands at the front door of the church and shakes the hands of each member. A man asks about the boy's lack of attendance, referring to him as Charles.

Doctor Proffit replies, "Oh, he fell yesterday during a hike. Bless him, he's afflicted with a broken shoulder bone. The doctor is coming by later to fix him up. Pray for him."

After everyone is gone, Doctor Proffit points at me, then the exit. We are the last to leave.

I know he is lying. There will be no doctor. We drive the short trip by to the house and again park in the garage. As the doors shut, I feel panic. The realness of my situation begins to sink in. There was a calming aspect to the ritual of the church. I know all the songs and routines. The actors are new, but the play is the same. We sit in the car quietly. I dare not move without explicit permission.

Doctor Proffit clears his throat and says, "As far as you're concerned, that boy fell on a hike. Even if you were to tell someone the truth, they won't believe you. Most wouldn't care what happened to a faggot anyway. You're lucky you're with us. Some of them would rather just kill you. They won't if you're under my protection."

Who I am to them is so revolting, they can only vocalize my existence as a vulgarity. For my entire life, I was simply Naomi. Now I am 'Naomi, the lesbian.' Whispers of a community are predictably pointed toward rarity. When one says a word designed to separate over and over, even those who are considered marked start to believe it. In my mind, I remain Naomi. That's all I need to be. Why would who I love change such an elegantly uncomplicated definition?

"Get you'ins inside," Patty states curtly. Again, it is Doctor Profit through the door first, then Patty, and last me. As I enter, I notice the bamboo cane has been neatly tucked away, back in its corner like a tool used, and returned to a drawer. That's all it is to Patty. A hammer drives nails, a can opener opens cans, and a bamboo cane controls. Simple.

I don't have to change after church, as I would have at home. In my closet, there are five identical, plain blue dresses, and nothing casual.

"Go to your room," barks Patty.

I sit and wait. The house is quiet enough that I can hear the faintest whimper through the wall. I don't dare investigate. Several minutes pass.

"Girl, get over here," Doctor Proffit calls from the hallway.

"I want you to see the consequences of your actions," he says.

He's standing in the hallway looking into the other bedroom; the one where the boy named Charles stays. Charles lay on his bed, which was against the back wall. He was on his left side, with his back to us. There is no doubt, his right shoulder was injured. I'm just glad he's alive. The pain was so intense he shook with each breath.

"You'll have to help me set his collar bone," Doctor Proffit says.

"Get up, boy!" he shouts.

Charles raises himself up with his left arm. His right arm is tucked seamlessly to the side of his body. Charles slowly turns and places his feet on the floor. He and the sheets are drenched in sweat.

Doctor Proffit turns on the light.

"Boy, take your shirt off, get on the floor, and lay on your back."

Charles slowly works his shirt off using his left arm. Then he crawls quite deliberately to the floor, left side first. Doctor Proffit approaches Charles from the left and swings his right leg over him. Straddling him, Doctor Proffit pushes both of Charles's arms toward his body using the inside of his dress shoes. He then sits down on top of the trembling boy, placing his knees against the outside of his elbows as a form of incapacitation. I can see where the cane hit. The crook of Charle's neck seems to sag where the collar bone has broken. The tip of one of the two halves of bone pokes upward, creating a small skin tent over its sharp point.

"Now, kneels behind his head. Hold the bump with your right thumb, then use your left forefinger to dig into the crease of his neck. Now bring your fingers together slowly."

I felt the broken tips grind together.

"Harder now."

Charles begins to hyperventilate. He moans and flails from side to side like gaffed tuna.

"Do it!"

I push harder until the crunching gives way to a hideous, deep click. Charles releases the most piercing, animalistic scream I had ever heard come from a human. Doctor Proffit stands and walks back a few feet. Charles rolls onto his left side while using his left hand to clutch the injury.

"Leave now. Go help with lunch."

A few minutes later, Patty, Doctor Proffit, and I sit down to eat at their rectangular dinner table. Each of them sits on either end of the table, I in the middle of the long portion of the table. I assume the chair across from me is typically occupied by Charles.

We eat in silence after the blessing. It's fried chicken, butter beans, a biscuit, and sweet tea. I help clean up as I would have at home. I typically do the dishes. My mom cooks, and my dad does nothing. Like church earlier, these are nearly identical lives, much like a dream where you experience a life similar to your own, but everyone and everything you know is utterly bizarre and terrifying. The one addition in this new life was the boy.

"Girl," Doctor Proffit says while pointing at me. "Go to your room for the rest of the night. You are instructed to read Genesis chapters eleven to nineteen seven times, pray, then go to sleep. Do not, for any reason, leave your bedroom until we instruct you to. That includes going to the bathroom. You can just hold it."

I grew up in the church. I already know the verses. It's the story of the fall of Sodom, and Lot, the most righteous of Sodom's citizens.

In my short life, I have become acutely aware of immunity to irony where faith is involved.

Due to the sin of Sodom's citizens, Lot's family is instructed to flee by visiting angels. Prior to realizing he's speaking to angels disguised as men, Lot offers up his two daughters sexually, as a favor to them.

Directly after Lot's family leaves Sodom, God destroys the city with brimstone. The fleeing party was Lot, his two daughters, and his wife. Lot's wife, whose name is never given in the Bible, looks back, even after being instructed not to. She is turned into a pillar of salt.

Afterward, Lot and his daughters live in a cave. Both daughters supposedly plot to have sex with their father while he slept, a proposition that sends my bullshit detector to its zenith.

Both became pregnant.

The irony is, Lot and his family are allowed to escape Sodom because he is the most righteous man there. Today, he would be considered a sex offender.

Lot's wife's sin: looking.

6

I finish reading the chapters assigned to me in Genesis, even though I know them thoroughly. I don't want to get caught off guard if they decide to question me about a minuscule detail.

Now I'm supposed to pray. I haven't prayed on my own in two years because I have yet to see any proof of the existence of the Christian God, or any other god, for that matter. However, tonight I pray. But it's not for forgiveness. No, I pray for my death. I go to sleep with the sincere wish not to wake up.

In my dream, I'm sitting next to Tiffany in the park. Her almost translucent white skin and long red hair are so real, I reach out my hand to her. At this moment I am happy.

A sharp, wide stream of pain sears my face from cheek to cheek across my closed eyelids. Tiffany is erased and I'm back in the Proffit's house. I see a belt raised high above me, primed for a second strike. I sit up quickly and dodge the encore.

It's Doctor Proffit.

"You will wake up every morning at four-thirty by instinct from this day forward. If not, I will awaken you with my belt at five. Do you understand?"

I nod in agreement.

"It's five AM now. You will get dressed and be ready to go in ten minutes."

"Ready to go where?"

"Wherever I say."

When five-o-nine rolls around, I am sitting at the kitchen table. Doctor Proffit's simple attire consists of plain jeans and an off-white pinstripe button-up shirt. I'm limping because of the large bruise Patty left on my right thigh. It's a purple outline of her cane. At least I can feel my foot again.

"Car, now," Doctor Proffit says to me like I'm an abused, unwanted dog. "Get in the back."

I open the rear passenger-side door and sit down. This time I'm able to fasten my seatbelt.

When we back out of the garage, it's dark. Sunlight is about an hour away. Doctor Proffit turns left out of the driveway. In a few feet, we cross a bridge over the river. About twenty yards on the other side, we reach a T-intersection. Their house is close enough to still be visible out the back window. We take a right onto the main road. The road meanders up a slight incline. We ride for about twenty minutes through the thick morning fog. I keep watching for a road sign. Eventually, I see what appears to be a sign indicating this was North Carolina Highway Eighty, whatever that means. I don't exactly have a map.

Since we've been in the car, he's said nothing. I just listen to the hum of the tires. After about twenty minutes we pass an old stone school, then hit another T-intersection. In front of the car sits a tiny post office. We turn left, then we get out onto a straighter traveling road. The sign states we are on U.S. Highway Nineteen East.

After another few minutes of silence, I catch a glimpse of a small town in the distance. When we get closer, I notice a sign welcoming us to Burnsville. We veer right onto a road that runs parallel to Highway Nineteen. The signs say it's Main Street.

We stop in the driveway of an old bungalow with peeling white paint. The porch light is already on. Someone is awaiting our arrival. In front of us sits a white Chevy truck that looks to be about twenty years old. The screen door on the front porch opens to reveal a lady with white hair shaped into a permed dome of churls. The engine comes to a rest and Doctor Proffit opens his door and gets out. He opens my door.

"Get out."

The searing welt across my eyes from earlier compels a quick response. We take a short walkway to find ourselves at a set of old concrete stairs. We climb up to the porch up to the lady with the white curly hair. She is tiny, probably just under five feet tall.

"Is this the girl, Vernon?" she asked in an almost compassionate tone.

"Yes."

That's the first time I've heard Doctor Proffit's first name.

He addresses me almost like I was a human. "This is Mrs. Maddie Bellew. Her late husband, George, was the pastor of Solid Rock for over fifty years."

"Hello, dear", Mrs. Bellew says in a reassuring soft tone. "Why don't you come in?"

Maddie's house smells of rose water. There is floral wallpaper barely visible through a festoon of old portraits. The furniture is pristine. It looks like a display from a well-appointed nineteen-fifties dollhouse.

Maddie disappears into the hallway to our left. We stand there in silence. After a few minutes, Maddie's tiny voice beckons, "Come on in, we're ready."

We walk toward the hallway to find Maddie standing next to an open room. It's the first door on the left of her short hallway. I catch a glimpse of three other doors further down the hallway.

The room appears as though it was originally designed to be a bedroom. It's completely white, except for the oak floor. In the center sat what looked like an antique examination table from the turn of the century. The metal has been repainted a dull green and the seat reupholstered in a black synthetic material. Affixed to the wall are a couple of wooden cabinets with glass faces. Below them is a short counter whose centerpiece is a large enamel sink. On the ceiling, the light of bare one-hundred-watt incandescent bulbs emits a sickening yellow hue.

"Have a seat," Maddie says.

She motions to Vern and mouths something I can't decipher. Doctor Proffit nods his head in agreement.

I climb up onto the examination table as Doctor Proffit slithers into the hallway.

Maddie, now in a threatening demeanor, says "Dr. Proffit is going to stand in the hallway. Don't get no sass, he gives an awful whoopin'. Now, lay on your back.

I do as I'm told. The bright lights are blinding and leave flashes behind when I close my eyelids.

From the foot of the table, Maddie commands, "Put your feet flat on the table with your knees up.

I hear two metallic creeks. Then I feel Mrs. Bellew's cold hands around both of my ankles. She slips off my shoes and socks, then throws them aside, against the wall. She places each of my feet into something cold. I feel leather straps go across the tops of my feet and behind my ankles. They're so tight, I begin to lose feeling in both my feet.

I look over to my left. Close to my knee is a small stainless steel surgical table. On top of it sits a metal box with flecks of rust on it. It has one rocker switch and a dial. Connected to it is a power cord entering on the side visible to me and a smaller black line exiting the other toward my feet.

When I saw the examination table, I naively thought I might be here to have my leg looked at. But when Maddie flips the switch of the rusty metal box to on, I know something truly terrible is about to begin. And there is nothing I can do to stop it.

It whines with the high-pitched electrical sound of a small transformer. Maddie turns the knob to the right, increasing the horrifying tone. She disappears between my legs. I feel her push my dress up above my knees. Her frail hands pull my panties down. I hear the slice of a pair of scissors. I can no longer feel my underwear. They have been cut off.

Mrs. Bellew reappears. She lifts her hand, revealing a hollowed-out wooden dowel whose bottom received the wire leading from the box. On the end is a thin looped wire. As it heats, the wire begins to smoke off whatever material remained plastered to it from the prior use. I start to squirm and cry uncontrollably. I feel like I should be bracing for some kind of injury. Is she going to brand me like livestock?

"Stop. Please don't. I won't do it again," I beg.

"Shush your cryin' now. It don't hurt long."

In dread, I begin to move my feet toward myself so that I can stand, but they won't budge. I then sit up in an attempt to fight her off with my hands.

Maddie steps back and says, "If you don't quit, I'll have Doctor Proffit hold you down and I'll burn out both of your eyes with this."

She holds the red-hot loop near to my cheek. With my eyes closed, I can feel my skin heat up and about to burn. Then it abates. I open my eyes, to see the smoldering iron loop moving away from my face in Maddie Bellew's tiny hand. Then, like a burrowing creature, she disappears under my dress again. This time she has a glowing hot instrument. I want to scream but I know she will do just what she said, burn out my eyes. And after that, she'll continue to do whatever this is, regardless.

"No. Please, God, don't!" I sob.

"You've got one part right, God," she says while I feel her rub a cold alcohol swab across my genitals.

I wait for the trap door to drop.

White-hot unyielding pain from the burning loop carves itself into me in an upward sweeping motion as I thrash and scream. I feel like I'm going to puke. I dry heave. Through my tear-filled eyes, I see Maddie reappear with a half-pint Mason jar in her hand. She pours a clear liquid from a plastic bottle into the jar. Placing the bottle down, she again reaches between my legs and brings up something bloody and pink, then drops it into the glass jar. After tightening the lid, she holds it to my face.

"See, all better. The first step to recovery is the removal of temptation. Don't you'ins worry now. I only gots the bit that matters. First girl, I took too much and cauterized her urethra shut. She died of kidney failure a few days later. Turned yellar. Bad way to go."

In the jar floats my clitoris. The hood and some of the hair are still attached. The top looked like the end of an infant's pinky. It's a mangle of cooked flesh, scooped out by an electric melon baller. The pink coloration fades and begins to turn white as the cartilage and skin die. I vomit down the front of my dress. I'm in unending agony as Maddie places her new trophy out of sight. The burnt flesh gives off a faint whiff of bacon underneath the overpowering chemical smell.

She painfully rubs some kind of salve across the searing wound. I'm becoming exhausted. I lie there without fighting as she bandaged me up.

My feet are unstrapped. Maddie helps me stagger off the table. On the way out she hands Doctor Proffit a blister pack of pills, and written instructions. I lie down in the backseat of the Buick. The ride home is a blur of light chopping through gaps in trees at high speed.

The next few days are a haze of bed-laden suffering, excruciating urination, and antibiotics. I am forced to sit up in bed and read Exodus repeatedly. The logic is that homosexuality is mental servitude we need to be freed from. But all I can think about when I read it is escape.

7

As Charles and my injuries heal, we are expected to assist with daily chores. I typically do dishes and laundry. Charles's tasks are mowing grass and trash duty for the entire facility.

We are despised here. It's worse for Charles because of his duties away from the house. Students throw trash at Charles and mock him with slurs as he gathers bags to pitch into the back of the school's old yellow Toyota truck.

Most of the pupils are here of their own free will. The entire student body is white. The majority were homeschooled or attended local Christian schools until eighth grade. They are then enrolled at Solid Rock from ninth to twelfth grade. As their parents see it, Solid Rock is one of the best finishing schools if one wants to attend a high-profile Christian college. Aside from Charles's trash duty, our interactions with the students are limited. Isolation, overall, isn't healthy, but here I'm glad for it. We are exempt from their classes. Our retraining is based on physical attrition.

Charles and I work side by side in silence for five months, under the watchful eye of God's self-appointed prophet.

After all that time, I am informed we are going to be allowed to labor, unobserved, outside of the house. This was likely prompted by the weather. Yancey County is brutally cold from November to March. There is almost no chance of survival if we were to run off. I also imagine having lackeys to work out in the elements suits Doctor Proffit and Patty just fine.

The day after students leave for Christmas vacation, we are given our first unsupervised work outing. We are to clean the girls' dormitory.

Doctor Proffit drops us off in front of the building with cleaning supplies. He informs us to walk straight home after we've finished.

Charles is a quiet boy who doesn't respond much to Doctor Proffit's yelling. He doesn't like looking others in the eye. When he glances at me, I feel as though I'm receiving the highest compliment. I had begun to assume Charles was mute. The only sounds he ever makes are during his nightmares or if he's in pain. Those sounds are mostly moans and screams, with no decipherable words.

Seconds after we enter the dorm alone, Charles looks at me and says, "Do you know why I'm here?"

I catch my embarrassing gasp by placing a hand over my mouth.

"No," I say while shaking my head and pushing the blank stare from my face.

Plainly, Charles says, "Because a man had sex with me."

"Did you love him?" I ask.

"No!" Charles says vociferously.

"Who was he?"

Charles mutely looks at his shoes, humiliated, before mumbling, "my youth pastor."

He continues, “I don’t like the idea of sex at all. It means you have to touch someone else, and I don’t care much for that.”

“Where are you from, Charles?”

I stare at him for about ten seconds, then his eyes avert. Common courtesy tells me he’s had enough, and I decide not to push him further.

Around noon we hear a car pull up. Patty walks in and sets down a plastic bag containing our lunches. She says nothing and promptly leaves. No one else comes by for the remainder of the day.

As we finish cleaning, I look through one of the windows to see daylight waning. We begin to walk back home. As we get closer, we hear Patty screaming inaudibly through the walls of the house. Charles and I stop. We don’t want to walk in on whatever this is, but we have nowhere else to go. We are expected home.

The front door of the house opens, and a girl I recognize from church runs out completely naked. Her name is Daisy Chambers. She and her grandmother sit on the third left pew. Daisy is about two years younger than me. She is blond and pale, like almost everyone up here.

Daisy’s white, barely developed figure stands out against the darkening background. As she gets to the bridge, we hear the deep click of a bolt being shoved into a rifle chamber, then the resound of an old Garand. I see the round strike Daisy in the middle-left of her back. When the bullet exits her front, she slumps and falls backward.

“No! You fucking bitch! You didn’t have to do that!”, I hear Doctor Proffit scream.

I see the outline of Patty as she lays the rifle against the house. She fired the round.

We stay still in the shadows along the dirt road. Doctor Proffit runs toward the girl. The gurgling coming from Daisy's punctured lung only lasted a moment. Doctor Proffit kicks her tiny, floppy body. She is undoubtedly dead. Doctor Proffit walks back to the house. The garage door opens. The Buick rolls out with no headlights. It traverses down the short distance to the bridge. The car comes to a halt next to Daisy's body. She lies where the centerline would have been if the state actually bothered to paint one. The trunk pops, and Doctor Proffit exits the car. He opens the rear passenger door. A dark sheet is produced from within. Doctor Proffit throws it over Daisy and rolls up her slight remains. He scoops up the unfortunate parcel and tosses it atop the stained mattress in the trunk.

The task seems unpleasant for him but no more so than cleaning up dog shit off the living room floor. He isn't rushing to hide what happened. He appears to have no fear of consequences or remorse, just inconvenience. It probably has something to do with the deacon who always comes dressed in a police uniform. His name is Alton Morton. He's the sheriff of Yancey County. The short, doughy deacon is named Brent Shoals. He is also the music director and a teacher. I still don't know the name of the man with a bald head and pointy nose. He's only present on Sundays, but not every Sunday.

Charles and I slowly walk backward, knowing full well we could easily end up inside the trunk with poor Daisy. Our boundary line was the edge of darkness provided by the scrubby brush we huddle next to in the ditch opposite the river. I've heard the locals call it 'The Toe River.'

Shaking, we stay like quail in the brush, waiting for a dog to flush us out. To our relief, the Buick slowly backs into the driveway of the house with the lights still extinguished.

Without warning, our safety recedes as the headlamps come to life and turn in our direction.

“Charles!”, I whisper in a quiet exclamation, “If he sees us, they’ll just dig a bigger hole! We need to get back to the girl’s dorm. Run!”

Charles is quick over a short distance, which keeps him a few feet in front of me. His steam, however, begins to run out as the headlight’s illumination bares down on our heels. Charles’s body gives out about fifty yards from the front door of the girl’s dormitory. He pants, hunches over, and grasps his side. I do the only thing I can and tackle him face-first into the yellow, dead grass. The car glides past, kicking up a cloud of dust in its wake. With the light ahead of us, and the dust as cover, I seize the back of Charles’s shirt and snatch him up to his knees.

“Back door, Charles. Go to the back door.”

As we round the corner, I hear the car door shut. We arrive inside just in time to see a shadow, cast by the car’s headlights, walking towards us through the window.

“Shit! We’re covered in dirt. He’ll know. Hit me, Charles!”

“What?”

“Hit me as hard as you can! Do it!”

The first punch bloodies my nose.

“Again!”

The second creates sharp pain in my left eye.

I slap Charles across the face as the door opens. Then I push him to the ground.

With Charles on his back, I shout, “I hate this son-of-a-bitch. Don’t ever make me work with him again!”

My face is swollen, red, and pounding. Charles begins to cry, not from physical pain, but rather, betrayal. He believes I mean those words. I had to make a choice. Broken hearts mend. Graves are eternal.

"Charles, you fucking pussy. Go get in the car and wait while I deal with this cunt," Doctor Proffit huffs.

After Charles is out of earshot, he says, "Do you want to be a man or something?"

"No," I respond.

"Liar!" he screams.

"Naomi, you're boyish in every way." He slides in close and whispers in my ear with his moist, hot breath. "Though, what I've been wondering is, do you fuck like a man?"

8

His hands shoot up between us and grab me by my throat. I'm pushed until my back is against the wall next to the door. I want to hit him, but strength is draining from my arms and legs. My eyes and lungs feel as though they'll burst. As darkness enters my periphery, he drops me to the ground. I'm ass down with my back against the wall. Doctor Proffit lowers his weight onto my knees. His legs wrap around my frame. I feel as though the bones in my legs will break. I scream.

"That won't help, only compliance and atonement will. You've been here long enough to know why my surname is Proffit. I am the last divine vessel for his prophetic word before end-times. Only through me can you talk to him."

Out of his left pocket comes a well-worn Buck 110 skinning knife. The old blade is opened slowly less than a foot from my eyes. The metal crunches minute particles of dirt trapped inside. The tip was chipped off years ago, leaving a blunt, flat end to the belly.

"Give me your hand."

I raise my right arm, never letting my eyes off the golden ends of the handle.

"No, the left one."

"But I'm left-handed."

"I know. It is the devil's hand. Left-handedness has always been a sign of evil. Demonic entities deal on the left. Satan baptizes his followers to his left. Homosexuals and lesbians have a higher percentage of left-handedness for a reason. Even the filthy Muslims know enough to use a bare left hand to wipe their asses. But Naomi has no shame, she writes with it, eats with it, and I bet you used to masturbate with it. That's not as easy as it used to be, is it?"

"Raise your hand in front of your face and spread your fingers. If you don't, I will make an incision in your stomach and pull the intestines out inch by inch through the little hole."

Shaking, I raise my left hand, which ironically gives me flashbacks of sitting next to Tiffany in English class. She's brilliant, and a chronic hand raiser.

"It's time for confession. Don't lie, I will sense it. God himself talks directly to me. I already know the answers, I just want to hear them from your contemptuous lips."

My hand is between our faces; the palm turned toward me. The knife blade is gingerly placed on the skin between my pointer and middle finger. The broken tip of the knife almost touches the end of my nose.

"Do you feel that? It's the bolster on the back of your fingers. The blade is kept sharp enough to skin an animal. It's almost four inches long. All I have to do is pull it back slowly."

He is quiet, then shouts, "Question one! Are you a man?"

"No."

"Correct. Safe for now. Question two, do you want to be a man?"

"No."

"Liar."

The blade is moved slightly, which opens a small wound. I gasp in shock, as a trickle of blood runs down my palm. I've cut myself before, but I've never had another person purposefully and maliciously cut me, especially someone who was just party to the murder of a little girl.

"Yes!", I shout, giving him the answer he wants.

"He says you don't believe your own answer."

"Who?"

"The Lord, of course."

He bears down on the knife and swipes it all the way back. Screaming, I look up to see a gash that exposes a deep white valley. I rock back and forth moaning. I bang my head against the cinderblock wall, anything to take my mind off of it.

"Next question," Doctor Proffit says, snapping his fingers.

The knife is placed between my middle and ring finger.

"Are you a virgin?"

"No." I sob, even though I am.

The knife is swiped again, and again in a sawing motion by Doctor Proffit's right hand as his left holds my wrist in a death grip. My screams echo off the walls. This continues until the gash is halfway down my palm, giving my opened hand the appearance of a gruesome Vulcan greeting. Fresh, warm blood pours out, down my forearm, and into my lap. I am too tired to wail any longer. The sight causes me to lose consciousness.

"Wake up, whore!" I hear while being slapped awake.

"Okay. Okay. Yes, I'm a virgin!"

"Right. Sex with girls doesn't count, so you are still a virgin. See darlin', all you have to do is tell the truth. Now, give me the hand he uses for his glory."

"Huh?"

"Your right hand, now."

I wait for another cut, instead, he places my uninjured palm on his right knee. He slides it towards him until I can feel his erect penis through the pants he is wearing.

"That's what a real woman wants, isn't it?"

I nod through the tears in feigned agreement.

"Keep your hand there. Two more questions."

The knife is placed between the ring and pinky finger of my mangled left hand.

"Are you going to be nice to it?"

"Yes," I say, nodding softly.

"Good. Last question. Are you going to tell?"

"No, no, no, never," I whisper while shaking my head vigorously.

He whispers in my right ear, "I believe you, but it doesn't matter anyway. No one here cares. I just wanted to hear you say it."

Doctor Proffit gently runs the tip of his tongue along the back edge of my right earlobe.

Again, he grabs my throat violently with both hands. This time the back of my head is slammed into the wall over and over. Doctor Proffit lets go and rises to his feet. I slump over on my right side. I watch as he stands over me. I'm immobilized by the loss of blood and head injuries.

First, he removes his Coke bottle glasses and stuffs them in his front left pants' pocket. Then off comes his red flannel shirt. Daisy's blood was still faintly visible against the camouflaging sanguine background. A yellow-stained white t-shirt was removed and thrown out of sight. Boots are slipped away, followed by pants. Finally, he slides his worn tighty whities down slowly, almost as if he thinks this is titillating for me.

His penis is half-erect and partially absorbed into a bulbous gut, the scrotum hangs loose and low. What stands out most to my blurry vision are the brown shit streaks contrasting with the white of his underwear.

I wait to be pounced on and sodomized. He wouldn't want to get me pregnant, then another fuck-toy would have to be thrown onto the rubbish pile before it's used up. I know they will eventually kill us. I just don't know when. Perhaps I'll die tonight. At this point, being dead sounds like a relief. It's how I'll get dead that worries me.

My hair is seized and I find myself looking at the ceiling, my back on the floor. I'm not able to get my bearings prior to having Doctor Proffit's penis dangled inches from my face. It's stained with Daisy's dried vaginal blood. He must have raped her right before she was murdered. She escaped before he could finish. She is dead and useless now. He just wants to cum in someone, and I'm convenient.

His hands go under my neck at the base of my skull and tilts my head backward.

"Open your mouth."

So I do. I have no choice. With that, the head of his penis is gradually placed through my chapped lips. I gag. I can taste the copper flavor of the dead girl's blood and smell Doctor Proffit's unwashed asshole. My head stays tilted back. His scrotum rests on my nose and eyes. His thumbs are pressed lightly on my throat, just below my jawbone.

"Relax, it will make it better for both of us."

I labor to inhale with a nose full of snot while choking as the head of Doctor Proffit's penis rests on my uvula. It's gradually pushed through, into my esophagus, despite my choking and muted screams.

"Cry more. The humming of your voice box feels so good."

I can't breathe. I desperately gag for air as Doctor Proffit inquisitively feels around with his thumbs under my mandible.

"I want to feel it through your skin. Oh, there we go. He presses lightly and massages his own penis through the skin of my throat. Gradually, it's pulled back but remains between my teeth. I consider biting down hard. I begin putting pressure on it. Then he lays the knife blade across my throat.

"If you bite, I will slice open your throat and watch my dick go in and out of the hole while you bleed out. Do you understand?"

I mumble, "uh-huh".

"That's some fine talking. Now sing *Amazing Grace*."

"Amming mmaccee ow wuueet d ound"

"Excellent. You're being such a good girl. Don't stop."

He then jams his penis into my throat again. It goes in and out further until his scrotum bounces off of my nose. My head grinds into the floor. I struggle to breathe during each pull-out. I don't know how long this has been going on. The rhythmic banging lulls me into the same disengaged place I went while my father beat me unconscious. For a moment, I feel as though I'm watching from afar. Abruptly, it stops and I reintegrate into my consciousness to find him still dangling above me.

"Give me your hand."

I lift my uninjured right hand.

"No, the sinful one."

I don't hesitate. He can take the knife out again at any time. The palm of my nearly bifurcated left hand was turned toward his crotch.

"This is going to hurt."

My middle and ring fingers are pulled apart, pulling the V-shaped incision into a wider opening. I am too tired to make a noise in protest. He wraps the v-wound around the shaft of his penis and squeezes it tightly to form a makeshift vagina, that he proceeds to grind through. At least I can breathe.

"Oh, God I'm close. Open your mouth. It's just like communion. The body of Christ and mine are one. You must partake of him for your forgiveness. The injured palm is placed over my mouth. My middle finger goes to the left side of my nose, the ring finger goes to the right. The v-laceration drips blood into my open mouth, as the mouth-raping begins again in earnest, this time through the gaping wound. His vile, pale, gelatinous legs tremble with bizarre pleasure twice a few seconds apart until I feel warm, salty, viscous fluid, squirting in pulses into the back of my mouth.

"Don't you dare spit out God's gift!" Doctor Proffit screams.

He pulls me up to my knees and kneels in front of me.

"Open, let me see your communion. Don't drop any. Stick your tongue out. Slowly swallow all of it. Say, 'Thank you for the body of Christ.'"

My words are jumbled, but I repeat his repulsive sentence.

"My child, you are forgiven. Now go into the girl's shower room and wash off."

9

My forked left palm is so painful I barely notice the swelling on my head and face, nor the sickening taste of blood, bile, and semen.

"I'm too dizzy to walk," I whisper at the highest register I can muster.

"You'll have to crawl, my child."

I tuck my left palm under my right shoulder and begin walking on my knees. The frigid concrete grinds itself into my knees. I waddle about twenty paces past the bunk beds. Then comes the smooth, clean tile of the shower room. I stop and regain my strength. When I look down, I see something I recognize as my body, stained red from the right armpit to the corresponding knee. Blankly, I look over my shoulder and glimpse what appears to be a bloody snake trail with round bulbous impressions where my right knee left its mark like a thumbprint.

I slide my way into the communal shower. I disrobe and start the water. I try to get as much blood from my face and scalp as I can without soap or hot water. There's no towel. My hair, which I am forced to grow long, is still wet and lays like thousands of ice strands down my neck.

I try to rise to my feet. Two attempts fail, but on the third, I'm able to get up. I walk slowly back to the bunkroom of the dorm. I see Doctor Proffit down on his knees praying, not for forgiveness, no. He's praying in tongues. It sounds like garbled horseshit.

Dripping wet, and still bleeding, I am able to dress, carefully and methodically, with one hand. I don't bother putting my left hand through my shirt sleeve, opting to keep it tucked under my right arm, inside my shirt. I can't tie my shoes. They'll have to flop around, loose on my feet.

"Let's go, Naomi."

That's the first time Doctor Proffit has ever called me by real name. I think he believes we are now somehow closer. I never want to hear my name come out of his mouth again. I intentionally slow down to illicit a response.

"Girl, I said move!"

'Much better,' I think to myself.

"Faster, girl."

I make it through the front door of the dorm and to the car.

"In, girl," Doctor Proffit says as he points to the rear driver's side door.

I open the door and take a seat next to Charles. He's never been good with unspoken cues, but he knows I've been raped as soon as he sees me. The facial expressions of repulsion and shame following being raped are unlike any other. Charles is personally familiar with that disengaged state. He visits it often himself. Contained within is a metallic flavored dialogue of doubt and self-blame. 'What did I do wrong?' plays on repeat inside that part of my mind.

His long stare at me lets me know he now realizes why I acted the way I did towards him. Shortly after pulling onto the school's dirt road, Doctor Proffit has to slam on the brakes to avoid hitting a large buck running across the road from the river side, toward the barren garden. A loud thud and the feeling of having the seat kicked reminds us that Daisy's body is right behind us.

In a few minutes, we arrive at the Proffits' house. He pulls the car into the garage and initiates the garage door to shut. We wait for Doctor Proffit's command to exit the vehicle.

He addresses both of us. "You two little bastards have sentenced yourselves to work together for a very long time. I will not have any discord in my house. You will learn to get along. Do you understand?

"Yes, sir," we echo.

"Get out Charles, tell Patty to call Maddie, shower, then go to bed."

As Charles disappears into the house, Doctor Proffit says, "Let's go, we need to drive the truck. It hasn't been driven in a while."

I know well why we aren't driving the car. There's a dead girl in the trunk.

I cringe as we drive over the bloody spot where Daisy lay just an hour ago.

We arrive at a house I am familiar with, Maddie Bellew's. I'm too weak to be afraid. I know she may kill me. And I don't care. I long for release from this existence. But my concern is Charles. What will become of him? There's nothing I can do to stop what is happening to us. However, if I continue to live, he won't have to suffer alone.

Just as before, Maddie is waiting on the porch backlit by a bare bulb.

"Let me see it, child.", Maddie demands.

Slowly I pull my hand out from under my right armpit, catching the lacerations a few times on the fabric.

"Oh my, the Devil's hand. I see, Pastor. Is she finished?"

"Yes, she has taken her communion."

Looking at me, Maddie says, "You know where my operating room is. Head on back and lay down."

Upon reaching the chair, I give out. I get lost in that distant part of me again. I come to staring at that vile sadist, Maddie Bellew, as she fumbles over my hand.

"Oh, you're awake. It's going to take some time to fix this."

Maddie walks away momentarily. She comes back with a bottle that says ether on it and an old rag. Maddie spills a little on the rag, closes the bottle. She presses it against my face. I lose all sense of time as it loops and brings forth skipping imagery I can see with my eyes open or shut. I don't have a choice now. My eyes begin to close.

When my eyes open, I'm lying face up looking at a bright, clear sky, illuminating the lush, comfortable grass underneath me. I turn my head to the right and see a dense forest. To the left are rolling hills. There are no houses or roads. I look up and scan the sky for jet contrails. None. Strange. There are no lacerations, no pain, only peace. I'm dead.

I feel someone behind me. They kneel behind my head and begin to speak. It's a soft, familiar voice.

"Naomi, don't be afraid, it's Tiffany.

Her face dangles over mine. Gorgeous, long red hair tickles my nose.

"I've missed you. You know I love you," she says.

"Yes, I've always known."

"There is something I need you to do."

"What?"

"Kill him." She repeats it louder, "Kill him, Naomi!"

Her disembodied face begins to drift into the sky as I hear what sounds like a stampede of feet heading my way through the forest. It grows louder, drowning out Tiffany, whose face is floating further away.

I sit up to see a group of a dozen or more mature chimps charging towards me. In front is a two-hundred-pound alpha-male with canines exposed. They're already on top of me. The dominant chimp's mouth comes directly for my face. I close my eyes and put my hands and scream in a pitiful attempt to scare them away. The chimps pass through me like a hologram. They became silent and translucent, now frozen in time.

They're gone now, and all that remains is a cold, dark room.

I realize I'm back on Maddie's operating table. My battered body is too numb and tired to move. I sense something wet. I'm sitting in a puddle of warm urine. In my humiliation, all I can hear is Tiffany's voice repeating, "kill him, kill him, Naomi, kill him!"

10

The initial shock and fear that I feel waking up on Maddie's table, covered in urine, soon gives way to an emotion I thought I knew but hadn't truly met until now. It's pure rage firing through every synapse of my brain. It burns heavily across my chest and boils when it reaches my bowels.

My left hand is completely covered by a cast. I sit up and slide my feet off the left side of the urine-soaked surgical chair. I pull the cast to my chest and attempt to stand. I'm still under the influence of the ether, causing my legs to collapse beneath me. I barely catch myself with my right hand, which softens the fall. I continue to roll to the right and onto the floor. Now on my back, I can see that it's dawn. The light begins to show under the door crease and around the edges of the poorly hung blackout curtains. I observe the sliver of light grow slowly. Listlessly, I enjoy this small moment as I watch light waves from the oldest dancer in our solar system put on its regular performance. I think about all the unlimited spaces in the universe where my body could exist. I feel momentary solace knowing all of those spaces still exist somewhere. I place myself in all of them, an eternity in a brief pause. This ends and I hear footsteps heading for the door. It's Charles. His expressionless face is swollen where I slapped him earlier.

Behind him, I hear Doctor Proffit order, "get her up now Charles, the girl is your ward until she heals up enough to go back to work." Charles turns around and glances at him. "Don't look at me, boy. You're the reason she's hurt. Suits the both of you to be condemned to one another's company."

Charles lifts me up to a seated position, then to my feet with his support. When Doctor Proffit is out of sight, Charles turns to me and gives an overstated wink with his left eye to let me know he knew why I slapped him.

"Okay Charles, I got it, stop doing that."

His face goes back to its normal state. When Charles uses facial expressions, it's as though he has memorized them and plays them back with the volume up too loud.

I lean on his left shoulder as he supports the bulk of my weight. Our walk to the car is rushed to the point Charles has to drag me a few steps. I am laid down in the back seat. Charles sits up front, most likely for the first time. We drive the sickeningly twisty way home. I am put to bed. I sleep the rest of the day away in a dreamless state.

When I wake, I am utterly catatonic. Sounds buzz like warbles mixed into an unending stream of faint white noise. This is the extent of my awareness now.

My mind works, but I can't perceive the world in any meaningful way. It reminds me of the stories I've read about how Voodoo priests created 'zombies'. They would use the dried organs of pufferfish, which contains neurotoxins that cause the imbiber's nerves to tingle and become numb. Cardiovascular function and respiration slow, giving the victim the appearance of being dead.

The body is buried, only to be dug up later that night. The person is awoken from the coffin and prodded back to the practitioner's house. The 'zombie' then becomes a servant, drugged up and drifting through existence.

That is me now, following the rape. I eat, shower, and go to the bathroom. I know Charles is here, as I feel someone guiding. I can feel his otherness out there, which makes me feel safe and not completely alone.

Around Easter, the haze begins to recede. One day, I become aware I am sitting on the couch next to Charles. I look over to see him reading his Bible.

In a shaky weak voice I say, "what the fuck just happened, Charles?"

"Don't say that, it's profanity!"

Charles has a lot of contempt for himself. He knows the church is full of shit, but he doesn't put down his faith. It has become apparent to me that Charles is likely autistic, like *Rain Man*, but less severe. It's drawn him into a dissonant vacuum. Take the cursing, for example. Charles can be rigid. His peculiar demeanor has added to the reasons society feels obliged to reject him. Charles's inability to feign stereotypical masculinity perpetuates the perception that he is gay. In truth, Charles is asexual. He finds touching others extremely uncomfortable. But, if someone could be non-sexual, but still considered gay, doesn't that mean it's an innate berth of his being and not based on a specific action? How cold simply existing be an 'abomination'?

I hold my left arm out in front of myself. The cast has been removed at some point. I can't remember how or when. My palm is very heavily scarred and weak, but it's fully functional.

I turn back to see a surprised Charles.

He whispers, "where have you been?"

"I don't know. Somewhere gray. It wasn't completely dark and silent, but it wasn't an awakened state. I felt trapped inside the color gray itself. Flashes of static bounced around the background. My mind itself was somewhat coherent but shielded from the outside. But I could feel you there, regardless."

"That's okay," Charles says.

After a long silence, I begin to cry. Charles reaches for the tissue box on the side table and places it between us. Within a few minutes, the tears run their course.

"Charles, we have to leave before they kill us."

"How?"

"I don't know. I just know we have to. You can't let them know that I've come to."

"They seem pleased with the state of things. It's the happiest I've seen them in a while. They have the sympathy of the church for taking care of us, especially since you supposedly fell and hit your head while cleaning the girl's dormitory. Kind of like how I fell and broke my collarbone while out hiking."

"No shit," I say rhetorically.

"Again, with the cursing."

"I love you Charles, but you're going to have to get the fuck over it."

I feel bad for lashing out at Charles. I wink at him, and he does his super obvious wink back.

"How about every time I make a joke, I'll wink to make sure

you know," I say.

He shakes his head in agreement while responding with "Okay."

"One thing, Charles, you don't have to wink back."

"We sit in silence for about an hour before we hear the Buick pull up. It's six o'clock but Patty orders Charles to get me ready for bed then go himself.

Charles walks me out of the bathroom once I'm showered. He then returns for his. I hear Doctor Proffit comment to him after he exits the bathroom following his own shower.

"I know you're hungry, but you can deal with it. I'll let you have a big breakfast. I know how you like to eat, piggy."

I lie in bed staring at the popcorn ceiling. I map the stars in my head that I can remember and transpose them in my mind across the little white bumps. I imagine I'm back with Tiffany watching the Perseids.

Through the wall, I hear a rap at the front door. It is Sheriff Morton, also a deacon at Solid Rock. I don't hear the sounds of dinner being served, just a conversation.

The Sheriff begins, "we got to talk about the girl. Her grandmother has been absent from church for months, and there's a lot of talk about her looking for a place outside Yancey County. She won't talk now, but if she leave, old Mrs. Chambers might cause us problems."

"What do you suggest, Sheriff?" I hear Doctor Proffit ask.

"I think I might go have a word with her. There's no need for anything else at the moment. I plan on it being mighty easy due to her age. I'm sure that's all the convincing she'll need. She's been grievin' hard. Maybe she's forgotten about fulfilling the prophecies.

"Maybe. I'll go with you to make sure."

"Whatever you want, Pastor."

They exit out the back. They must be taking the police cruiser because I don't hear the garage door open. Sleep comes, and with it, my first return to darkness since my awakening hours before.

11

At 4:30 the next morning, I hear the general waking commotion. I dare not move. Plates clink, water runs, toilets flush. Before long I hear Patty stick her head into Charles's room

"We're done. Get her up before she soils the bed again."

While in the gray, it seems I was able to hold my pee, but only for a little while. That explains why my mattress smells like old urine. I hear the garage door shut.

"They're gone," Charles says.

"Thank you for what you've done for me all these months, Charles. I only have two friends in this world. You're one of them."

"No one has ever called me their friend before. That's good. It's good to have friends."

In Charles-speak, that translates to, "You're my best friend."

Charles microwaves instant grits and mixes in deer sausage. There is a freezer in the garage packed with venison. Yet another donation from the flock.

Our days go on like this, seven days a week into the summer. Even on Sundays, we stay in because of my assumed pervasive catatonic state.

Not long after coming to, I ask Charles about the youth minister.

"I'm not supposed to talk about that," Charles replies, as though it's a practiced line fed to him by an invisible person. Silence, as usual, follows.

An hour later, Charles turns to me and says, "Brad Kershaw." Firmly.

"Who is Brad Kershaw?"

"He's the youth pastor you asked about," Charles says softly, as though he has done something wrong.

Charles continues, "That's the man who had sex with me. Because of it, I've been here for about a year and a half. I arrived on either November first or second, nineteen ninety-two. I don't remember because it was dark when I arrived."

"Our church always has a fall festival on Halloween. This involves setting up booths in the Family Life Center. That's what churches call their gyms so it sounds more tithe-worthy. It's billed as an alternative to the demonic holiday. Our parents could rest assured the apples weren't filled with razor blades or that their child won't be sacrificed on some devil-worshipping metal head's altar."

"Like any active youth member of our church, I was expected to help out in some way. Mr. Brad is not only the youth minister, he's the pastor's son. He was twenty-three at the time and had recently retired after playing two years of minor league baseball. Brad is a hero figure at our church. He bears the visage of a Nazi youth, six feet tall, with blond hair and blue eyes."

Charles sighs.

"Let's just say, he's never been referred to as unattractive."

"Brad played for four years at Liberty University, where he

earned a bachelor's degree in youth ministry. His short professional career was nothing of note. He was shuffled around between teams on the Carolina League. That kind of pedigree and resume can get you a long way in the small-town church hierarchy."

"I know exactly what you mean," I say.

"Yeah, it's nothing more than a high school cliche, isn't it? Brad married the previous summer to a girl he met in college. That marriage fell apart in less than a year. However, it's never to be spoken about."

"What happened that Halloween?"

"Brad made sure I was able to help out with the hell house. I'm a decent artist, so I got to paint murals of botched abortions, hellfire, demons, and the like. This meant spending extra time after school during the week preceding the fall festival. That year Halloween fell on a Saturday. From four o'clock to nine o'clock Monday through Thursday, I helped set up decorations. Other youth group members did the same. None of them dare speak to me for fear my curse will rub off on them."

On Friday, I found that no one else had shown up. The Family Life Center's lights were out except for Brad's office. Most of the center is made up of a basketball court, except for along the right-hand wall as you enter. The wall contained a kitchen, to the left when facing it, two restrooms, and Brad's office located in between. As I walked into the dark building, Brad summoned me from his office.

"Come in here, Charles, I want to show you something."

I peeked inside to find Brad at his desk clicking away on an electric typewriter. He reached into the small pull-out drawer under his desk, never taking his eyes off the keyboard. There, he materialized a tattered, coverless magazine. Brad dropped it on the desk and asked, "Why did you have this?"

I knew it wasn't my magazine, so I replied, "That's not mine, Mr. Brad."

"Open it," he demanded, as he drew his attention away from the keyboard.

Inside the magazine, the first picture I saw was of a naked man on top of another.

"I could tell your parents I found this on you. What do you think would happen? Just imagine their embarrassment to have an abomination for a son. It won't matter what you say, no one will believe a little weirdo who walks funny, bouncing on his heels like some kind of girl. You really should be ashamed of yourself, Charles."

My mind seized. I was unable to reconcile what I knew was a lie coming from someone I was supposed to trust. My better instincts got a hold of me after about ten seconds. Those instincts told me to back away slowly, which I began to do. Brad Kershaw was very fit from his years playing baseball. After my second step backward, Brad leaped out of his chair. He cleared the desk and was on top of me before I could step back a third time. He beat my face so badly I couldn't see through my swollen eyes. I heard the crack of my nose break transmitted through the walls of my skull. Soon, I was trying to hold on and breathe through the darkness. I felt warm blood run from my nose and mouth. At some point, Brad stripped me naked and pinned me over the front of his desk. I felt the cold wood across my naked chest. He raped me. I was already in agonizing pain, and it hurt so much. But screams and cries only made him laugh during the act. He said, "stop pretending to cry. I know you like it, girly-boy."

Just as he finished having his way with my body, I heard him address someone standing in the doorway. It was old Pastor Kershaw.

Pastor Kershaw sobbed, "Oh no, Brad, not again."

I heard the clink of Brad's belt and felt the stickiness of our sweaty skin being pulled apart. Brad yanked up his pants to face his dad.

"Son, why? We've prayed so hard for you." There was a momentary pause before Pastor Kershaw screamed, "it's him isn't it, Brad? Why does the devil always send these homosexual sirens to temp your resolve?"

Crying, Brad replied, "I tried to fend his temptation off. See how I beat him? This little reprobate used Satan to tempt me. I fought him off, but I was unable to resist. Daddy, please forgive me!"

"It's not my forgiveness you need to seek."

Brad continued to cry, "I know, I know, but I can't. You have to get rid of him. That boy cannot be around while I heal. Charles Laboda has satanic powers."

I remember feeling myself being lifted, then the occasional sounds of the road. When my swollen eye slits opened, I caught my first glimpse of Maddie Bellew. It was the Monday following Halloween. Maddie didn't talk to me, and I wasn't there but a few minutes after waking up. She treated my wounds and reset my nose. The next voice I heard was Doctor Proffit shouting, "Get up now, boy!"

Stumbling, I followed his shadow to the car. He opened the back door and I lay on my back across the seat to avoid hitting my nose.

From that day until now, I've been Doctor Proffit's go-get-boy. I fetch for him and do as he demands. Since I've been here, he has never done to me what he did to you, but Brent Shoals, the deacon, has; twice, in fact. Even though I didn't receive a beating from Brent, it hurt all the same. Both of the times he raped me, I was doing exactly what you were. I was cleaning the boys' shower room.

No one cared to ask where the bruises on my arms in the shape of fingers came from or why I walked funny. I was in excruciating pain from the tears in my rectum. For days after, I wadded up toilet paper and stuffed it between my cheeks to absorb the blood."

"I'm going to kill him," I respond to Charles. One day I will engulf his life in suffering. He will become it."

12

"We need to escape. We need guns," I say to Charles.

"Is it really necessary that we acquire firearms?" Charles states in a soft, monotone voice. Charles could be that way sometimes, becoming a detached-hyperlexic when stressed.

"Very much so. Are you going to ask for forgiveness when Vernon catches up with us? Look me in the eye, even if it's uncomfortable. If they catch us, they will kill us. It will not be a quick death, either. I assure you of this, Charles. Doctor Proffit almost seemed sad the night Patty shot Daisy, not because Daisy died, but because he didn't get to finish raping her. Solid Rock has a firing range. They have to store their guns somewhere.

"The student guns are locked in the stone cellar under the church. I've been down there. They have eight old .38 service revolvers, six .22 rifles, and four double-barrel twelve-gauge shotguns; three side-by-side and one over-and-under."

"What else is down there?" I reply, knowing Charles would have a detailed manifest of the basement in his memory.

"Five boxes of clay pigeons, a machine that pitches clay pigeons, a twelve-volt deep-cycle battery to power it, twenty-three boxes of twelve-gauge birdshot, ten boxes of 500 count .22 caliber full-metal-jacket rifle rounds, twenty-three boxes of 50 count .38 hollow-point rounds, twelve rucksacks, two-hundred and three MREs, a fire extinguisher, broom, dustpan, a stack of black silhouette targets and a first aid kit. It's locked up tight behind a custom-made door constructed of three-quarter-inch plate steel. The only people who have keys are Doctor Proffit, Sheriff Morton, and Brent Shoals. Even if you could magically steal Doctor Proffit's keys, which you can't, you'd still have to get out of the house undetected. Then you'd have to run the half-a-mile there, then run back loaded with supplies. It's impossible. However, when I was home mending from my broken collarbone, I overheard Doctor Proffit and Brent Shoals discussing purchasing thirty-round magazines. I found it odd because those don't fit any of the guns located in the church's basement. There was a pause in the conversation. Then I heard Brent read aloud a sequence of numbers. It sounded as though he were reciting it for a teacher. Then there was a click and the sound of a large metal door opening. The only explanation I can deduce is that there is a very large safe in their bedroom. The point being, why go further than you have to? It's likely that all the guns and supplies we need are right through that wall. I remember the combination."

A moment later, we hear the garage door open. An air of catatonia washes over me.

In walks Brent Shoals. In my fugue, I'm not aware of the 'when', just the 'is' of existence. My mind ignites with an explosion of electricity. I realize it is the first Monday of Easter break. Brent taught music during the week and spent the weekends helping prepare for Sunday service. He's got an empty schedule and open space in his brain to dwell on his repressed desires.

Brent is visibly shaking and jittery. He walks past me and stands in front of Charles, who is seated to my left on the couch.

Brent stutters, "Get up. The boys' shower room needs to be cleaned right now."

Charles stands and points his gaze down to his dirty old sneakers. With shoulders slumped, he begins to shuffle off to a methodically orchestrated rape fantasy come to life for a man who teachers the word of Christ five days a week, then sings his glory on Sundays.

In an unplanned natural instinct, I stand up and put myself between them and the door. I've grown two inches in the last eight months and am now six feet tall. And I've been working out, doing push-ups, and jumping jacks while the Proffits are gone. I raise my left hand and punch Brent across his forehead in a downward motion, grazing his brow and the bridge of his nose. Brent slumps forward and covers his now bleeding nose. He stumbles back onto the floor. Brent seems like an overturned turtle, with his white stomach exposed for the hawks to see.

I leap forward and onto him, driving my right knee directly into Brent's chest. All the air is pressed out of his lungs. He struggles to breathe. As Brent squirms, I slide my knee up further pinning him to the floor. I feel my kneecap grind against Brent's Adam's apple. Bone on bone. I am in control for the first time in my life. Now, what began as a defensive action becomes a slow, deliberate execution. His hands flap, willowy, and light at my face. Brent's mouth gapes open, and I begin to see his eyes glaze over.

Charles cries out, "Please Naomi, don't kill him."

I ease away from Brent's unconscious body and take a deep breath.

"He's alive. Are you happy, Charles? Do you think he'd extend us the same courtesy?"

"No he wouldn't, but we are better than him."

"They're going to kill us. That's what's next, Charles. Unless we make the choice to do something about it. We need to open the safe, arm ourselves, and make a run for it."

"Where should we go?"

"The woods. That's our only option. We tie Brent's arms around the base of the toilet, gag him, open the safe, and arm ourselves."

"Guns! Are you serious?" Charles says, his voice getting louder and higher in pitch.

"Yes!"

Charles is a tame city boy. I, on the other hand, have had a gun of some sort in my hand since I was six. Out there, it's just a part of life. Bullets bring food to the table.

I stand and grab Charles by the hand. "They'll never hurt you again. I won't let them."

Charles's gaze is still at his shoes. His face drifts upward and he looks me in the eye for the first time voluntarily and replies, "okay."

"It's one o'clock. We should have till about four before Patty comes home to start dinner," I assure Charles. "You're good with this kind of stuff. How do we get into their bedroom?"

Charles thinks for a minute.

"The weakest point of a door is next to the handle. You're big enough to kick it down, but you'll risk injury. I say we go get Doctor Proffit's large toolbox from the garage and use it as a battering ram by swinging it at the doorknob. The momentum and weight will provide you with a greater mechanical advantage with less risk of injury."

We leave Brent unconscious on the floor, in the middle of the living room. As we go through the door from the house to the garage, I look to my left and pick up Patty's cane with my now scarred left hand.

"What are you going to do with that?" Charles asks.

"I'm going to beat her to fucking death with it."

"No, no, you are not going to do that. I told you, we are better than them."

"No Charles, you are better. I just want to watch them all die."

"That's not very Christ-like is it, Naomi?"

"Fuck Christ's opinion! I don't see him here to kick the door down and save us, do you?"

In the corner lies the toolbox. It is right on top of the work table. Convenient. I grab it and run as fast as I can toward the door. I drop the cane in the hallway. Holding the heavily laden toolbox with both hands, I slam it into the doorknob, knocking the door open on the first try. Their bedroom is a room like any other. I kind of expected Moses's tabernacle after all the forbidding of entrance upon pain of the rod. The furniture is typically shabby, like the rest of the house, except for the giant armoire that sits in the corner, sharing a wall with Charles's room.

"The safe has to be in there. Where else could it fit?", I say.

It's locked.

I swing the toolbox at the crease where the two doors meet. One smack and the wood around the small lock splinters, revealing what looks like metal through the hole it made. Two more whacks and the door swings freely, revealing the mother of all goddamn safes.

"The house must have been built around this damn thing. That's the purpose of the house, Charles. I figure there's something either worth a fuckload of money or an equal fuckload of prison time inside this thing."

Charles doesn't react. He has a stark, distant gaze. He rocks a little while reciting the directions.

"Naomi, you'll have to turn the dial. I don't have the steadiest hands."

Charles's lips move as he closes his eyes.

"Turn the dial four times to the left. After the fourth pass, continue turning until you reach thirty-six. Now, turn it to the right three times. Stop on twelve after the third turn. Then two times to the left and stop on twenty-two. Turn it right once and stop at forty-five."

Once the dial is set to forty-five, I stop and pull my hand away. Suspiciously, I turn the handle. Nothing happens.

"Oh fuck, Charles. It won't open."

"Oh yeah, one last thing. Turn the dial to the left until you reach the nineties. You'll feel a bump. Roll through that bump until it goes slack, then abruptly stops."

There aren't the obligatory safe opening sounds heard in movies, but the handles on the door spin free of the locking mechanism.

"Charles, I'm going to need help opening it."

I huff while pulling the door. It begins moving, millimeter by millimeter. Charles grabs hold of the wheeled handle to my left and we pull together. I gingerly peek in the safe and notice a white light switch on the left, just inside the safe. I switch it on. Fluorescent lights on the ceiling of the safe pop on to provide an ambient glow. There's nothing but iron walls set in a concrete floor, which is about four feet by four feet. The safe is about six and a half feet tall, so I can stand up completely inside of it. In the center of the concrete floor is a manhole cover. Charles notices a tool in the back left corner. It's a galvanized iron rod, about two feet in length. The triangular handle has been formed into one end. The other end of the rod is bent at a right angle. The bit after the bend is roughly three inches in length.

Charles says, "I guess that's how you get the cover off."

I pick up the tool and insert the tag at the end of the right angle into a slot cast in the manhole cover. Charles and I pull together. The cover lifts slightly, only to crash down as our muscles fail us. We try once more with the same result.

"Let's try to lift and pull at the same time," states Charles.

We lift as high as we did before, then shift our weight to the right. The tool is snatched from our hands as the metal disk wobbles around in circles. Eventually, it works its way to the left rear corner of the safe's interior. A custom-made metal ladder welded from angle iron has been encased into the side of the concrete tunnel.

"We need flashlights," Charles states.

"Yeah, what store are we going to drop by to pick some up?"

"Check the bedside table drawers."

I slide open the top drawer on the left-hand side table to reveal an old family Bible and a modern Glock pistol with a large flashlight on the rail. It's a mid-sized nine-millimeter; model nineteen. My father is a survivalist who is obsessed with guns like this but could never afford one himself.

I rack the slide back halfway to check the chamber. There's already a cartridge in it, so I let it slide back into place so as not to eject it. I'm used to shooting small .38 revolvers. The increased number of rounds makes this gun heavier than its polymer body would suggest. I remove the magazine and count the rounds. There are fifteen, plus the one in the chamber, making for a healthy sixteen. There's no backup mag or box of ammo, just a pistol-shaped flashlight. I push a button on the side of the rail light until it clicks. It illuminates the room with a blinding white light. I immediately hit the switch again to turn it off.

"I'll go down first, okay Charles?"

Charles shakes his head slightly to indicate he heard me. I have no pockets in my dress, so I carefully climb down the dark tunnel with the gun in my left hand. I grasp the best I can without shooting my face off. At the bottom, I kneel down and turn on the blinding glow of the rail-mounted light. I'm in the corner of what appears to be a concrete room. The flashlight on the pistol catches the glint of a metal light switch faceplate to my left. When turned on, a series of fluorescent bulbs begin to pop on overhead. Their light is starkly blue, giving the concrete chamber an almost clinical feeling.

These people are even worse than I imagined. They're planning something terrible. The left-hand side of the chamber is lined with dozens of illegal M-16 rifles. On the right, at least twenty sets of hand and leg cuffs dangle from the wall. There are MREs, first aid kits, and flats of plastic water jugs stacked atop one another. All the way on the back side of the room stands a steel door, which is barricaded from whatever is on the other side. A four-by-four acts as a crossbar. I lay the gun on the floor, lift the four-by-four, and place it against the wall. I pick up the gun, pull the door inward, and shine the light beyond it. A natural cave, whose end I cannot see is in front of me. The beam cast by the flashlight sparkles off the silica in the wall, softly dispersing it. I pause to absorb it all. I am beginning to relearn how to be free and to appreciate the beauty of what I am seeing as my own, with no one else's filters. I'll never go back.

13

When I arrive back at the bottom of the ladder, I shout for Charles. There is no reply. A cold surge of fear sweeps through my nervous system. I shoot up the rungs, the gun in my left-hand clinking against the metal every time I take a step. Peeking out of the manhole, I see Charles's back to me. He is frozen, staring at whatever had just entered the doorway. I fumble out of the hole and to my feet. I run toward Charles. Looking over his shoulder, I catch a glimpse of a very bruised and disheveled Brent Shoals.

In his left hand, Brent grasps a fillet knife Doctor Proffit uses for cleaning trout. Brent doesn't speak. He bolts towards us. I step around Charles's right side, lift the Glock in my left hand, and sound off one round, striking Brent in the abdomen. He lands face-first in front of Charles. Moaning, he lifts himself upward after hitting the ground and flails the knife outward, slicing Charles on the inside of his left thigh. Charles screams as I pull him away. He crumples against the wall inside the safe. I didn't act fast enough to keep Charles safe. I promised I would keep him safe.

Brent isn't dead, merely in a lot of pain and paralyzed from the waist down. He squirms on the floor, with the knife bearing

Charles's blood still in his hand.

"Throw the fucking knife away, Brent," I command.

Meekly, he flings the knife about a yard to his right side. I keep the bastard's head in the pistol's sights as I walk toward his shattered body. I stand over him and point the muzzle directly at the back of his head. Brent curls his hands over where the bullet would enter his skull in an impotent attempt to shield himself.

"Brent, tell me where the cavern leads, and I won't kill you."

"Okay," Brent cries, snotting all over the carpet. "It's about two miles long. The only other exit empties out into the woods."

"The woods where?"

"Nowhere."

"There's no such thing as nowhere."

"It leads to an abandoned stone road."

"Is it just the one tunnel, Brent?"

He doesn't respond.

"Well, motherfucker, I guess you've spoken your last words on Earth, then."

I leap into the air and come down crushingly onto Brent's upper right arm. When the bone breaks, it sounds like someone stepping onto a snail, only a hundred times louder. Brent squeals and hyperventilates. Further streams of tears and snot extruded from his face.

I reach for the knife that lies to the right of Brent's now broken arm. Expecting to be stabbed in the back he cringes and raises his left hand, half covering his skull. It's now Brent's only functional appendage. I toss the Glock toward Charles and pull Brent's face off the floor by grasping the hair on the back of his head with my right hand. I use my left to place the sharp edge of the fillet knife against his throat, up toward his chin.

"Tell me how to exit the cave on the other side, or I swear on Daisy's grave I will kill you."

I pause for a second before leaning over and whispering into Brent's ear, "It isn't much effort to drag the knife a little. I could do it now."

I move the blade a few millimeters, turning the infrequent dribbles into a small stream, which steadily drips onto the shitty Berber carpet.

"Now!" I shout, with my mouth directly next to his left ear.

He squeals like a pig at slaughter.

"The tunnel forks off four times."

"How do I get through to the other side, Brent?"

"At the first split, go left. At the second, take a right, then at the third take another right. At the final one, go left."

I let go of Brent's hair, and his right cheekbone smacks against the floor.

"You got that, Charles?" I say, turning my head in his direction. I see Charles sitting with his back against the interior safe wall. Both of his hands are wrapped around his injured thigh.

"It hurts, but I'm not bleeding much."

"Okay," I mouth nervously.

Then comes the most horrifying noise: the garage door. Patty is home.

Brent begins to scream, "Help, Patty!"

I swiftly kick him in the back of the head twice. He shuts up. I'm not sure if I knocked him out or he just didn't want to get kicked again. Patty's footsteps seem frantic now as they ascend the garage stairs.

I hand Charles the gun.

"Stay here."

He nods in agreement.

As I move into the hallway, I peep down to see the cane where I dropped it before. The door opens and Patty sees me. I revel in her appalled expression. Without a sound, she begins to remove her earrings. She places them in her purse, after which she hangs it neatly on the plain wooden rack mounted next to the door. Patty opens the storm door into the garage, and casually reaches her hand around the corner for the bamboo cane. Patty's hand shuffles about. There is nothing. She removes her eyes from me and opens the door fully to scrounge for it. When she glances back, Patty sees what she seeks in my hand. My mind goes cold. My ears ring and words disappear as I charge her, fully intending to beat Patty to death. Unexpectedly, she steps back into the garage and runs out the still open garage door. I don't have time to chase after her and I won't dare leave Charles too long.

I walk back into the bedroom.

"Patty's run away. We need to get as far away from here as we can.

"How?"

"Patty's car. She left it in the garage, alone with her purse, which is where she leaves her keys."

"No, that's what they'll expect. Right now Patty is alerting everyone. Phone calls are being made, men with trucks and guns are coming. They will run us off the road and our best-case scenario is that they execute us on site. In the tunnel, at least we have a head start."

"They'll be waiting for us at the end, Charles."

"Not if the safe is closed. No one but Mr. Shoals knows we've opened it."

"Yeah, but the door weighs a fucking ton.", I shout in nervous aggression.

"Not if we pull together from the inside, then snatch our fingers out of the way right before the door shuts."

"What about our fingers?"

"You can survive without your fingertips but you won't survive if you go out there."

Still bleeding, Charles gets to his feet.

"Naomi, we have to do something with Mr. Shoals.

Holding up the purloined Glock I reply, "I have his ticket to the promised land right here. All I have to do is punch it for him."

"No, that's not what we are going to do."

"Why not!"

"You promised this man his life. I've had to learn the hard way about spotting liars. Mr. Shoals is a blurter. He's out with it to whoever has power over him. Just a minute ago, that was you. He was telling the truth, and I expect you to do the same."

"For some reason, I don't give a shit. He's a rapist asshole who deserves to die! "

"Maybe, but you don't deserve to be a murderer."

"Goddamnit, Charles. Fine. What do you think we should do?"

"Help me drag Mr. Shoals into the safe. I'll take his left leg, you take the right."

Brent isn't a heavy man, despite being pudgy. He is short. It only takes two good, shared tugs to get his ass over the ledge of the safe. Once at the manhole, we slide his feet in and lift him into a seated position. Then we let gravity do the work for us and push him down the hole. Luckily for Brent, he didn't hit his head on the way down. His fall was broken by his now vestigial legs.

Charles's line of sight whips toward the window. He hears a sound I do not.

"Patty's back and she has someone with her."

"Who?"

"It's Sheriff Morton. I can hear the radio on his belt. You might win a shootout, but he's the first of many to follow. We have to go down the shaft."

Standing inside the open safe, we position ourselves to pull the door shut. Charles squats below my longer reach. We curl our fingers around the safe door and begin to pull. It moves slowly at first, then we gain momentum. At this moment, Charles and I step into the safe and move our fingers out of the way just in time. Charles lets go right before I do and tumbles backward. I watch my fingers slide through the crack with no more than a millimeter left to spare. The door whooshes shut as I land ass first onto Charles.

We hear the muffled sound of Alton screaming, "Sheriff's department!"

I descend the ladder first. Charles's blood drips down onto me from his wounded leg.

When both our feet are on the concrete, we get a good look at Brent. His face is almost unrecognizable. His nose is flattened, eyes swollen shut from the impact, but somehow, even with a nine-millimeter round through his gut, Brent is still alive.

"Come on, we have to put Mr. Shoals on his side at least," commands Charles.

"Okay, if you're sure we have time."

"I'm certain. I may not be well versed at picking up on some things during conversations, but I analyze interactions in my mind. Given enough time around a person, I get an idea of how they will respond to certain situations. It allows me to avoid beatings.

"How do you know they won't check the safe?"

"I've spent the last two years allowing them to believe I'm a moron. And they think you to be inherently incapable because you're a girl. They'll scour the woods for hours before even considering this possibility."

"Let's get this fucker on his side, then," I say.

When we kneel down, one on each side of Brent. I notice how much blood is dripping from the cuff of Charles's left pant leg. His jeans are dark. In the rush, I hadn't realized how badly he had been injured. Charles said nothing. He is more worried about this son of a bitch than himself.

The two of us extend Brent out and lay him on his right side the best we can.

"Brent will be lucky to make it, but it's not your fault," I assure Charles.

"I know you're right, but I can't help but feel guilty."

"That's why you're a better person than the rest of us. But, you need to let me look at your leg."

"Later. We need to head out."

I pick up an empty OD green rucksack off one of the shelves and stuff in as many MREs as I can, along with a first aid kit, and hand it to Charles.

"Are you going to take one of those things?" Charles asks, pointing at the M-16s.

"Why shouldn't I?"

"Because I know you."

I half-laugh while my eyes become transfixed on these equalizing weapons. I don't know if I'm laughing because Charles is right or because there is only one path for me now, and he knew it before I did.

"I won't go with you if you do. I'll stay here with Mr. Shoals and wait for whatever comes."

"Are you serious?"

"Am I not always?" Charles replies.

"But, why?"

"Take the pistol for self-defense, but those weapons are for one thing, killing many people quickly and efficiently. I know you'll do just that given the opportunity."

"What in the hell are these crazy fucks doing?" I ask aloud.

"I suppose preparing for some kind of war, whether it's real or imagined, I can't be sure."

"It's real enough to them."

I grab a second rucksack and begin to stuff it equally with MREs and another first aid kit. Embossed on the exterior of each of the ammo crates are the words, "5.56mm, 50,000 cartridges."

"No nine-millimeter rounds," I say, pointing to the crate.

"Sixteen rounds," Charles whispers, as though he is talking to someone not there.

"What?"

"You have sixteen rounds in the pistol. More importantly, what's on the other side of that doorway?"

I shine the light into the cavern. The beam illuminates a glistening tunnel of white stalactites. The cavern has a well-trod path. A small clear stream, no more than two feet deep, runs down its left side. After we both pass through the doorway, I turn back and catch a glimpse of the blood trail Charles is leaving behind.

Charles hobbles as he walks behind me. In my peripheral vision, I catch the sight of him dropping to his knees. I turn, only to see him continue to fall face first. Charles's flesh emits a sickening thud as the right side of his skull percusses against the rock floor. I scream louder than I ever have in my life. I run to Charles, dropping to my knees at his side. His eyes are open, but still and lifeless. There is a sighing noise as the last breath Charles will ever take exits his corpse. It gives his body a brief reanimated quality. But Charles is gone.

14

The shrillness of my scream resonates down the cavern and echoes into countless disembodied shrieks. As the final reverberation rings in my ears, tears begin to stream down my cheeks. Unfortunately, this alerts the posse to my location. I hear them growing closer. Then the footsteps are in the concrete room behind me. Quickly, I cover the light mounted to the rail of the Glock with the palm of my right hand. My left pointer finger instinctively finds its place beside the trigger thanks to my father's training. I slide backward on my rear. I sit with my back against the left corner where the cave meets the bunker wall. When the door is completely opened, it creates a triangular cubby hole for me between it and the cave wall. Holding my breath, I watch through the crease between the wall and door as the darkness is shooed away by the glimmer of a flashlight. I hear Doctor Proffit's penny loafers click as he walks through the entryway. They stop briefly as he observes Charles's body on the ground. I hold back tears of rage and begin to pray. I ask God to keep me hidden and safe.

'Dear God, let him keep going. Allow me to stay hidden.'

He begins walking further into the cave. After about a dozen slow steps, I hear the footsteps halt and turn back.

The gleam of a black Maglight shines on the floor right in front of my hidey hole.

'Fuck you, God,', I think to myself.

The door is jerked back with forceful anger. I release my right hand from the Glock's mounted light. We both blind one another with competing beams. My ears ring as I fire the pistol. There is a metallic explosion as the round enters the lens of the Maglight Doctor Proffit is holding above his right shoulder, level with his line of sight. The resulting shrapnel sprays across his face. I see Doctor Proffit fall backward. He's on the ground covering his right eye, writhing in pain next to Charles's body. He screams, alerting the others.

I jump up to run away. It's then I feel the toes of Doctor Proffit's right shoe in my shin. I stumble. As I fall, I let go of the pistol to catch myself. I see the light on the Glock in front of me, beaming out into the cave. I pull my knees up, dive forward and grasp the composite grip with my right hand. Just then, my pack is grabbed up from the floor with me still attached. I try to free myself from the rucksack. My left arm breaks free first. As my right begins to slide out, Doctor Proffit pulls the shoulder strap into a tight loop around my wrist. I panic and try to pull away but realize I can't get my hand free without dropping the gun. I pull the trigger instead.

Blood and fragments of Doctor Proffit's left femur pelt the wall. Twice in a row, I have dealt the Prophet real pain. His screams blister the cavern. With my wrist released, I tumble away and land on my back. In the process, I smack my head against the cavern floor. In pain, I turn my head left to find I am lying next to

Charles's body. The two of us are face to face for the final time. I tilt my head up to see Sheriff Morton fumbling down the ladder. Before his wobbly feet touch down, I'm off. As I run, the light from the gun shows my way, as it bobbles up and down across the crystalline structures. Realizing what happened, Sheriff Morton fires off two rounds in quick succession. Luckily for me, his shots are wildly off. The cave meanders to the left, which puts me out of the Sheriff's direct line of sight.

I run across the slick rock with purpose. Gyroscopically, I glide until my side begins to ache. I bend over and wheeze for oxygen.

I stay hunched over for about a minute when a presence became apparent behind me. Out of the darkness it sweeps around and grabs my right wrist, pulling me forward. This new pilot rights my flailing trajectory. Instead of going left at the first split, we travel a new course through the tunnel to our right for a couple of minutes.

The light temporarily illuminates the figure with each stride. In the brief flashes I get, I can tell that it is intimidating in size. It's at least seven feet tall and appears to be covered in black fur. The hand grasping mine seems almost human, but not exactly. I can tell that its strength is far greater than any person's.

It stops and turns toward the distant, heavy, fast noise clambering in our direction. When it seems as though Sheriff Morton has reached the entrance of our divergent shaft, he again begins to sound distant. Did he go left instead?

Charles was right about Brent. He's a weak man. After the threat passes, I realize our new path saved us, not because Charles was wrong about Brent's honesty, but because he understood Brent's character. Doctor Proffit knew, as soon as he saw Brent lying there, that he had told us everything. Sheriff Morton was just following Doctor Proffit's direction.

The creature releases my right hand. I place my right hand on the rail-mounted flashlight attached to the Glock and press the two disengagement buttons. I slide the light off and point it toward the creature. I don't want to point the pistol at it. For some reason, I have no natural fear of it, just curiosity. It leans down and looks me in the eye. Their eyes are golden but shaped like a human's eyes. It appears almost chimpanzee-like. The face is thinner and longer than a chimp, and the chin more pronounced. Besides the face, the rest of its body is covered in black fur.

It doesn't speak. But I can feel its intent. My mind fills in the thoughts. Somehow, I know her name is Mara and she means me no harm. Despite having no secondary sex characteristics, it projects itself as adamantly female in my mind.

We wait for the ruckus of people following behind the Sheriff to fade. After ten minutes, there is silence. I know a posse will be waiting for me at the exit of the cave to unload a bevy of bullets and buckshot into my torso. In no rush to meet my inevitable fate of death by firing squad, I continue walking down the wrong cavern. Mara falls in line behind me and follows quietly. After five minutes of walking, the cavern becomes progressively narrower until it's no more than a yard wide. What else am I going to do? I keep going. I'm in shock. The implausibility of Mara's presence is muted by the terror of Solid Rock's henchmen. The cavern reaches a dead end. All that remains is a rock wall ahead of us. Water from a stalactite drips down, which creates a puddle that takes up the last few yards of the tunnel.

'I suppose I won't die of thirst,' I think.

As I step closer to the puddle, I run the light up and down the walls, looking in vain for a non-existent way out. Pointing the light down at the puddle illuminates its bluish-clear water, the beam doesn't stop. It shines like a white path into a translucent, inland abyss of freshwater. Confused, I kneel down to peer further.

From behind, I feel a push, then the cold shock of the near-freezing spring water. Instinctively, I swim toward the surface. As I panic for breath, I release the pistol and light into the deep. The beam of the flashlight continues to illuminate a path upward. Bleary-eyed, I smack my forehead against the rock ceiling. I reach my hands up and probe the granite above me. I propel myself along as though I were an acrobat walking on my hands across a dark, upside-down floor. I move quicker now, slapping at this rock barrier in an attempt to preserve my life.

Then, my left hand pierces through into an open space. It's a small hole into a pocket of air. I poke my head up into it and take a huge breath of cold fresh oxygen. I grip the edges of the hole and rest. It's small. I slide my arms up further into the pocket. I'm able to get my shoulder through and hold myself up by resting my elbow on the cave floor. Exhausted and afraid, I wait in this position for several minutes. I can't be sure I'm not about to receive a shotgun blast from the dark. After continued silence, I build up the courage to pull myself up. This is also provoked by the numbness creeping up my legs. I push up with my arms and pull my body out of the hole. I curl up into a fetal position and rock back and forth in an attempt to warm and comfort myself. I am alone now and am afraid I will die in this cave. I ponder the pros and cons of death from exposure versus multiple holes bored into my body.

I stand and begin to map out the room. Just behind me is a wall, so I follow it counterclockwise. Nothing but rock, then another puddle. I kneel and place my hand into the water. There is no bottom, which means it probably leads back into the deep underground aquifer. I continue examining the wall with my hands. It curves around. I feel a void in the rock. It's about six feet long horizontally and about two feet vertically. It feels rough like it has been carved.

As I probe around inside, it seems like a human-sized cubby. It's empty.

Above it, I feel another, and above that one, another again. It's three atop one another. I continue to find another empty three, and then finally comes the last three, for a total of nine.

I shuffle my hands around inside bottom cavity of the last three. It's empty; However, the middle one has what feels like a moist leg wrapped in clothing. I run my hand up. I recognize the texture of fabric. As I reach further to the left, I place my hand onto a skull, still wrapped loosely in its remaining, rotting, moist skin. I'm so exhausted with fear that I can't even feel aghast at the discovery. In the top bunk lies a bare skeleton, wrapped in similar clothing. This body seems much dryer and older. In the top two sepulchers, in the center, are bodies that have fairly intact skin. The other five are empty.

It occurs to me there was no way the bodies could have been brought through that tiny hole by large grown men. This means the other puddle leads to an exit. My survey of the dark crypt brings me back to where I had begun, which was next to the circular opening I swam up through. I am freezing, so I strip down to get the cold clothes away from my skin. I drag them with me. I am exhausted, naked, and trembling. I crawl into one of the empty sepulchers. As soon as I lie back, I begin to fall asleep.

I awake gasping for oxygen after hearing Tiff's voice yelling, "Kill him!" Everything goes quiet again. I'm not sure how long I've been asleep. Prolonged darkness is disorienting for the sighted.

I reach over and pick up my still damp clothes, stand, and begin putting them on. The despair and fatigue that set in while I was beginning to drift off has been replaced with a rested sense of righteous indignation. Furious, I hurry on my stupid fucking prairie dress. I am determined to get out.

I guide myself around, still barefoot. As I pass by the last set of body-cubbies, as I think of them, my bare toes feel water. I slip on my shoes and slide my feet into the horrible cold again. This time I find the bottom once I'm shoulder deep. I hold my breath and put my face into the piercingly cold water. After a few feet, I reach my hand into another opening. I peek my head out to find myself outside. In the distance is brilliant starlight set against a moonless canvas framed by the Black Mountain range.

15

When I step out of the water, I find myself on the edge of a paved road. Across the blacktop, I see what appears to be a golf course. In the distance I make out the silhouette of Mara standing quietly on the green, waiting. I don't understand how she got out, nor can I comprehend her existence. But I am so exhausted that I accept this warping of reality. If I were drowning, would I reject the hand of impossibility coming to my rescue because I couldn't comprehend it?

Mara stares back at me like a living shadow and I know I should go to her.

I walk across the quiet road and over a small wooden fence at the edge of the property. On the grass, my shoes squish with each step. I'm not afraid. I am fascinated and transfixed as I draw closer. I stop about two yards from her. Now, she appears as nothing but a dark outline, pitch black, with fuzzy edges, as though she is somehow controlled by the static in the air. I don't need to speak. We are bound together in a way I do not understand.

I follow this shadow across the golf course and head toward the silhouette of the mountains ahead. On the other side, we hop another small fence, then enter into a thick spruce forest. Dodging through trees, we begin to rise in elevation. Drained of energy from my ordeal, I become winded within minutes of trekking up the steep incline. I am wet and cold. I can't go on. My knees buckle and I collapse forward. I lessen the fall with my outstretched palms.

My father, Amos, could best be described as a survivalist. He became obsessed after reading *The Turner Diaries* and delved headlong into the militia movement. Amos trained me to be in a constant state of preparedness for the inevitable, which, to him, was a breakdown of a cohesive society by way of race riots and wars. This, of course, is all bullshit. But the bushcraft skills he taught me are invaluable, regardless of the intent.

I pick myself up and begin to ascend again. Mara doesn't budge. I pass her and keep climbing, not only to survive but to prove myself to this creature. I take no more than five steps before I fall backward toward a patch of sharp rocks. Before I realize I am falling, Mara is there. I feel as though I jump-awakened from a freefall dream, only to land softly in my bed. She picks me up and places me back down where I began to tumble.

Mara disappears into the brush for a few minutes. She returns bearing dried pine straw, kindling, and a shoulder stacked with dry firewood from a dead locust tree. She intends for me to start a fire. She hands me a flat dry piece of wood, a long straight stick from the same dead locust tree, crispy dry straw, and a small bundle of kindling. I test the kindling by breaking a piece in half. It snaps, making a crackling noise, which faintly mimics the sound of a fire. I think back to the many tutorials my father boringly dragged me through. His forays into insanity involved training periods lasting months. Most were brought on by what he heard on AM radio shows. They sold him fear and unease, then offered solutions that promoted disengagement and hatred.

Mara sits down on the ground in front of me with her legs crossed, waiting.

I poke around the area in search of a sharp rock. I find a small, flat, black stone with an acute point. Right away, I set to work. I put my right foot onto the flat piece of wood to hold it in place while I cut out a notch. Then I sharpen the end of the long stick. I take the dried straw in my hands and crumple it up. I fluff it and pinch a spot in the center to catch an ember. I place the sharpened tip of the long stick into the newly carved notch of the flat board, which is still being held in place by my right foot. I lift my hands at the top of the long stick and place it between my palms. I push down hard while spinning the stick back and forth as though I were rubbing my hands together. As my hands work down close to the bottom of the stick, I return them to the top and repeat the process. Within a few minutes, my hands become shaky and weak. I push as hard as I can each time, unwilling to stop until my hands involuntarily fall away.

The most wonderful sight appears: an orange glow. For a few seconds more, I drill even harder to grow the ember. Acting quickly, I pick up the board and hold the notch over the fluffed-up straw. I give the side of the board a tap with the drill stick. The orange glow falls home into the divot I made for it earlier. Lightly, I close my hands over it and blow slowly. I don't dare squeeze too tight. Smoke begins to billow. I make the mistake of breathing in over the bundle, inhaling a lungful of smoke. Wheezing, I turn away, unable to control my breath. The smoke begins to dwindle. While still coughing, I begin to shake my prize back and forth slowly to continue oxygenating it. The smoke comes back, like a mist at first, then auto-ignition.

I place the baby fire on the ground. I feed it small bits of twigs at first. It grows into a modest little fire in short order. Warming by the amber glow, I still shiver. Mara jumps up again and waltzes off into the woods.

In the distance, I hear wood snapping.

Upon Mara's return, she brings me three branches. Two are of equal length. Both have broken off forks on one end, making them look like two large slingshots. The other pole is as long as I am tall. I jam the single end of one of the shorter branches into the ground, as does Mara, in synchrony with me. Both stand freely now, with their slingshot ends up in the air. Together we place the long stick atop, cradled inside the forks, to create a kind of spit. But it's not over the fire, rather near it.

I strip naked. I am relieved to have the wet clothes away from my skin. I place each garment over the long stick next to the fire to dry.

I begin to worry about the blaze signaling my location. I'm only about two miles from Solid Rock. In early spring, it's not abnormal to see a few campfires along the dark ridges.

After an hour or so, my clothes are completely dry and smell of campfire. After dressing myself, I scatter the fire and stomp out this thing I coddled only a short time ago.

Though I drank plenty of water while down in the caverns, it has been more than a day since I last ate. Despite being weak, I stand and follow Mara as she continues to climb. I make it no more than five minutes before falling to my knees. I can go no further. As I continue to kneel, attempting to will myself forward, I feel warm hands on my back. I am gently lifted up. Mara wraps my arms around her neck and places my legs around her torso. She carries me like an ape would its young. We continue to ascend. As my face lies in this shadow creature, the rhythm of being carried against warmth eventually lulls me to sleep.

When I wake, it's daytime and I am alone. I am lying in the woods, just feet from a dirt road. Before walking out onto it, I check nervously in either direction. All around me: nothing but forest. No cars or houses. The only sounds are of the wind shuffling leaves lightly. Being early spring in the Appalachians, it's a rather damp day. It's the kind of rain that never pours, just dribbles on you. The sun's rays shine through enough to tell me it's about ten o'clock in the morning and that the road runs east to west. From my position on the side of the road, the west is to the left and the east to the right. The path presents a decision that will lead to two different lives. Go east, back towards civilization. I can alert the authorities and eventually go back to my parents. Chances are, they will believe the church's narrative. I will be shamed by my family and Pastor Howell. I may even find myself, prisoner, at Solid Rock again. West leads to high elevation and deeper backcountry. Water will be plentiful, but I'm beginning to weaken. I am strong but lean and sinewy. I have so little body fat that dying of starvation will only take a few weeks.

Even though my freedom is no more than a day old, I cherish it and will never go back for anything.

16

Into the western fog I go. The road is bare of cars or foot traffic as I walk on until the sun is at its highest peak of the day. Not long after noontime, I come across a structure of some kind, hidden in the mist. It sits where the dirt road ascends to the left, into switchbacks.

As I grow closer, it begins to take the shape of a cabin, perhaps forty to fifty years old. As I move toward the wood line bordering this property, what strikes me is the intricate dovetailing at the cabin's corners. Someone with a keen eye built this place and that concerns me. Ducking back into the woods, I begin to formulate a way to bypass the dwelling without being seen. But my stomach begins to growl in protest. I know there has to be food in the cabin. I continue walking through the woods toward it. I stop at the wood line of the property. It's a fairly level lot for the mountains. The cabin sits on the highest point. Behind it is a large garden, and a wooden fence about three feet in height. Outside the fence roam a dozen or so small laying hens. There is a simple red wooden barn, big enough to park two tractors inside. A dirt driveway meets the bend in the road, leading to the house through a well-worn course

There are no cars in the driveway and no movement. I think I might see if one of the doors is unlocked. I know it's risky, but I'm set on getting in and stealing as much food as I can run away with.

Calmly, I begin walking across the yard toward the cabin as if it is mine. I reach the front door and walk up the five wooden stairs. The covered porch is equally as wide as the cabin. I turn the old bronze handle. It's locked. I run down the stairs and head to the back. There I find the backdoor, located up three wooden steps. Clutching the door handle, I grimace as I'm met with another locked door. I turn around, ready to give up when I notice the short wooden fence concealing winter greens: mustards, kale, and cabbage.

It's as though my stomach has taken over my brain. I run toward the gate, fling open the latch, and let myself in. I grab the cabbage closest to me and bite into it like I would an apple. Normally, the idea of doing this isn't necessarily repulsive, but it certainly wouldn't sound pleasant. After a few more nibbles, I look up to see the boots of a man. Worse, he is between me and the gate. I am weak and not sure I can hop the fence. I continue up the boots, which become denim jeans, then a plaid shirt. The man has a long white beard and round wire-rimmed glasses.

"You don't have to steal to eat.", the man says in a soft baritone voice. "We will gladly feed you, my wife and I."

A dusty, calloused hand reaches down to help me to my feet.

"My name is Albert Sillman, but most people call me Al. What might your name be?"

"Naomi," I declare softly.

"Come on up. I'm not going to hurt you. We need to get you fed. You look awfully scrawny for a growing girl."

I no doubt look like a lanky lost fawn.

"You seem to have been through a time. Why don't you follow

me on into the house? I've got some bread and molasses. That should tide you over until we can get a proper meal on the table."

Terrified, I turn into a pillar of salt.

"It's okay," he reassures me. "If you want to wait, my wife Milly will be back soon. She's out in the woods gathering ramps."

Without conscious thought, I find myself running toward the fence. Drained, I feebly attempt to jump over. My left foot goes up, and I'm in the air. I almost make it over the diminutive garden fence, but my right foot clips the top. I'm sent quickly to the hard ground on the other side. I get the wind knocked out of me and take a nice bash to the right side of my noggin. Dazed, I lie there with a face full of grass. I'm not knocked out but I'm unable to flee any longer. I think about the way Charles looked, face down like I am now.

"Milly!" the man shouts. "Come quick, there's someone who needs our help!"

It's not long before the man, who calls himself Al, makes it to my pitiful shell. Soon, a set of smaller feet join him.

"Oh dear," the soothing woman's voice exclaims. "Let's get her inside."

I feel her hands on my head. She's protecting my injury as Al rolls me onto my back. Scooping me up under my arms, she lifts my torso as Al does the same with my feet. It's a short walk to the back porch. Al puts my feet down as the woman, Milly, stands me up. They support me as I stumble up the stairs. We pause for Al to unlock and open the door.

My new charges lay me supine on a brown couch in what appears to be their living room. The two disappear into the kitchen. I wouldn't say that I have given up, but I am so incapacitated by fatigue I can no longer affect the events around me. Running is out of the question. The power of control over my existence and future fades. I begin to accept that what happens now isn't up to me.

The inside of the cabin is dark in a cozy way. The stained wood surrounds and comforts me. There is something about such an environment that is native to mankind. Low whispers echo out of the adjacent room. The conversation must have been simple, because in short order, Milly walks through the swinging door with what appears to be a metal mixing bowl. She kneels by my side and places the bowl on the coffee table.

"There, there. Let me put something cool on that goose egg."

She places a small folded towel, soaked in cool water, across my forehead. It has been so long since an adult has been kind to me that I am terrified. She's not like Charles. This woman is capable of lying to me. I'm on edge as the cloth reaches my face, I turn away and cover it with both arms. My reaction is programmed and unconscious. When nothing happens, I begin to regain my composure. I turn back to see the woman dismayed.

"Lord, what has happened to you?"

I quietly shake my head in response. She begins to place the cloth on my forehead again, this time a bit slower.

"There," the woman named Milly says.

She backs away slowly and sits down on the closest of two recliners. The recliners sit caddy-corner to the end of the couch where my head is. Behind me is the front door. To my left is a coffee table. My feet point toward the swinging door that leads to the kitchen. I look across the coffee table to see a wood stove with two glass doors. Passing to the right of the woodstove would place one in a hallway.

Milly appears to be in her early sixties and is no more than five feet tall. Her hair is kept up in a bun, which is capped by a simple bonnet. With no preamble, she picks up a crochet hook and continues working on what appears to be the beginning of a brightly colored Afghan.

The man, Al, comes through the door with a plate and glass. He sits them down next to the bowl on the wooden coffee table. Al, like Milly before him, walks away quietly and takes a seat in the further recliner. I turn my head to look behind me for unknown threats.

Unlike most people, their chairs don't face a television. There isn't one. Rather, the center of attention in the house is the wood-burning stove. Its fire burns lightly to take the spring chill out of the air. I look back at them. Millie works away silently as Al skims through an old Bible, his reading glasses perched on the end of his angular nose. In his lap sits a notebook that he occasionally picks up to take notes with a yellow no.2 pencil.

The threats I keep looking for do not materialize. I am hungry, though. With a bit of initial disorientation, I get myself upright. On the plate are homemade bread and thick molasses for dipping. In the glass, lightly sweetened tea, with a slightly minty aftertaste.

"So where might you be coming from?" inquires Milly in a doting manner.

"Nowhere," I reply. "Why haven't you called the police or something yet?"

"Because we don't trust them," Al pipes up angrily. "The Sheriff's department is nothing more than a private police force for Vernon Proffit. I'd bet dollars to doughnuts, you're the missing student from Solid Rock boarding school. But you don't look like a runaway to me. You look like an escaped prisoner. That's why we're not calling." Al unintentionally raises his voice, "Vernon Proffit treats women and girls like chattel! And another thing...."

"No," Milly interjects. "She's been through enough and you're on your soapbox again, Al." Milly looks at me, "I'll get you some proper food after you get cleaned up. You don't have to talk to anyone until you're ready. I have some clothes from when my daughter was your age. You're a bit tall, but we'll see what we've got. The shower is over there," Milly says, pointing toward the hallway.

"Okay," I whisper.

Milly has a very slight German accent but Al sounds like he is one generation removed from a household where Yiddish was spoken.

After I finish scraping the plate clean, Milly asks, "Are you ready to get cleaned up?"

I nod my head in agreement. She puts her hand out and helps me to my feet. I feel like a gangly monster next to this diminutive proper country lady.

"Come on, now. I won't let you fall."

I'm not sure she could catch me, but I want to trust her good intentions. Their bathroom is simple. Despite the small interior, there is an old clawfoot tub. I turn the knob labeled 'H' and a few seconds later, I am greeted with glorious hot water. I have had nothing but cold showers for two-thirds of a year. I soak myself in that beautiful tub for a half-hour. When I finish, the water has turned brown like Stoney Creek back home. I let it drain, then shower off the residue. After turning off the shower, I wrap myself in a clean towel.

Milly knocks at the door.

"I have some clothes. Can we see how they fit?"

Without warning, Milly opens the door, slides in, and shuts it behind her. In her hands is clothing about my size. The bra and underwear seem to be about right. Milly holds up a long-sleeved black t-shirt.=

"This one is from my daughter's stupid Madonna phase. She had to wear everything long." Holding up a pair of acid wash jeans, Milly continues, "she ordered these horrible things from a J.C. Penney Catalog. They were too long for her. I never approved of this manner of dress, but Mr. Feminist over there," she points to the door, "feels differently. For now, we'll compromise, as it looks like these are the only clothes we have that will fit. I think we have a pair of old sneakers about your size. I'll leave you to it."

After getting dressed, I feel my chest tighten. I sit down on the closed toilet seat, with my left hand over my heart. It aches for Charles. I begin to cry, quietly. Grimacing, I stuff those emotions back down into myself, hidden away, where they belong only to me. Looking into the mirror at my bloodshot eyes, I catch a glimpse of Mara behind me. I turn around and come face to face with her. She dissolves into a haze, dispersing herself out of reality. I look back at the mirror, hoping to see her again, but she is gone. For a second, I see my reflection with her golden eyes superimposed over mine. The next time I blink, they vanish.

17

Leaving the bathroom dressed in borrowed clothes ironically gives me the sense of being my old self again. I've never perceived myself as completely female. I loathe dressing in so-called 'feminine' clothing and never understood why it was so goddamn important to others how I present myself.

Al and Milly's house looks as though it were built and appointed sometime in the nineteen-fifties. The furniture is antique but in pampered condition. The smell is like an old library book: wise, stable, and reassuring.

The movement of the floorboards under my feet alerts Milly that I've exited the bathroom. She comes hustling out of the kitchen.

As I exit, dressed in my new clothes, someone else's old clothes, I look over to my right to see Al, still absorbed in his Bible, unaware of our comings and goings.

Milly meets me in the hallway.

"I warmed you up some chicken and dumplings. It's good and hot. I made you some more sweet tea, too."

The kitchen has an intricately carved wooden table with custom glass laid across the top. Milly catches me looking down at the image, a giant oak tree. I trace over it through the glass with my left index finger.

"Al is a good carpenter and woodworker, isn't he? He built the entire table, carving and all. The oak tree depicts the tree the table itself is built from. It died years ago, and Al thought this was the best way to honor it. He's extremely sentimental. Al learned the woodworking trade from my father."

I turn to my left and smile at her as she places the bowl of dumplings and iced tea on the table. Then I see a look of horror come across her face. Her eyes are locked onto my left hand. I stop tracing. In a whisper, Milly asks, "Did he do that to you?"

"Yes," I reply at the same volume. Tears begin to run down her face as she excuses herself to the bathroom. A few minutes passes. She emerges and walks directly over to Al. She leans into his ear. There is some chatter back and forth, then I see him shake his head in agreement. At this point, I'm closing in on the bottom of the bowl.

In a forced happy tone, Milly asks, "Would you like another bowl?"

"Please," I responded in the same soft voice as before.

After pouring me another glass of tea, Milly excuses herself again. She takes a seat next to Al and they return to their muffled conversation. Mesmerized, I gaze at them the best I can through the kitchen doorway, partially obscured by the swinging door. I try my best to read their lips to no avail. I can tell by Al's body language that he is furious.

"I'm going to kill him this time, Milly!" Al shouts, loud enough for me to hear, as he springs from his chair with a clenched right fist. Al storms off into the hallway. Less than a minute later, he emerges with an old double-barrel shogun. The stock is worn and slightly faded from the years. Milly doesn't budge from her chair.

Right as Al is halfway to the front door, Milly chimes in with a mother's voice. "Stop right there, Albert Sillman," she commands. "The Sheriff will have his boys string you up from a tree in short order. I know you're aware of that and don't care what happens to you, but have you thought about what it would do to me? When you are before the Lord, the first thing he'll ask will be, 'Why did you abandon your wife, Albert?' What are you going to say to him?"

"I'd say to the Lord, 'In a hot-headed moment I made victims of all the people who loved me.'"

Al stands there in contemplation, the shotgun still in his grip, with the muzzle aimed towards the floor.

"Turn around and put it back right now, Albert," Milly commands while pointing toward the hallway he just exited.

With no protest, Al does exactly as he was told, which to me, is fucking amazing. I'm used to Amos slapping my mom for her tone, let alone if she were to command something of him.

I feel a bit guilty. I've become a source of tension in what seemed to be a peaceful household. Pretending not to notice, I stare down at my bowl of chicken and dumpling, attempting to not exist. Albert doesn't return right away and Milly just keeps crocheting. This tells me all I needed to know about her. She is a woman of substance, who knows herself better than anyone I've ever met. And she knows Al better than he knows himself. She centers herself in a mantra of crochet and continues going forward.

Upon hearing my spoon hit the bottom of an empty bowl, Milly puts down her work and shuffles her way into the kitchen.

"All finished?"

"Yes, Ma'am."

"How about you come with me to the living room and try your hand with a crochet needle? You can put your bowl next to the sink."

Reluctantly, I leave the isolation of the kitchen and join Milly. I sit at the end of the couch closest to her chair. Sitting catty-corner to her, I feel uncomfortably close. In a large wooden bowl on the coffee table rest three balls of yarn colored white, red, and green.

"What are you making?"

This is the first full sentence I've spoken to anyone but Charles in about four or five months.

"It's a Christmas-themed Afghan. It's going to have candy canes and Christmas trees on it."

"But it was just Easter?"

"I like to get an early start."

After a few minutes of instruction, I am making my first chain stitch. My mind calms as it grows longer. About the time the snake of yarn touches the floor, a door opens in the hallway. Al walks out, having obviously just finished sobbing. He sits down next to Milly. She puts her yarn and needle down.

Al looks in my direction and says, "if a man can own someone's greatest vice as well as their salvation from it, he can own that person. Never forget it." He pokes his finger toward the direction of Solid Rock in the imagined distance to drive home the point.

"Vernon Proffit did that to you?" Al asks, pointing at his own left hand, indicating my scar.

"Yes."

"You're one of his throwaway girls, aren't you?"

I nod my head in agreement.

"You've made it farther than any of the others. You're the cause of the ruckus up the road the other day, aren't you?"

I nod my head again.

"Good for you," Al says passionately while making a fist.

"I shot them, both Vernon Proffit and Brent Shoals."

"Are they dead?"

"I'm not sure about Brent. He's more than likely dead, though he wasn't when I left. Doctor Proffit is very much alive, but he'll never walk properly or see out of his right eye again. That's for sure."

"Never refer to him as 'Doctor' again. He's a charlatan. His certifications are from unaccredited correspondence courses. A person doesn't need a degree to be smart. But he has neither education nor decency. He's clever and more socially astute than anyone I've ever met. That's how he maintains control over the region. If they find you, they'll kill you, and us for good measure. Vernon owns all of Yancey County. It may as well be a sovereign state. The federal government doesn't really exist up here, except for in the post office. Not in law, though. Under normal circumstances, in a typical suburb, we would have called the police and child protective services. Here in Yancey, it would be like calling Vernon's direct line. He owns most people in the county, one way or another. They clamor to dash their own children at his feet on Sunday but buy and drink his liquor incognito Monday through Saturday. The rub is, they don't know the second part, nor would they believe it even if faced with irrefutable evidence. They trust him that blindly. His tendrils run through anything his people touch. If there's moonshine being made down in a holler, some of that money will see its way to Solid Rock's coffers through Sheriff Morton. Even if we took you to Asheville, he'd track you down. I assume he has some kind of custody agreement with your parents?"

Glass-eyed, I nod my head.

"He's the Erlking."

"What?", I respond puzzled.

"The stealer of children. He tempts them with the promise of a better life. It's a narrative of self-importance that makes an impressionable listener feel as though they are living on the verge of end times. If God chose Vernon, and Vernon, in turn, chooses your child, it would be as though God himself called you for a special purpose. An unobservant parent might ignore the warning signs until one day they find their child is dead. Exactly like the child in the Goethe poem."

Over the past eight months, I had almost forgotten that books other than the King James Bible exist. I feel as though my mind has atrophied since the rape.

Al continues, "The poem tells of a spirit who stole a child from a neglectful father while they traveled through the Black Forest."

"He did that to our daughter," Al says while pulling both of his palms, open toward his heart. "Vernon drew Hannah in with stories that made her feel important. We were pleased with her exuberance to attend a church with a classmate. Our negligence cost us her life. We don't even know the whereabouts of her body. She would be twenty-two in June. There's a young man out there who would have been our son-in-law that we'll never meet. There would have been grandchildren whom we will never know. Now they'll never exist and here we sit in a silent house. Jesus told us to forgive. I cannot. I am not a perfect man and if forgiving Vernon made me so, I'd rather stay flawed."

"What was your daughter's name?"

"Hannah Sillman," Milly responds. "Hannah had a friend from school named Josephine. Hannah never attended church. Our family always worshiped at home. We do not require the approval of a larger audience. In fact, we avoid churches if we can. Our relationship with Christ is our own. However, Josephine attended

Solid Rock and wanted Hannah to attend with her. As I said, one's relationship with the Lord is private. It wasn't our place to define Hannah's for her. After a few weeks, I noticed Hannah shunning her city-style clothes for more conservative, long dresses. I was glad for this. After a few months, she refused to join our nightly Bible study. Then one day, she just wasn't there anymore."

"This was nineteen-eighty-six," Al interjects. "Hannah was about your age then."

"I'll be fifteen in July."

"I think that's enough for now," Milly says, putting up her palm. "It's late in the afternoon, and I'm certain you haven't slept properly in days."

"No ma'am.

"You can sleep in Hannah's room. It's the first door on the left. I'll fetch you a nightgown."

Milly goes ahead of me and rummages around in Hannah's chest of drawers. It looks as though she is still alive, just in stasis. Her underwear drawer is neatly arranged and the bed is made. All the outdated posters on the wall tell a different story. Their edges have begun to curl inward and turn yellowish. The headboard on Hannah's twin bed has been intricately carved into a collage of dozens of flowers, each one a little different in the smallest ways. It is humanizing to be clean and safe in a warm bed. I haven't had this feeling in so long it is unnerving.

At four-thirty the next morning, I wake up screaming, fighting off a non-existent attacker. With a mother's grace, Milly slides into the room. She sits at my side, holding me.

"Brent killed him," I said.

"Who?"

"Charles. They killed Charles," I say through sobs.

It's the first time I have let my emotions pour out unhindered since before I arrived at Solid Rock.

"Would you like to tell me about it?"

I don't respond.

"That's alright."

I begin to doze again. I wake up around seven-thirty, to the smell of breakfast. I have scrambled eggs, bacon, grits, and two pieces of toast.

18

On the surface, it's easy to discount the Sillmans as simple. They're anything but. Al is a depression-era baby, born in Crown Heights to two German Jews fleeing the upwelling of anti-Semitism. Milly was born to the Amish.

The story goes something like this. In nineteen-fifty-three, directly after graduation, an eighteen-year-old Albert Sillman set off to drive across the United States in an equally aged black Packard One-Twenty sedan. This was met with the general disapproval of his rather Orthodox parents. Al got no further than Pennsylvania Dutch country before, late one evening, his Packard left him stranded along the roadside. Eventually, young Albert was picked up by an Amish carpenter, Eli Bontrager. Eli was the widower father of an only child named Emily, or as she's more affectionately known, Milly.

Al spent the first night in the barn. The next morning, Al joined Eli for breakfast in the main house. There he met sixteen-year-old Milly for the first time. They each haven't left the other's side since.

In the course of a year, Al had accepted Jesus as his Lord and savior, Milly as his wife, and took up the family craft of carpentry

One would expect their daughter to come along in short order as well. But the two remained childless. "The Lord," Milly says, "gives when he wants, not when you want." Al was never able to convince her to see a specialist about their inability to conceive. "It is God's will," Milly would say. Then, in the spring of nineteen-seventy-two, Milly found herself pregnant. Milly told me she foolishly thought that becoming a mother at thirty-five would mean she'd be wiser but admitted to me that she was "so very wrong." On Christmas Day, nineteen-seventy-two, she gave birth to Hannah Sillman. Hannah died somewhere between Friday, June fifteenth and Sunday, June seventeenth, nineteen-eighty-six.

Hannah slept over at Josephine's house that Friday and Saturday. Hannah was to attend church with Josephine Sunday morning. When the Sillmans arrived to pick her up Sunday afternoon, they found Josephine's house locked and quiet.

Assuming Hannah was still at Solid Rock, they drove their green nineteen-fifty-nine Chevy Apache down to the church, only to find the entire property empty.

Milly and Al drove back up the dirt road to Vernon's house to ask if he'd seen them. No one was home. Again, they returned to the church. After pulling back into the gravel parking area, figures began to exit the woods in all directions, encircling the truck. Al stepped out of the driver's door as the circle of people tightened. When they came shoulder to shoulder to form a solid circle, the congregation and students of Solid Rock stopped, and in unison, they began silently pointing their fingers toward the Sillmans. Sheriff Morton and three of his deputies cut through the mob from each quarter.

Al and Milly aren't imposing figures. Al is five-foot-six and Milly, five-foot-one. They're both slight of frame. Even so, Sheriff

Morton and his deputies felt it necessary to throw both face-first into the gravel and cuff them. Bruised and skinned up, each found themselves separated and placed in solitary holding cells at the tiny Burnsville police station. Over the next five days, they were starved and only allowed water. On the afternoon of the following Thursday, both Milly and Al were brought into the Yancey County Sheriff's interrogation room. Across from them sat the alcohol-bloated face of Sheriff Morton.

A series of a dozen or more polaroid photos were spread out before them. Each showed pictures of pre-pubescent girls naked and forced to perform sex acts on one another.

"These Polaroids were found in your possession, Mr. Sillman," said the Sheriff.

"Where's my daughter?" yelled Al.

"I don't know anything about you'ins having a daughter Mr. Sillman," replied the Sheriff. Public records don't show no birth certificate and no one in town remembers her. This make-believe daughter of yours never ain't real. But, these photos look right real to me. I want you to pick up each one and looks at them closely."

Sheriff Morton pulled his pistol from its holster and placed the muzzle to Milly's temple.

"Pick them up now."

Reluctantly, Al did as he was told. Retching, he held each photo, looking at them in detail.

When Al was finished, Sheriff Morton said, "Now you understand the weight of evidence we gots against you'ins. Your fingerprints are all over these. Anyday we just may decide to file them charges, unless of course, we don't. I don't knows about you'ins, but I hears them fellas at the central prison in Raleigh don't take kind to no child molesters. Shit, most of thems got at least a dozen little bastards runnin' bout. They'll steal and murder each other but kids, to their credit, are the one thing that's off the table. They'll make you their prison bitch. Eventually, they get tired of raping the same person and smashes his skull open on the cell floor. They's mostly already in for life. What's the difference to them? With you locked away or dead, Milly might have an accident. You never know? I'll hang on to these. Just you remember, I don't want to hear you'ins talkin' bout no imaginary girls, and the North Carolina SBI won't have to know about your little secret."

Dazed, the Sillmans were told they were free to go. Outside they found their truck parallel parked directly in front of the sheriff's station with the keys in the ignition.

The first few weeks at the Sillman's were quiet. They gave me a wide berth when I needed it and comforted me when the nightmares came. Milly continued to teach me to crochet. I became accustomed to the concept of learning to do things 'just because.' The first crochet project I completed was a simple dark blue scarf after only a few weeks under Milly's tutelage. I didn't need a scarf, I just wanted one. Even so, I felt guilty and selfish for making it. How can someone who let their best friend die deserve anything?

19

It's the summer of nineteen-ninety-five. I have been with Al and Milly for a little over a year now.

I've been working in the garden most of the morning. As I use a triangular hoe to weed, I begin to think about the turned earth and all the bodies buried in it through so many millennia. My mind goes back to the caverns. 'Hannah's body,' I think. I realize that one of the two girls entombed there would have been her. I drop the hoe and fall to my knees. I crouch forward and cover my face with both hands and begin to cry. Milly, watching from the kitchen window, rushes out the door. I feel her arms around me.

"What's wrong? she asks softly.

"I know where she is. I know where they put Hannah's body." I breathily say through my tears. I feel as cold and numb as the stone surrounding their corpses. Milly doesn't press me for information. Instead, she leads me into the house and insists I have a shower and start my new crochet project. It's going to be a plain grey Afghan.

Al is out picking up a fifty-pound bag of starter feed and grit for an upcoming clutch of blue silkie bantams. When Al's truck pulls up, Milly exits the house to meet him at the barn. There, it will be guarded by an old one-eared, white Main Coon named Miss Penelope, who mysteriously enters and exits the barn from a passage known to only her.

As I focus on my crochet project, I try not to think of the rotting carcasses entombed in the cave. My fingers work autonomously, allowing my mind to drift to a quiet place.

I hear Al enter the back door. He sits down in his recliner, which puts me diagonally across from me where I sit on the couch.

"I have no doubt God himself has brought you to us," he says stoically.

I no longer have beliefs of my own, so I just nod in recognition of his statement.

"I want to know where Hannah is, but only when you're ready to talk about it."

"Tomorrow," I say.

I crochet in silence for the rest of the day.

Tonight, in my dreams, I see Hannah. She's dressed in a white burial gown, with long straight brown hair, Al's hazel eyes, and Milly's plain features. She stands there awash in a sliver of moonlight cutting through to the forest floor.

"Hannah?"

The young woman nods her head.

"Don't want for my remains. They will only bring misery. I no longer need what has been left behind. I am peace."

"You're at peace?" I question.

"No. I am peace."

Hannah turns and walks into the darkness between the splinters of moonlight. I try to follow, only to find myself incapable of movement. I wake up at four-thirty screaming. Milly comes to my bedside to console me. I say nothing of my dream.

I drift off, waking up four hours later to the smell of breakfast. I dread the impending conversation. I slide on my jeans and one of the many random white t-shirts I have taken to wearing. I remain barefoot, as I do most of the summer.

Pa is already at the table, half-finished with breakfast. I know he won't initiate the conversation, so the obligation to bring it up is mine.

I sit across the table from him and say, "Let me tell you now. I want to get this out of the way."

Pa places his fork down.

"The night I escaped from Solid Rock, I passed through a tunnel whose entrance was accessible at the bottom of a large safe in Vernon's home. It leads to a room where the church is amassing food rations, restraints, and illegal guns. Beyond the room, it's a labyrinth of caverns. Swimming through an underwater cave, I found myself in some kind of burial chamber. It was dark. I felt around the rock wall. There were nine cavities chiseled out of the rock wall for corpses. Four contained bodies. I know they're human. I felt their skulls. They had on clothes.

I escaped through a second underwater passage that placed me on the edge of Buck Creek Road, right across from the golf course. We can get in that way."

Milly, from the stove, responds, "You can't. It doesn't matter anyway. It's merely a shell. Her soul resides with Jesus now."

"I know Milly, but she's my little girl," Al responds.

"Let her rest where she lies. We'll see her again, but removing her will surely come back on all three of us. Putting us in danger is not your choice.

Pa gets up from his half-finished breakfast and walks out the back door.

20

Two years are a quiet time for me. The stillness and removal of the outside world has allowed my mind to grow exponentially. It's the spring of nineteen-ninety-seven, and I'll be eighteen this summer.

The Sillmans taught me to grow my own food, butcher livestock, forage, and hunt. Al and Milly are brilliant people. Homeschool became as much a part of my day as chores or bushcraft.

The days have spilled out in a line, like a ball of Milly's yarn rolling across the floor. As it does, it rides a groove like a needle in a record. The path is the same, there are just mild sonic variations each day.

My groove has been something like this: math and house chores with Milly in the mornings, lunch, then literature and science lessons with Al in the afternoons. In the evenings, Al and I usually worked outside. Following dinner, there's a Bible study, which I was never obliged to join. I declined once, afterward receiving no condemnation or further questions about the subject. Unlike Pastor Howell, they're not obsessed with the 'What happens when you die?' question. Rather, they are more focused on the now and what they could do to better the lives of others; so, they did

The calm ended with a cough. It was small at first, then like a campfire, it grew and consumed. The creature's waste was the bloody sputum Milly began spitting up. She grew weak, her skin became a sickly yellow, and a series of lumps appeared around her neckline. These were the unmistakable symptoms of lung cancer. She never smoked or worked in a factory around harmful particulates. Nature did it to her for no other reason than plain bad luck. Al pleaded with Milly to allow him to ask Sheriff Morton if they could travel to Asheville for medical treatment. She declined, saying "I'd rather die than beg of those men. Besides, it's the Lord's will and I miss my Hannah."

Milly went about her life. She taught my math lessons, crocheted, and prepared the garden for spring. She lived the way she wanted until the end, never needing more than she had. For her, as a very structured woman, Milly was defined by her daily comings and goings. And those went on as long as she had breath to bring life to them.

Milly died March, twenty-eighth, nineteen-ninety-seven. It was a Friday.

She had gone out earlier in the afternoon foraging for early Spring ramps, while Pa and I did our lessons. She came home thirty minutes later, sweaty and panting. Al took her to bed. That evening, she called me to her bedside.

She told me, "I only found two ramps, but there's a patch that's going to come up between the two acorn trees. You know the place. Look in on them in two weeks. There should be plenty by then. Watch after my silkies, won't you?"

She dozed off not long after.

Al lay in bed, holding her as she struggled for air. I heard Milly's prolonged wheezing from my room as I settled my numb body into bed for the night. I quietly cried under the covers. Around three in the morning, her gasps became further and further apart. Eventually, her breathing slowed to a low whisper. Then there was nothing.

We buried Milly under an ancient oak tree in the backyard. Her body feeds its roots, and the tree's shade protects her silkies.

21

It is July twentieth, nineteen-ninety-seven. It's an emancipation day of sorts, at least psychologically. I am eighteen today. Were I considered alive, I wouldn't be under the auspices of anyone, as all adoptions and parental rights have become void. But here I remain, a prisoner of the ever-watchful eye of Solid Rock and my love for Al.

The day will come when I have to make a run for it, just not today.

During lunch, Al says, "I have a birthday present for you."

This is new territory for him. Milly was always the one who gave me birthday presents and baked a cake.

"I want you to have Hannah's identity for your birthday," Al says.

"I don't understand."

"Technically, Hannah isn't dead as far as the federal government is concerned. No legal documentation was made of her passing. How could it have been? Sheriff Morton wouldn't allow it. One day my daughter was dead, that was it. The community and the county went on pretending she never existed. Under duress, we had to do the same. To the outside world, her birth certificate and active

Social Security number deem her to be alive. The rumor spread by Solid Rock after your escape was that you died of exposure. Sheriff Morton has no doubt made this true on paper. When it comes to their cult, I've found the most reliable information can be found in their rumors. And the biggest rumor is that there are other communities like Solid Rock and they have begun organizing. If you resurface as Naomi Pace, they will hunt you. As for me, I'm trapped here. Leaving would mean facing child pornography charges. With their claims and my fingerprints on those photos, it wouldn't take long before my mugshot is flashed across every television as a wanted pervert. That's okay, though. This is where I want to be. It's where everything I've ever held dear or loved is located. That includes you."

Al pulls an envelope out of his front pocket and hands it to me. I open it to find Hannah's birth certificate and Social Security card.

As I look up from the documents, Al says, "I already consider you my daughter anyway."

"I'm not ready to go anywhere."

"When you are, I'll do what I can to help you escape. The church has eyes everywhere. It's a risk. The only guarantee is that once you're out, we'll never see each other again in this life."

"I know," I say, sniffling. "Hannah would be twenty-five today, I'm only eighteen."

"I suppose you'll always look young for your age.", Al says with a mischievous glint.

The summer passes solemnly. The garden gives up all it can to be canned, and as the weather turns, the spring roosters start disappearing into my dumplings with regularity.

It's late October of nineteen-ninety-seven. Tonight is the first snowstorm of the season.

Al and I are sitting in our usual spots: me on the couch, Al in his recliner, next to the empty one where Milly once sat.

The wood-burning stove bounces its light gently onto the Afghan I am finishing. Milly began it in the weeks before her death. It's light blue, like the sky on a warm summer's day. The pattern creates a bright sun right in the center. Looking down at it, I realize something. When I first met Milly, much of her crochet work was predominantly Christmas-themed. Hannah was born on Christmas Day. Now it makes sense in a way that makes me feel as though I knew it before but didn't get around to telling myself. About a year after my arrival, Milly began doing summer scenes as well. I was born in the summer.

I haven't thought about my escape in a while. I've put the thoughts of Mara out of my memory. In time, she has faded into a figment of imagination experienced by a desperately tired and hungry little girl. From behind my crochet, I look at Al and say, "I saw something I can't explain the night I escaped from the cave."

"What did you see?" Al says, as he puts his Bible down.

"I don't want you to think I'm crazy."

"Never."

I tell him about the visions of Mara during my escape. Al locks on to every word.

"Why do you call her Mara?"

"I don't know. It just seemed to be her name."

"That's peculiar. Do you know what Naomi means?

"No."

"It means pleasant. Naomi was the name of Ruth's mother. She was strong with the Lord until a famine in Israel forced her family to flee Moab. During this time, she began to tell people not to call her Naomi, but rather, Mara, which means bitterness. Your Mara sounds like a golem."

"I don't remember that in the Bible," I respond.

"It's not in the Bible. Golem means 'partially formed.' In the Talmud, Adam is referred to as a golem before being given a soul. Without it he was incomplete. Eastern European folklore is rife with golems. In most of those legends, the golem is made from dirt, like Adam. Unlike God, humans can't create souls, so the golem form is under the control of its maker. The purpose of the golem is almost always as a protector of the Jewish people. It's like a purposefully spread rumor, hopefully warding off potential attackers."

"I'm not Jewish," I reply.

"Are we not all children of God? My ancestry makes me no more chosen than any other mortal. The spiritual viscera we are made from is carved by our deeds, not our lineage."

"I've always assumed you knew, but I'm a lesbian. Your God says I am an abomination."

Pa holds up his Bible and says, "this book says a lot of stupid shit. Those are flaws of man. What you have to read is the intent God had before mortals spoiled it with their need to stand above one another. It's the same with racism. Some choose to stand on others' heads rather than hand in hand, just so they can occasionally feel a brief shudder of fleeting power. It's all nonsense. None of the excuses for hate or violence reached for in religious texts have anything to do with God, in whatever form you wish to view it. The only message God ever wanted to convey to us was love. It doesn't matter who you choose to love, only that you do it selflessly."

My mind returns to Tiffany. She's been so far out of my reach, I have placed thoughts of her far away so that it hurts less.

Al continues, "the rituals to create a golem involve using virgin soil, which if taken literally, would mean soil that has never been plowed or grown in before. Fresh spring water is needed for purifying. Usually, there are long, long prayers that must be memorized and repeated to perfection. The final, and in my opinion, most important stipulation is need. I doubt God would grant someone a golem to do their dishes just because they can repeat long prayers aloud. Politicians often make a public show of their prayers, but it doesn't mean they get anything done. In your case, I'd say you had more than enough need. I believe when Charles fell, he made an outline in the virgin dirt. The clean water dripping from stalactites above purified Charles and the outline. Unknowingly, a chain of events was set into motion, and you were provided this golem. Like all golem, she will only appear during times of genuine need."

Something changed on Al's face after saying this. It reads like a man surrendering.

"We've got a lot to do tomorrow. You should get some rest," I say.

"I will in a few minutes. I'm going to finish my verses for the night."

I leave for bed, telling Al, goodnight.

When I pass by my dresser on the way to bed, I run my hand over the top of it, which has become a bit of a ritual for me over the past few months. In the top drawer sits the envelope with Hannah's birth certificate and Social Security card. They are my tickets to a new life free of Solid Rock.

22

In the morning, I find Pa just as I left him, only now he is dressed in a fresh set of overalls instead of his usual plaid pajamas and a white t-shirt. Though, he is still reading his Bible.

"Did you go to bed?" I ask.

"I'm afraid not. All I could think about was that Hannah's body should be next to her mother's, not in some dank cave along the road."

"You're right, but what would happen if we took Hannah's body out of the cave? When Vernon kills again, he'll notice a trophy is missing from his collection. Or worse, you'll be spotted removing her."

"I know. But, Milly is gone, and the Lord has provided you with Mara as a protector. The only person left for Vernon to hurt is me."

"Mara isn't real. She's just the byproduct of a scared child's mind." I reply, dismayed.

"I have faith. There is no other way you could have escaped. It shouldn't have been possible. I've already made my choice."

I look out the kitchen window. There is a mound of dirt sticking out of the snow, underneath the oak tree where Milly is buried.

"It was her dress. That's how I knew it was Hannah. All I could think about was the day Hannah was born. I delivered her here, at home. I was the first to hold her, even before her mother. I couldn't get the vision of her as a newborn out of my head. But instead of a baby in my arms, I saw her infant carcass laying on a cold granite slab, stiff and blue."

"I don't blame you one damn bit," I say. "I would kill him if I had the chance."

"So would I. What does that say about me as a Christian?"

"I don't know, but it says a great deal about you as a father. You're not Christ. Some things one person does to another are absolutely unforgivable. We just don't have the capacity."

Then comes heavy banging on the front door.

"Sheriff's department! Open up!"

Then comes an unmistakable bellows-like voice. "Open up, Albert. We have a warrant!"

"It's Vernon! I say to Al in a whisper, still standing right outside the hallway.

"That's not Vernon, child, that's freedom. You are protected. Go. Get Hannah's documents and run out the backdoor into the woods before they see you."

Al stays seated, reading his Bible, unflinching.

Frantically, I turn and run back through the hallway, past my room, and straight into Al's. I know the old Mauser bolt-action rifle he uses for deer hunting rests in the back corner of the closet. I fling the door open and push through the clothes until I find it. I pull the bolt out halfway to see if it's loaded. Shit. It's empty.

Just then, I hear a kick at the front door. It causes me to turn my head back toward the commotion. I think I catch a glimpse of

Mara out of the corner of my eye. 'The nightstand,' I think.

Yanking the drawer open, I find a box of seven-millimeter cartridges. There are only four rounds. I push four into the top-loading magazine, one at a time. Then I chamber a round. I flip the large safety lever down and head back toward the hallway. The front door lock breaks loose with a kick. It swings open to reveal a deputy. I level the rifle and fire, hitting him center mass just before the foot he used to kick the door touches the floor. He crumples and lands facedown, revealing Vernon's blood-spattered face, his right eye covered with a patch. He is lucky to be standing off-center. The round went straight through and would have ended Vernon as well.

Al hasn't moved. He sits there quietly, having only put his Bible down. He intends to sacrifice himself for me as a distraction.

Before I can pull the bolt back to chamber the next round, Vernon unholsters his sidearm and lets off one round in my direction. The hot metal slices open a gash on the left side of my neck. I twist in the direction of the bullet and fall to the floor.

Just before Vernon can pull the trigger again, Al jumps on him, taking both of them to the floor. I hear a muffled gunshot. The blowback out of Al's back is enough to paint the log rafters. With the weight of his dead body on Vernon, I have a chance to escape.

Before running out the back, I shove open my bedroom door and reach into the top drawer of the dresser. I pull out Hannah's documents and stuff them into my front left jean pocket. Vernon is still struggling to get out from under Al. I raise the Mauser in Vernon's direction. I hear another car pull up and several voices. The deputies outside think they've come to arrest a harmless old man but don't yet realize what's happened. I could kill Vernon, but the gunshot would alert them. I can't win a shootout against so many. But I know, by the look of bewilderment and embarrassment on Vernon's face, that he would never mention to them that I'm still alive. It would severely weaken him in their eyes.

I make my way out the backdoor and quietly shut it behind me. As soon as the bolt in the door clicks, I take off running. I jump the fence and run through the fall greens, then over the backside of the fence. I pass Hannah's grave to my right and take a left toward the barn.

The barn is no more than eight hundred square feet. In the back, behind Al's faded red Allis-Chalmers tractor, is an enclosed room the size of a modern walk-in closet, where feed is kept. I wedge myself behind the feed bags against the back wall. I pull the bags over the gap between the wall and the rest of the stack. I lie on my back with the rifle pointed up, waiting for a face to peer down upon me. When the door to the feed room opens, I am greeted with two sets of footsteps. Vernon and Sheriff Morton.

"I doubt there's anyone else around here," Vernon says to the Sheriff.

"Okay, pastor," Sheriff Morton replies. "I'll see to the house, then".

"Yeah, go ahead, Alton. Oh, say do you think you could get one of the deputies to bring me one of the gas cans. I'd like to burn this structure down myself, privately, if you don't mind. You and the others take care of the house.

"If that's what the Lord is telling you'ins to do, then I don't question his providence. I'll send Deputy Ray with the gas.

A half a minute or so after Sheriff Morton left, Vernon addresses me directly.

"I know you're in there. Just so you are aware, girlie, I've got my pistol drawn, in case you want to jump up and do some stupid shit. You won't stand a chance coming from around the top of the bags with a long gun and I wouldn't stand a chance peeking over those bags. You probably have that rifle chambered and ready for me don't you?"

"You're goddamn right!" I announce loudly.

"Throw it out and I'll kill you fast. Either way, I'm burning this building down with your body inside. It's your choice whether you want to die from a gunshot to the back of the head or to burn alive."

"They'll ask why you shot the gun. You'll be exposed as a fraud when it's seen I escaped you years ago."

"It doesn't matter. They believe anything I tell them. As long as they don't see you, they will believe. I intend on making you ash, never to pester me again."

I continue to stare up with the rifle shouldered. I dare not stand. I won't give Vernon the enjoyment of my surrender.

The door opens.

"You wanted this, sir," a young, meek-sounding Deputy Ray says.

"Yes, thank you, son. Now, go on back to the house and help them search it before it's burnt down."

Upon the deputies' exit, Vernon says, "I suppose you've made your choice."

Vernon pulls the door shut. I hear a heavy rattle around the handle. It sounds like it's being pulled tighter against the frame. There is a series of deep metallic clicks on the other side, followed by creaking wood. I know the sound. It's a lever chain binder. One chain end was on the handle and the other was probably affixed to the heavy old tractor, effectively sealing the door. I hear a splatter, then the sound of an empty metal can hitting the ground.

The fast ignition of the accelerant pushes its backdraft under the door, changing the pressure in the room so violently it causes my ears to pop. My hearing is muted and ringing. Searing heat collects around the room until I begin to sweat profusely. As the ringing begins to clear, I hear frantic scratching from above, as though something was on top of the bags trying desperately to get in. When she let out one of her awful, low-pitched meows, I know it's Miss Penelope. I raise my right leg and kick the bag over me aside. A fluffy white blur lands on my chest and runs with no regard over my face.

Tilting my head back, I witness Miss Penelope claw up a board on the side of the barn. It acts like a railroad barrier lifting, which allows her to slip under, but closes as she flees. I feel a flash of smugness now that I know Miss Penelope's secret. I slide on my back a few feet, head first, in the direction of the loose board. Al must have bumped it with the tiller a few years back. The board is completely loose. The one above it is wobbly. I push the bottom board up and out of the way, then grab hold of the board above it with both hands and jerk it to and fro. The board bounces millimeters between the nail heads and the frame as I struggle. The old, rusty nails begin to give way until I'm able to push the board completely off the side of the barn. I throw the rifle out first, then work my way between the board and ground. As I make it through, I feel pain as the rough gravel and soil are pushed into the gash on my neck. I worm through the hole and come out the backside of the barn covered in mud. I am out of sight and only four yards from the wood line. I clutch the rifle off the ground with my left hand while I get to my feet. I look both ways and see no one.

Without hesitation, I go for it. If not for the roar of the house and barn ablaze, everyone would have heard me barreling through the downed autumn leaves. The sparse trees offer little cover as I race through the forest. The elevation begins to bottom out as I come to the stream running behind the draw. I crash through knee-high water. When I arrive on the other side, I'm greeted with my target, a large rocky outcrop. I stop and squat behind them. Now I'm covered from their direction and can hear anyone approaching from behind or the sides. I can either clear out before they see me or take them off guard. I still have three rounds in the internal magazine. I slowly remove the bolt and let the previously spent cartridge fall out easily. I pick it up and stow it in my right jean pocket. I can't risk leaving a clue about which direction I traveled in case I don't engage them. I push the bolt in and advance the next round.

23

By midday, the smoke from the Sillman's house slows to a dark, stringy trickle. The noise subsides as the fires are sprayed down and sifted through. There is nothing left for me. I must move forward. But Al and Milly gave me the greatest gift, love. As his last act, Al sacrificed himself for me and handed me my future in the form of an envelope.

I follow the flow of a small stream. I know it well. About five miles down, the tributary will join the North Toe River, but not before going past Bakersville. I can't exactly roll into town and not expect to grind up against members of Solid Rock.

With about six hours of sunlight left in the day, I realize if I hike hard enough, I can get a few miles south of town before nightfall. I pass Bakersville, mostly keeping along the river and out of sight. There are occasional vacation rental properties along the way, but most are empty and are more likely to be occupied by tourists from Atlanta or Charlotte.

I'm about two miles south of Bakersville now. I've been drinking water straight out of the river all day. In most circumstances, this is a bad idea, but I'll risk stomach distress to allow me to move along quickly. The further away I get the safer I will be. It takes Giardia about three days to hit you hard, so I'll deal with diarrhea at that time, hopefully when I am further afield and able to rest.

But now, I am hungry. Wild edibles are sparse in late October. Hunting is an option if the opportunity arises, but sounding off a round makes me nervous.

About two hours before dark, I spot a clutch of hen-of-the wood mushrooms at the base of a tree that has fallen parallel to the river. I pluck about a quarter of the bunch free. It's roughly larger than both of my hands. I take refuge behind the fallen tree on which the mushrooms grew, squatting down with my back resting into her dying trunk. Hen-of-the-wood kind of tastes like a swimming pool when it's raw and I'm not at starvation's door by any means, so I put it aside to build a shelter.

I pack a thick bed of fallen leaves against the backside of the tree. I use downed branches to build a lean-to roof above the leafy bed. I pick what fern leaves I can and weave them like shingles to create a roof over my tiny new home. With just a little sunlight left, I scrounge around for loose dry firewood. I'm able to put together a hand drill set to start a fire. I use a clump of dried old man's beard I snatch off a tree to catch the ember. I can't help but think of Mara. The last time I saw her clearly, I was doing the same. This time is different. I don't need her help.

I locate the fire just outside the foot of my lean-to and put a few rocks around the flame to keep it tame. To make a cooking surface, I use a nice big flat rock I lean against the fire. Even after cooking them, the mushrooms still taste like dirt. I build up the fire and I tuck myself away into my leafy nest while clutching Al's rifle. I begin to find sleep easier than I expected. I think it's because the one thing I feared the most had already happened. Now I can no longer dread it.

I don't dream. Instead, everything goes dark, then it is morning. My fire has dwindled but there are enough embers to ignite fresh firewood within a few minutes. I pluck another handful of hen-of-the-wood and put it on my cooking stone. After eating, I disassemble my campsite and disperse the fire, hoping to leave as little trace as possible.

When I reach the intersection between the North and South Toe Rivers, I have to come dangerously close to Burnsville. Worse yet, the river runs right past Solid Rock. I move on downriver, pushing myself hard until mid-afternoon. Before getting too close to Solid Rock, I take a respite. I lie in the tall grass out of sight until nightfall. As darkness falls, I know exactly where I'm headed: Maddie Bellew's.

An hour after darkness has fallen, I am on the move again. The thought of breaking into Vernon's house, opening the safe and retrieving an M-16 and as much ammo as I can carry crosses my mind. Delicious as the thought is, I know it's a suicide mission. And it's likely, out of an abundance of caution, the combination has been changed.

I move into town guided by moonlight. I stay in the wood line until I'm behind the small road where Maddie's house sits, only about two blocks from the courthouse and Sheriff's station. The entire enclave is in a state of hibernation, huddled indoors, mostly asleep, avoiding the chill. A light dusting of snow still laces the ground from two evenings ago. Pain and fury block out any sense of frigidness I should feel. As I approach the back of Maddie's house, I consider boosting myself through a window. But, on second thought, I figure trying the direct approach. I walk around the house, up the front steps, and turn the doorknob.

Many associate the concept of leaving your doors unlocked in small towns with naivete, but in Maddie's case, it's downright hubris. She's the widow of a well-known pastor and confidant of the prophet. Who would dare harm her?

I don't make the same mistake: I lock Maddie's front door behind me after I enter. I quietly make my way to the back door and do the same, then return to the kitchen.

The fluorescent light above the sink shines dimly across the green, laminate countertop. I make myself at home and rummage through Maddie's refrigerator. I find the remnants of a chicken pot pie. I snag a bowl from the cabinet, scoop in the remainder, put a moist paper towel over it, and nuke it for two minutes. I pour myself sweet tea from Maddie's antique aluminum pitcher and help myself to a seat at the kitchen table. I make certain to sit on the side opposite the hallway, so I can keep an eye out. With a round in the chamber, and the safety off, I put the rifle down on the table. The muzzle is aimed across the kitchen at the hallway entrance.

I feel perfectly at home, waiting silently for my guest. The day ahead is Monday. Maddie has already made her twice-a-day Sunday appearance at Solid Rock and won't return again until Wednesday evening. I don't have to worry about her comings and goings. There is a calendar featuring pictures of old churches, next to the kitchen wall phone, outlining her entire schedule.

The gunshot gash on my neck is really beginning to ache.

I shuffle through her kitchen drawers and cabinets. I locate the junk drawer. It's filled with odds and ends, loose pens, screwdrivers, and such. To my delight, I find a vintage roll of duct tape. "Good for you," I whisper to myself, as I hold it up at eye level.

Also in the draw are eight index card boxes, each designed to hold five hundred cards. I pick one up and return to my seat. The cards aren't dated or in any discernible order. Curious, I get up, and have a look through the other boxes. The stock begins to look older the further back the box is inside the drawer. The cards in the furthest box felt as though they would transform into confetti if handled roughly.

I take all of them, clutched to my chest, to the kitchen table. As I flick through, I examine each card, then throw them one by one onto the green linoleum floor. By the time I get to the last box, the floor is awash in whitish-yellow index cards. Halfway through that final box, is a white sliver in a sea of otherwise curled tips. Flipping ahead, I pull it out and hold it up. It's a list of names. I believe these are names of living girls Maddie is grooming for Vernon. The card reads longways. There are more than twenty names aligned all the way left. Hyphens follow each name. Following the hyphens, some have the letter 'M' or 'V'. Others have both or none at all.

Around four in the morning, I hear an old iron bed frame creak, then tiny, slow footsteps. The bedroom door squeaks as it opens. Maddie makes her way into the bathroom, not yet realizing this is no normal morning. I wait. She goes about whatever her morning routine is. The toilet flushes, water runs, finally the old bathroom light switch makes a loud click as she turns it off.

Maddie doesn't notice me at first. She's on autopilot, her eyes pointing down as she enters the room. Then she notices the eruption of recipe cards scattered across the kitchen floor. Maddie's head pops up and she shuffles back a bit. Assessing the situation, she is unable to calculate a response. She freezes, which is her only real option. I hold the name card out longways in my right hand.

Calmly I say, "What do M and V stand for?"

I flip the card around.

"I don't have my glasses on," Maddie replies.

"You know damn well what I mean, Maddie Bellew. The girls. What do the letters mean?"

I can tell by her silence she is concocting the most convincing lie her mind can muster at this early hour.

"Don't even, Maddie, you know what I'm talking about. Why these girls, and why the M and V?"

Her stunned silence continues.

Louder, in a commanding tone, I say, "Goddamnit, I'm going to reach under the sink, pull the pliers from your tool kit, clamp them down as hard as I can on your earlobe and pull it straight from your skull."

"M indicates that the girl has reached her menses. V is for virgin. I always inspect the girls for hymens. Those without are dealt with harshly by their mothers because she has shamed them. It's a woman's job to quell the desires of her own daughter."

"Pull up a seat," I say, as I kick the chair in front of me across the floor in her direction. Maddie shuffles sideways to her left until the chair is fully behind her.

As she sits, I say, "Keep your hands in your lap."

The muzzle of the rifle is pointed straight at her stomach. Maddie is in her mid-eighties and rather frail. I don't need to take all the precautions. I can easily overpower her, but I don't want to hurt her. At the moment, I need something.

"You're going to clean and sew up the gash on my neck," I say, standing up.

Maddie is repelled, putting her hands out as I come around the table. I click the safety on and place the rifle against the wall behind me, then pick up the duct tape as I round the edge of the rectangular table.

"Put your hands backward, through the bars of the chair's backrest."

There is no hesitation this go-round.

I lightly bind Maddie's hands with just two wraps of tape. With her hands immobilized, taping her legs, thighs, and midsection to the chair is easy. After sliding her to the edge of the table, I wrap the tape around Maddie's already bound left leg, making complete circles around her calf, the chair leg, as well as the table leg. With the three now one unit, she's not going anywhere.

"I'm going to get what we need. If you scream, I'll cut your tongue out."

Upon entering the makeshift operating room, memories come back in a rush as the stench of chemicals enters my olfactory system. The operating table is in the same spot it occupies in my mind, retaining an obelisk-like permanence. Briefly, I am a little girl again. Then I see the little girl I was, and I want to protect her.

I gather together, on her rolling stainless steel tray, a curved needle, black thread, forceps, long cotton swabs, and a bottle of alcohol. I pick up a scalpel but don't place it on the tray, opting to keep it in my left hand. I roll the cart into the kitchen, bringing it to rest on Maddie's right side.

"I'm going to untie your hands now. You need to behave," I say, pointing my finger at her like the headmistress of a one-room schoolhouse. I peel the tape from Maddie's wrists, then pull my seat out from under the table and move it toward her. I switch the rifle to my right hand and put the muzzle right up to Maddie's chest. I then turn and begin to straddle the seat. This allows me to get close to Maddie while letting me lean my chest into the backrest for support. As I lower myself onto the seat, the gun lowers and comes to rest on the corner of the table, pointing right at Maddie's midsection. I keep my forearm across the stock, my index finger on the trigger. Now my left shoulder faces her, with the wound accessible on the same side of my neck.

"It's a bad fucking way to die," I say, looking down at the rifle.

She begins to blink furiously, which I suppose is what she does when nervous.

"I can't do this here," she says.

"Why not?"

"It's going to be sloppy. My hands shake. It would be better if you were lying down."

"Calm yourself. I'm not going to kill you if you give me the three things I came for."

"What do you want!?"

"Sew me up first, and you'll live to hear about the second."

Maddie sees fit to stay quiet and get to work after that.

The alcohol used to clean the wound runs down my neck, mingling with the blood soaked into my shirt. I choke back a scream. Maddie uses the long swabs to get deep inside the wound to scrape out all the little bits of grit that came along with squeezing out of Miss Penelope's secret door. After the first rinse, I block the rest out the best I can.

"How am I going to cut the stitches?"

I pull my left hand up and let the scalpel flash a glint of light across her face. Maddie audibly gasps in fear. At first, I think it's the blade, but then I see the true impetus of her gaze. It isn't at the scalpel, but rather the horrid scars on my hand. She shuts her eyes and shudders involuntarily. Our momentary silence is broken by the sound of a stream of piss running off the seat of her chair and onto the floor.

"I thought you went already."

"I did. Sometimes I don't get it all out at one time no more. I feel like I have to pee but nothing comes out. I'm eighty-five years old."

"I don't give a shit, Maddie. Being old doesn't excuse you for what you've done. As far as I'm concerned, as long as there's breath in the body, there's time for comeuppance. You can just sit in the piss. The main focus of your life right now should be sewing me up."

Twenty shaky minutes later, I end up with nine sloppy stitches. Seeing that I've already made a habit of collecting scars, what's another if it means I'm alive?

Maddie gently puts the needle and forceps down after I cut the last stitch.

"You're Naomi, aren't you?"

"Yes, I am, and no, you can't talk your way out of this, so shut off the act and just be the cunt you are."

Walking behind her, I say, "Put your hands behind your back. I reach down and yank both of her tiny hands through the vertical wooden bars of the backrest. I wrap the tape tight enough to cut off the circulation.

I find that I truly relish Maddie's pain. I am in control. Each whimper stokes an all-encompassing white-hot nuclear reaction within, followed by static up my spine, and ringing in my ears.

I straddle my chair, facing her again. I slide my chair up as close as I can. I get right in her face and say with a stony sternness, "Where is it?"

"Where's what?"

Tears of pain stream from her eyes and collect on her simple white nightgown. I feel the slickness of the urine on the floor with the tips of my boots. I lean over and begin to whisper into Maddie's right ear.

"Where the," then I continue in a yell, "fuck is my clitoris!?"

"The closet. The closet in the operating room."

I tape Maddie's mouth shut. The small closet is to the left upon entering the operating room. There are five shelves. On each, as well as the floor, are stored scores of preserved anatomy trophies in old pickle jars. It's a hodgepodge of moles, teeth, tonsils, appendixes, kidney stones, gallbladders, as well as fingers and toes that had been amputated due to irreparable lacerations. Each has premade canning labels adhered to them with surnames and first initials. I clink through the collection, from the floor up. I find it in the far right corner of the third shelf. It reads "N. Pace." It dawns on me how unfamiliar the name Pace has become to me. I have thought of myself as a Sillman for the past three years. At eighteen, three years is a huge swath of your already lived lifespan.

I slam the jar down onto the table in front of Maddie, just soft enough for it not to break. Its bang against the old wood reverberates through the house. I rip the duct tape from across her lips. I turn the adhesive part around and say, "Well, at least we took care of your mustache."

"Is that what you wanted?" Maddie says

"Not everything. I need to know a few things. I assume most of your jar collection are the fruits of backwoods surgery? I know why you take clitorises, but what's with the testicles?

"A few of them I took from queer boys. The rest were from the diversions. The boys that the Prophet's vessel might be courtin'. They can't sully his prizes, and each paid the price for challenging him by temptin' them girls."

"What happened to Charles's body?"

"Charles?"

"He was the boy who died in the cave the day I escaped."

"Oh, that fat miscreant?"

Furious, I stand and slap Maddie as hard as I can across her face with my scarred left hand. Maddie winces in shock. She spits in my face. Whipping the scalpel out, I slice through the tape securing Maddie's leg to the table. I place the toe of my boot under the front of Maddie's chair and slowly push it over backward.

Waves of pleasurable warmth ripple through me when the sound of her wrists shattering enters my ear. She ejects piercing screams. I rush to cover her mouth. As I stand her back up, I keep my hand in place over her mouth.

"I'm going to take my hand off your mouth. If you scream again, I'll push the chair back over. Do you understand?"

As she nods her head and I release my hand from her face.

"I'm going to repeat myself, this last time. Where is Charles?"

"In Hickory Hill Cemetery, at the end of the first row of headstones. He doesn't have a marker."

"One last thing."

"What?" Maddie says with effort through immense pain.

"Beg my forgiveness."

"I'm going to cut you loose, and I want you to get down on your knees and grovel for my grace."

I slap another strip of duct tape over Maddie's already red mouth. Using the scalpel, I meticulously free her from the chair. Afterward, I push the chair forward, which forces Maddie to her knees. She attempts to catch herself with broken hands.

"On your knees," I command as I snatch her up by her curly white hair.

Maddie balances herself. I let go and walk around so I can see her face.

"You can start now," I say, right before snatching the tape from her lips.

"When you kill me, I'm going to be swept up by the Lord. I kneel only to him and his Prophet."

"I take that as a no, then? What makes you think I'm going to kill you?"

I tape her mouth shut before grabbing Maddie's shattered right wrist and dragging her across the floor to the quiet soundtrack of her muffled screaming. Once in the operating room, I pick Maddie up and toss her onto the operating table where my clitoris was stolen so many years ago.

"I'm not here to kill you, just to take."

With that, I turn on the cauterizing loop.

24

Maddie's skin is so thin, it burns away like rice paper. I begin running the cauterizing loop along the bottoms of her feet, peeling away flesh, one strip at a time. I start with the big toes and work my way down to the heel. She is so weak, I don't even have to tie her down. I just hold her leg with my right hand and work with my left. The smell is atrocious. It takes an agonizing fifteen minutes to strip the bottoms of her feet to the tendons and muscle.

After untaping Maddie's mouth, I muffle her screams with my hand.

"Where do you hide the money?" I whisper. "I know you people don't use banks."

"In my bedroom closet," Maddie says weakly.

I tape her mouth shut again and leave her unattended on the operating table. In her closet, I discover a small fireproof safe. I take it back to Maddie, untape her mouth, and demand the code. She doesn't respond. I pry her left eye open and dangle the cauterizing loop millimeters away from the pupil. I immediately get a clear, deliberate response.

"Right thirty-six, left twelve, right six."

There's a healthy pile of cash, made almost exclusively of one-hundred-dollar bills. I am able to fold and distribute the bills between my front and back jean pockets. There's roughly twenty thousand dollars in each of the four. I even take the twelve cents rattling around inside.

"Is that all of it?"

"Yes," Maddie responds in a trembling voice.

"I believe you."

Without warning, I begin peeling the skin off of Maddie's palms. She breathes heavily and moans, but lacks the strength for a proper yell.

I pry open her left eye again and say, "I never promised not to hurt you."

To keep her in place, I press down hard on Maddie's head, then scoop out the cornea and lens of her eye. It kind of looks like a clearish melon ball with a hazel iris. Dropping it on the stainless-steel tray, I move my hand to pry open her right eye.

With little fight left, she shakes and begs, "No. Please," through low grunts of horrific pain.

"I'm sure you've heard that request from where I'm standing many times before. Did you stop?"

She doesn't say anything.

I begin to wonder if Maddie might not go into cardiac arrest before I can finish, but she persists as I collect another melon ball. I arrange the two irises on the table so I can look into her dead eyes while she still lives. I go back to work on peeling the skin from Maddie's palms. She incoherently mumbles and shakes. As I finish them, I see light around the edge of the blinds. It's twilight. My time is short. I pick up a hemostat and use it to straighten the cauterizing loop. Then I twist the hot wire five or six times to give it some rigidity. I grab Maddie and shove the searing wire into her left ear canal. Guttural sounds come now, more animal than human.

I lean down and whisper into Maddie's right ear. "I told you I was only here to take. I'm going to leave you alive, in the quiet dark where the only thing you'll sense is pain and the stink of your own burning flesh. Hell on Earth is wrought by monsters, some are born and some made. Don't be surprised when the ones you make bite their creators. That's their nature."

With that, I cram the hot spike down into the canal of Maddie's right ear, rendering her completely deaf. I stand there quietly and watch her squirm about. As she makes the slightest attempt to lift herself, I grab her face with my left hand, pry her jaws open by gouging my thumb and forefingers through her cheeks and separating the back molars. With my right hand, I pick up the hemostat and firmly grasp the tip of Maddie's tongue with them. Holding the hemostat with my left hand now, I pull her tongue out and begin working the wire back and forth; slowly severing the front half it to a chorus of gurgling. I toss it aside, onto the same table.

After I release Maddie, she begins mewing wildly in anger, thrashing about. I leave her there and return to the kitchen. There, I retrieve the Mason jar with my preserved clitoris floating about in it. I take it back to the operating room, remove the lid and drop Maddie's corneas and tongue inside with my clitoris. After sealing it, I place the now fuller specimen jar into the small fireproof safe that once housed Solid Rock's cash. I place it back where I found it, inside Maddie's bedroom closet.

Back in the surgical suite with Maddie, I unplug the cauterizing machine and wheel it and the tray into the hallway. I plug it into an outlet but leave it off. Stepping back in the operating room, I open the specimen closet to my left and begin sweeping the jars from their shelves, letting them burst across the old wood floors. They ring out like machine-gun fire as they break in series. When I reached the bottom shelf, the fumes become overwhelming. Smashing the last few, I rush out of the room and shut the door behind me. I lay the lead cord of the cauterizer over the door handle, dangling the hot end about six inches above the floor. Leaving it, I return to the kitchen and retrieve my rifle. As I head to the backdoor, I turn the knob of the cauterizing machine. I'm greeted with the audible click I still hear in my nightmares. Then I jack it to the max by turning the knob all the way to the right. The sharp tip glows as it sways slightly from the door handle. I flee out the back, closing the door behind me. I'm off into the woods.

Twilight is ending. I begin running east by way of Highway nineteen toward Asheville. Sticking close to the edge of farmer's fields, I do my best to put as much distance between myself and Maddie's house.

Al used a chemical called urea-formaldehyde to bond layers of wood together. Because of this, I learned that formaldehyde fumes are extremely flammable, but heavier than the atmosphere. They will creep across the floor in a thin layer and spread across the house. Formaldehyde fumes are particularly dangerous because of the low ignition temperature. The tip of the cauterizing loop will be plenty. It won't be long before Maddie flops off the table and begins to crawl toward the door. When she finally manages to open it, the hot loop will fall into the heavy fumes, then an energetic flash.

After a full out run for half an hour, my energy begins to drain. I'm roughly three miles away from Maddie's house now. I keep moving forward at a fast hike.

It isn't long before I hear it. A whooshing explosion. It sounds as though the house itself has burst like a balloon. Minutes later there are sirens.

The fire department will sift through the rubble and ash, eventually coming across the small safe. They, like the Sheriff's department, are proxies for Solid Rock. It will be remitted into Vernon Proffit's hands, where he will open it in private, assuming he will retrieve the churches' cash. Peering in with his one remaining eye, Vernon will unearth my presents.

The blast's thudding resonance is a new birth. I have taken two lives in less than a day. What difference does it make? Governments force eighteen-year-olds to kill for them, often for no real reasons at all. So, in a way, I'm not that much different than many people my own age. There will be no parade or condolences for removing the unrighteous with equally righteous violence.

I am full of Maddie's food, so I have plenty of fuel left in me for the remainder of the morning.

By early afternoon, I have covered the five miles to the border between Yancey and Madison counties. To ease the difficulty due to terrain, I take the risk and begin walking along Highway nineteen. When a car approaches, I try to profile them. Do they look like members of Solid Rock? If it's a large truck or humungous sedan, I duck into the brush. Otherwise, I stick out my thumb in an attempt to get a ride further up the road. Three cars come along in an hour. The first two zoom right past. The third is an early eighties canary yellow Volvo wagon with two kayaks riding on the roof rack. One is blue and the other orange. I see the faces of two young men become clearer as it approaches and begins to slow. They both appear to be about my age. The car is obviously a hand-me-down from parents, the remnants of a recent childhood.

The passenger is a skinny guy wearing a white t-shirt with a blonde buzz cut. The driver is plumper, with an olive complexion, and a plume of bushy red hair. The car stops near me, half on the road, half off. I approach the passenger door and lean over.

"Do you need a ride?" says the blond guy with an unusually thick southern accent.

"Yeah."

"Where are you headed?" The driver blurts out in a higher-pitched tone.

"Asheville," I respond, not knowing what else to say.

"Hop the hell on in, then," the driver responds.

They take no mind of the rifle as I lay it across the floorboard in the back. Neither mentions the blood on my shirt or fresh stitches on my neck. I have a seat behind the passenger, the butt of the rifle lying atop my shoes. Firearms are such a common sight up here, no one really thinks much of it.

The blond passenger turns around and introduces himself.

"I am Nate and that is Herschel."

Herschel waves his right hand in response as he pulls back onto the empty road.

"I assume your parents provided you with a proper moniker," Nate inquires in an eloquent southern drawl.

Herschel, interrupts, glinting at me through the rearview mirror, "don't encourage his personality disorder."

"Pardon?" Nate responds.

"He's such a hyperlexic queen," Herschel says to me, ignoring Nate altogether.

"Nate's a goddamn English major with a chub for all things literary. He talks like that almost all the pecker-loving time."

Nate turns around quietly and begins to light a cigarette out of a pack of Marlboros.

"I'm Hannah," I say with some initial discomfort adapting to my new identity.

"Would you like a cigarette?" Nate says while handing me a lighter and a single cigarette over his left shoulder. He doesn't even look back for a response. Coughing a little, I feel my nerves calm somewhat as I take the first inhalation.

"There was one hell of a mess back there," Herschel says. "There was a roadblock. The police told us there had been a gas explosion."

"Pray tell, how did you find yourself on the side of the highway this morning?" Nate says, not turning around.

"Escape,", I involuntarily say, wistfully.

I look out the window and take a small exhale of relief.

There is an awkward silence, then Nate chimes in. "From whom?"

"The Erlking," I say, not thinking.

"Who the fuck is this Earl guy?" Hershel blurts out.

Nate corrects him. "The King of the Elves. It is from a poem. In Germanic folklore, Elves are most often associated with the duties of persuasion on behalf of the demonic. Essentially, Hannah said she is running from an emissary of the devil upon Earth."

"Something like that," I reply.

Herschel and Nate quietly glance at one another, as not to be seen. I figure they're both thinking, 'Who is this crazy girl we just picked up?'

"That is absolutely terrible," Nate says.

He turns around to look at me again.

"It sounds like you have had a difficult morning."

Sensing I am in no place to talk, Nate turns the conversation back onto himself and Herschel.

"We have had a bit of a rough morning ourselves. Herschel and I are business partners, and we had a deal almost fall through."

"Almost?"

"One of our regional suppliers is experiencing shortages."

"What business are you in, exactly?"

I am biased in my opinion based on their age and Herschel's appearance, as he wore an unfortunate brown button-up collared shirt with short-sleeves and khaki shorts. His hair is a disheveled pouf of red curls. Nate looks military to me. He is skinny, but fit, with a dirty blond buzzcut. He wears a simple, crisp white t-shirt and a pair of jeans.

"Sales and distribution," Herschel says.

"Distribution of what?"

"This, that, and other things, you know? Don't worry about it."

"No, I don't. But that's fine."

Nate interjects. "You'll have to excuse him."

Directing his comment toward Herschel, Nate says, "we have discussed how you can be terse and rude to others. This is one of those times. Remember, you asked me to point it out the next time you did it."

"Goddamnit," Herschel mumbles under his breath, with the angery realization Nate is right.

Nate continues, "our supplier is being strong-armed into a less profitable contract with an alternative retailer. He informed us this would have to be the last time he did business with us. His new guys had already claimed an exclusive deal with him. Our supplier said he wasn't supposed to, but he sold us his products one last time. That gives us a month or so to make new arrangements with our other supplier. We have a meeting in Asheville this afternoon."

My confused look is interrupted by a loud crash and severe jostling, followed by a slight fishtail from an impact to the rear of the Volvo. Nate and I turn around, as Herschel accelerates, visibly frightened by what he sees in the rearview mirror. It's a faded, red, late seventies model Chevy truck that has been ridiculously modified, with enormous ground clearance for monster-sized tires. It has a homemade police bumper bolted to the front, constructed from square steel tubing. As the truck accelerates in pursuit, the tires deliver a high-pitched whine to our ears. We're somewhere in Madison county now. The truck lunges to the left and into the lane of oncoming traffic. A light tap to our left rear wheel from the side makes the car spin three hundred and sixty degrees more times than I can count. We come to rest on the left side of the road in gravel, facing back toward the road. The Volvo's rear bumper is only a couple of feet from a granite wall formation. The truck pulls off the road and heads right for us. I am afraid they will ram us, but they slow. The driver gently pushes their steel bumper against the front of the car, which pins it to the granite wall.

"Who the fuck is that," I whisper.

"Our competition," a stoic Nate responds.

I figured since they didn't ram the car at full speed, they don't want Nate and Herschel dead. However, they aren't disinclined to the idea. At best, the boys are in for a severe beating. I lean over and grasp Al's rifle with my right hand. I only have three rounds.

"Don't do that," Nate says.

Herschel stares ahead, mute from fear.

"Lie down on the floorboard, pull the seat cover over yourself, and be quiet. They likely won't notice you. They are only looking for us. If you get the chance, run."

I do as Nate said, not wanting to get involved in whatever is going on. All I wanted was a ride to town.

I hear the men approach. Both come to a stop at either front door.

"You'ins know don't nobody else buy from Tommy no more but us. Open them doors and let us have it and we won't kill you."

I hear the sound of a shotgun shell being chambered. The locks click open. There is grunting and a struggle. The other man says, "You fuckers knows better!"

The air outside the Volvo fills with a symphony of dense thuds and screams, then fades. Nate was right, the two men were honed in on them and didn't take notice of the lump covered by fabric on the floor. I lie here for at least a minute. I have learned to be afraid of men like them. Suddenly, the guilt of what Charles would think of me flows into my brain like liquid. What would he think of me cowering? Charles was a pacifist by nature. What lesser evil would he have me choose? What would Al or Milly think? Their voices bounce around off the interior of my skull. Then I hear Al's voice from when I first told him what had been done to me. "I'm going to kill him," Al had said. Milly stopped him, but at the time, I wish she wouldn't have.

I torque my body to the right and extend my hand. I slowly pop open the rear passenger door and gradually push it halfway open. I slink out feet first, on my stomach. Outside on my knees, guarded from sight by the door, I hear Herschel scream, "No, please don't! We won't do it again. No, no, please no!" Then there are shrieks and squeals of intense pain. Nate stays unflappable. Keeping low, I creep along the car and continue down the side of the truck. When I reach the cab, I stand up slightly to peer over the edge of the bed.

The scene begins to come into view. The tailgate is down. There are two men who appear to be in their fifties. The one to my left is bald, short, and obese. His face is round, cheeks, nose, and neck red and puffy. He's wearing a dirty, faded green SunDrop t-shirt and mud-stained jeans. The other man is much taller, even more so than myself. He has broad shoulders, with sharp features offset by a large mustache. He is naturally husky and appears strong, filling out his dirty, off-white work tee with bulk. The brown Dickies he wears makes me think he just came off of a construction site.

Nate is on his knees behind the tailgate. The tall man stands in front of him with the muzzle of a pump shotgun against Nate's forehead. I notice how much blood is on Herschel's shorts. Then I see how he is clutching his left hand against his chest. The short man has a pair of bolt cutters in his right hand and Herschel's severed left pinky in the other; all the while shoving it into Hershel's face.

"Do you see what happens when we lose money and time? The short man screams. "It means you lose something. The number of pounds equals the number of fingers. I know Tommy has a one-pound minimum, you both owe us at least one finger." He looks at the tall man and shouts, "get his ass up and put him on the tailgate," referring to Nate. "You'ins gonna be lucky to have one finger left to pick your nose with."

I click off the safety and begin to lift my rifle gently, keeping it right below the edge of the cab. Just as the tall man moves the muzzle of the shotgun away from Nate's forehead to lean over and pick him up, I center the crosshairs of the scope onto my target and fire a round into his forehead. His massive body becomes instantaneously limp and crashes to the gravel below.

I rack the bolt and turn the sites to the short man, just as he throws the bolt cutters in my direction. I raise the rifle and deflect it with the barrel. I fall backward, and inadvertently fire off a second round into the sky. As I roll over, I see the man's hand reach for the shotgun, as I peer underneath the truck. While still on the ground, I lift the rifle with my left hand, chamber the final round, tilt my head upward and pull the trigger. The bullet strikes the man through his right hand and into the shotgun's wooden stock, shattering it to splinters.

The man falls to his knees and begins screaming in pain. I scream as well, but in fury. I am barely aware of my actions until I'm already on him. I kick the obese man in the chin, which knocks him to his back. I strike him in the forehead as hard as I can with the butt of my rifle. Dazed, but not unconscious, he flails in pain. I put the rifle down on the tailgate and pick up what is left of the shotgun. I pump it until all five shells have been ejected. The stock has turned into a forest of spikes and shards of wood. I grab it with both hands; with the shattered stock facing downward. Frenzied, I step onto the man's chest full force, all the while stabbing at his neck and face with the sharpened bits of wood still connected to the shotgun butt. I transcribe my anger across his him with wood and blood.

I keep screaming, "Why did you do it?" over and over.

When Nate comes to his senses, he pulls me away from what is left of the man. Most of his facial bones are caved in completely. I look down to see pieces of the man's flesh embedded into the tatters of the shotgun stock. I feel Nate's arms around me from behind. He held on and says, "it's over now." My thoughts return me to the sight of Charles's dead body years before and I begin to cry. I throw the weapon down, turn around and hold my new friend as though I've known him for years.

Nate says to Herschel, "Take Hannah back to the car. I need to back their truck up so we can get our vehicle out of here. Herschel picks up his finger and takes my arm. I crawl into the back of the Volvo from the passenger's side and lie down. Herschel clutches his hand while he shuts the door before sliding into the front passenger's seat. I hear the truck start, then the metallic grinding of the vehicle's metal bodies coming apart. Upon returning, Nate opens the car door at my feet and tosses Al's rifle, the two discarded casings I fired from it, and what remains of the shotgun over my head into the cargo area of the hatchback. Shutting it again, Nate walks around the car and takes over driving. He says, "I retrieved everything I could, and wiped down the steering wheel where I touched it. I am not sure what to do in a situation like this, but I do know we need to be somewhere else post haste."

I have now doubled my body count. I find myself vacillating from feelings of, 'What's the difference?' to 'Good, those bastards had it coming.'

Let's see. I killed a crooked deputy serving as proxy law enforcement for a death cult, an evil woman whose favorite pastime was mutilating children's genitalia, and two assholes committing an act of torture on the roadside. Their deaths cause me less guilt than a jaywalking offense.

The rage I have felt for years has finally been released to the betterment of the world. The further we travel, the more confident I become of my liberation. I begin to feel drained and sleepy. I doze off, still lying across the Volvo's backseat.

25

We didn't make it to the hospital in time to reattach Hershel's pinky. On the way to try, he and Nate manufactured a tale involving a camping trip and chopping wood. The hospital staff didn't question it. The lie seems more likely than reality. We are deep in the Appalachians, with two national forests nearby. Camping accidents are a daily occurrence in this emergency room. They did, however, want to keep him overnight.

Nate still has to make it to the meeting. He asks me to go. Under different circumstances, I would say no, and be on my way. I've spent the last three years only speaking to two people. My ability to read others, especially young people from the modern world, has been extremely hampered. But who else is there better to trust than the man whose life I just saved?

Experiencing extreme violence together seals a connection that few others will understand. Soldiers often experience a similar bond. I had that with Charles.

We leave Herschel in a medicated stupor and make our way back to the parking deck in pensive silence. Nate drives, of course. I've only ever driven Al's tractor.

After both doors of the Volvo shut, I turn to Nate and ask, "What kind of business are you in, exactly?"

"Cannabis."

"What the fuck is that?"

"Marijuana," Nate states calmly.

"Do you smoke it?"

"No, but Herschel does."

"Neither of us set out to be drug dealers. We were just a couple of normal college kids, but extraordinary circumstances require congruent responses."

"I've known Herschel for two years, and he's more of a brother to me than my real brother."

"I grew up along a dirt road, in a doublewide, outside of Wilson. I've always been a bit different than my kin. I'm more inclined toward books than sports. The opposite is true of my younger brother, Gary. We are what they call, 'Irish twins,' born less than a year apart." Nate laughs to himself.

"He was held back a grade and has been perpetually two years behind me in school. Little merit was assigned to my good grades. Gary was always the favorite. He gravitated toward sports. You know, 'guy stuff.' Mind you, I do not have anything inherently against enjoying such activities. I just have no personal interest. My problem has always been with how their importance is unwarrantedly lofted. I have always loved fishing, but in eastern North Carolina, that's not 'guy stuff,' it is a cultural obsession."

"Gary has always been keen on church despite being, excuse my parlance, a whore. At least that's why they would call him if he were a teenage girl. To the wider community, when a boy does it, he's 'conquering' like he climbed a mountain. Why chastise the girls while praising the same boys they're having sex with?" Nate shakes his head.

"During my senior year of high school, I was accepted into the English program at State on a full scholarship, to the chagrin of my parents, who told me not to, 'get too big for my britches.' Or 'Don't think you're better than us now.'"

"My father has always been an abusive drunk. I never gave much thought to it until I met Herschel, who told me about his family. My father isn't much different than the other dads I knew growing up."

"Herschel's father passed away when he was fourteen. Now a widow, his mother scraped by. Diane, Herschel's mother, is a librarian in Little Washington. As you can imagine, it's not a lucrative career. Herschel and I were thrust together as university-assigned roommates our freshman year. Freshmen aren't allowed to have a car on campus. Diane was nice enough to offer me a ride home when she came to pick Herschel up for his first weekend away from school, about a month into the fall semester. I only agreed because Wilson is on the way to Washington. Before getting out of the car, in front of my parent's trailer, Diane handed me a piece of paper with her phone number on it. She told me I could call her if I needed anything. Then said goodbye, and that she'd see me Sunday evening."

"The weekend went by uneventfully. My father drank himself to sleep Friday and Saturday nights but rolled into church cloaked in an air of undeserved holiness Sunday morning. The pastor preached a sermon entitled, *Abomination*, He essentially said people like myself would be the downfall of western civilization. Though, I don't see what's so civilized about it." Nate lets out a sigh, seemingly exasperated with their shared stupidity.

"On the way home, my parents and Gary chatter about their sudden realization of the great, 'gay conspiracy.' I had known that I liked guys from the time I was thirteen. I struggled with those thoughts as if I were somehow programmed incorrectly. The term 'gay' wasn't an identity at my middle and high schools, but a taunt. I would repeat, 'Don't be gay. Don't be gay.' in my head, as though that might make a difference. I played and watched sports, went hunting and fishing; anything stereotypically considered masculine."

"I thought, maybe doing these things would help me like girls. They didn't. I fell in love with fishing instead of a girl." This brings a slight smirk to Nate's face.

"Listening to them drone on, I felt as though I was being shredded apart inside. At that moment in the car, I exploded."

"'You are all so hateful!' I yelled from the back seat, across from Gary."

"He said, 'What do you care? Are you a homo, or something?"

"Without thinking, I replied, 'What if I am?'"

"The car fell silent as my dad clicked off his holy-roller radio show."

"'So what if I were gay? Would you be so hateful to your own son?'"

"'You'd deserve hell, just like every last one of them,' my mother replied."

"'You know that ain't the way you were raised up,' my father added, suspiciously."

Nate grips the steering wheel, and grits his teeth, seething from remembering.

"What if people are born gay? What if you're wrong?"

"'God is never wrong,' my mother snapped. 'All those people make a choice to be that way. I have no sympathy. If God's law was carried out, we'd hang every last one of 'em and leave their bodies to rot in the public square.'"

"I corrected her, 'There is no public square in Wilson.'"

"'Smartass,' she shot back.

"Without thinking, I blurted out, 'It's better to be gay than hateful.'"

"My father screamed, 'You watch your damn mouth! Don't you ever talk to your mom that way again.'"

"Furious, I shouted back, 'She should not care what I say anyway, since I am one of those queers!'"

"Abruptly, my father turned onto a tractor pull-off next to a field of cotton. He briskly walked around the back of the car to my door."

"Dad snatched open the handle, reached down, and unbuckled my seatbelt. He grabbed me by my dress shirt collar and threw me headfirst into the gravel. I was pulled by my collar and pinned to the side of the car in a seated position. My dad held his left hand around my throat, while he pointed at me with his right index finger."

Nate stares blankly at the highway as if a vision of what happened is being projected onto it.

"'Are you a fucking fairy?' he asked, finger to my nose, as he screamed as loud as he could."

"Yes."

"The slapping and punching began. My mother and brother paid no mind to the beating, as I 'deserved' it. When it was over, my father left me on the side of the road. I had two black eyes, a broken nose, and an assortment of shoe-shaped bruises all over. He kicked me in the groin over and over because, 'If you ain't gonna use it right, you don't deserve it.'"

Tears gradually appear in the corner of Nate's eyes. He wipes them away, almost angry that they appear.

"By sheer will, I was able to walk a couple of miles to the nearest gas station, so I could use a payphone. I borrowed a quarter from a gentleman having a Coke and hotdog on the bench outside. I dialed up a woman I hardly knew and explained to her I was beaten and abandoned on the side of the road. A little over an hour later, her car pulled up to the gas station."

"Knowing I couldn't return home, Diane saw fit to take me under her wing as a surrogate mother of sorts."

"Living in the dorm isn't consistent. Their model is set up with the assumption students have stable home lives. We're forced to leave on long holidays and summer. I had nowhere else to go then, but she gave that to me. Whenever she takes Hershel home, I go as well. Every holiday, and the last two summers, I have lived in Diane's home. I have been treated with kindness I never knew before."

"Around Christmas last year, Diane was diagnosed with breast cancer after a routine mammogram. She was to begin chemotherapy and have a double mastectomy after the new year. Two days before the procedure, Diane's insurance company dropped her because of an acne diagnosis from her teens and twenties. They said this meant it was a 'preexisting condition' they're not liable for. The hospital asked for a fifteen thousand dollar deposit to continue. Needless to say, she didn't have it. Desperation set in. Herschel's Aunt Beverly, Diane's sister, knew a source up here in the cannabis business. The source is Beverly's boyfriend. Since Hershel was family, trust was easier to earn. We were in business in less than a month."

"Cannabis is exported by the ton from secret outdoor productions, or so-called, 'guerilla grows', throughout the Appalachian mountains each fall. During the rest of the year, it departs by the carload from indoor hydroponic operations. The region has the right climate, a history of moonshining, and all the distrust of the federal government that entails. Their market lacked reach, and we were on the ground at a huge university, in a cannabis-bare locale. There is plenty of disposable income and want for a quality product."

"As it stands now, Diane's recovery is going to be a long and expensive ordeal. We'll continue on as long as we have to," Nate says defiantly.

"You're gay?"

"Yes, I am," Nate says with no hesitation.

When Nate describes himself as gay, it's the first time I've heard the word used without it being slung about as an insult or accusation. Rather, for him, it is one part of his identity. I spent the years I should have been developing an understanding of my sexuality as a prisoner or in exile.

We head back north and eventually turn off into a suburban Asheville neighborhood. When we arrive at the house, Nate says, "Wait here. I am going to go in and let our supplier know what has happened."

Earlier, when Nate spoke of his supplier, I assumed we would be pulling up to a run-down flophouse of sorts. Rather, we are in the driveway of a two-story light blue house at the end of a cul-de-sac, in a neighborhood designed to make the middle class feel like the nouveau riche.

The front door opens and Nate disappears inside for about ten minutes. Nate cracks open the screen door and waves for me to come in. A deep woody smell, not unpleasant, hits me at the door.

"Is that what marijuana smells like?" I ask.

Nate and the man, who appears to be in his early fifties, look at me curiously.

"No," the man says. "That's Palo Santo wood burned as incense. I just like the smell."

He's about my height and rather scrawny. He has dark hair down to his shoulders, sprinkled with a small helping of gray. He is clean-shaven, with a sharp nose and black-rimmed glasses framing kind brown eyes.

"This is Zeke," Nate says.

I hold my hand out to him and introduce myself as Hannah. Zeke shakes it with a slight grip.

"It's pleasant to meet you, Hannah."

I can tell right away, Zeke is a bit of an eccentric. He's wearing what looks like thick pajama pants, with vertical stripes of red, orange, blue, and yellow over a background of purple. His button-down shirt is equally purple, with dozens of small identical pictographs of fish and neon pastels. He is barefoot.

The downstairs of Zeke's house is pine paneling and thick wall-to-wall green carpet. The living room's focal point is a conversation pit in the center. A very short, dark wooden table sits at the bottom. On it is a large digital scale, a silver tray, rolling papers, and an ashtray.

Zeke invites us down into the conversation pit. The three of us sit cross-legged, with Zeke on the broadside of the table, and Nate and I on either short end.

"I hear you found yourself in a mess of trouble this morning," Zeke says to me.

"Yes."

"Those were the Mace brothers. The taller man was Authur. The short, round one, whose face you mangled, was George."

"Moonshine doesn't pull in the cash it once did. A lot of shiners are turning to pot as supplemental income. After their father died a few years ago, the boys had begun playing rough. The older Mace always tempered their nature. Neither had the silver tongue of the late Mr. Mace, and business was failing because of it. They've grown a couple of patches of shitty weed in the past two years. Due to their failure, they have begun to levy threats against skilled growers."

"To expand their strength, they recently got tangled up with a group that claims to be Asatru called 'Odin's Oath.' They feign belonging to an ancient pre-Christian, Norse religion followed by the Vikings. But they don't actually follow any of its tenants. Rather, it's a cover for a white supremacist gang. Their rhetoric debases an entire religion, for whom most of the adherents want nothing to do with such hatred. Rest assured, you did humanity a favor. They were nasty, violent brutes who will not be missed."

Zeke turns to Nate and says, "Open the gate and drive the car into the back yard. Close it behind you."

I haven't said a word since introducing myself, so after Nate leaves silence falls over the room.

After we are alone, Zeke says, "Thank you for saving them. They're good boys. Herschel's aunt Beverly is my girlfriend. If he had been killed, I would never live it down. We're going to take care of this little problem."

Zeke stands and motions for me to follow him out the back door.

His backyard features a small deck built against the house. An old wooden privacy fence engulfs the entirety of the rear perimeter. The focal point is a workshop about half the size of the house and painted the same blue.

Nate pulls the car between the house and the shop.

Zeke slips on a pair of brown canvas flip-flops. I follow him down the stairs and to the car. He clicks a small black dongle, which opens a garage door on the shop large enough to drive the car through.

"Back the car into the garage," Zeke commands Nate through the Volvo's open driver's side window.

Nate pulls forward, then backs up slowly into the open door. I follow Zeke through the same door. He clicks the remote again to close it behind us. Zeke reaches over and flips on the overhead lights. The sudden illumination reveals a shop riddled with plate metal scraps strewn across a smooth concrete floor in some form of organization only understood by Zeke. There are hundreds of tiny metal animal figures welded from scraps sitting on shelves. There is one very large piece in the center of the floor, which is nearly complete. It's a cockatoo with chainsaw blades for its frill feathers. Zeke noticed the surprise splashing across my face in a wave.

Looking at me, he says, "It's an order for a lady with too many parrots and too much money. Mostly, I deal in these little guys. Foxes, rabbits, turtles, and such made of unwanted bits of metal I'm able to buy cheaply. I sell them at flea markets or to local shops downtown. It was a hobby. Now it's a bit of an obsession. I only sell them so I have room to make more.

Nate opens the hatchback, revealing the shattered shotgun and Al's rifle. The carpet is soaked through with the blood that remained on the shotgun's jagged butt. George's flesh is still present, gored and clinging onto the shards.

"Well, that's just grizzly, isn't it?" Zeke remarks. "The police have no love for the Mace brothers. They'll look into their deaths, but not too hard. Some of them would secretly like to thank Hannah if they were honest. Nate says he wiped down the Mace brother's truck. From what I understand, Herschel mainly bled on himself, and there's probably not enough blood present on the ground to identify him via DNA. They probably won't find the site before the flies drink it up. Not to mention, the Madison County Sheriff's department doesn't have extensive capabilities. The only thing that can link you to their deaths is in this trunk. If you get rid of that, you get rid of the problem."

26

Zeke goes back inside to change into work clothes, leaving Nate and me alone in the shop.

"Thank you for what you did back there," Nate says.

"You would have done the same."

"I would like to think so. But, if we are going to be real, the Mace brothers aren't the first people you have killed, are they? You did not hesitate and were absolutely brutal. How many people have you killed?"

"Just two other people in the past couple of days."

"In the last couple of days?!"

I didn't realize how outrageous that would sound until the words were in my ear from my own mouth.

"Yeah", I reply reluctantly.

"How many people have you killed?"

"Just the four."

"So you went your whole life without murdering anyone, only to commit four homicides in forty-eight hours?"

"I'm having a bad week."

"I concur with that assertion," Nate says as we watch Zeke step out the back door. He has donned thick tan overalls with a dark blue denim long sleeve shirt underneath.

Zeke's heavy boots gallop down the deck steps, then softly through the grass.

"Let's get to work, then," Zeke announces, as he briskly enters the doorway while rubbing his hands together. He turns briefly to Nate and asks, "would you mind closing the locking door please?"

When Zeke reaches the back of the shop, he opens up an electrical box and pops on three circuit breakers in sequence. The first one causes an air compressor with a tank the size of a small person to snap on in the far corner for a few seconds as it builds up pressure. The second turns on a huge overhead exhaust fan that causes metal shutters above it to slap open. Faint daylight trickles in around the edges of the rain cowling mounted above. The third breaker illuminates a red light on the welding machine labeled 'on'. The blue metal casing begins to emit a low hum.

Zeke addresses the two of us as a teacher would. "This is an arc welder. Some people call them stick welders since the rods they use are essentially coated sticks with flux inside. Every time I touch the lead with the welding rod in it to grounded metal, it creates enough heat to melt the two pieces together. That's where the air compressor comes in. The compressor blows air across a special carbon stick coated in copper. It heats up beyond steel's melting point, creating something like a mini open-air forge of sorts. It's called arc gouging. This is what I use to break a previous weld. It will completely obliterate any steel I hold it to, eventually turning it into a pile of dusty slag."

Zeke puts the shotgun into a huge vice at the shoulder where the gunmetal intersects the wooden stock. A metal clamp with a wire leading back to the blue welding machine is clipped to the back of the vice, grounding it. In Zeke's hand is a far more robust, red clamp. He clips the copper welding rod into this clamp at its midpoint.

Zeke warns, "You're going to want to shield your eyes. The UV emitted from the arc can damage your vision."

After saying this, he pulls down a green, full-face visor. It has a rectangular window of dark glass in front of the eyes so Zeke can see what he's working on. We both use our hands as makeshift blinders by tilting our heads down in a sort of frozen salute. As Zeke pushes the stick forward from the muzzle back to the stock, the metal slowly turns into tiny molten bits, falling to the concrete floor. Eventually, nothing but the shattered wooden stock of the shotgun remains.

Zeke heads back to the hatch of the Volvo to retrieve Al's Mauser. As the rifle barrel begins to melt, I tear up. It's the only thing I have left of him, and now I have to trade it for my freedom. Then I remember the papers in my pocket guaranteeing a new life. I begin to realize I will always have Al with me because he has gifted me every moment from that point forth by allowing me to take on Hannah's identity.

I feel a deafening wave thrust me to the ocean floor. The sand creeps into the static of my nerve endings, and I begin to come to terms with the dramatic shift my life has taken. A few days ago, I lived in calm, exiled from the world. Now here I am disposing of murder weapons. This must be what it's like when we're born. Our bodies are banished from a cozy, warm cabin into a cold callous existence of infinite choices, most of which lead to no importance at all.

At some point, I curl up into a ball, sitting on the floor. My forehead is pressed into my knees, arms folded around my body. Zeke doesn't notice. How could he with that mask and noise? Nate, seeing this, kneels down in front of me and wraps his arms around my shoulders. For a moment, I feel like I'm back in the cabin. Even if I'm not, I don't feel quite as bad. I haven't had a real friend since Charles was killed.

The welding stops and we stand up.

"Are you okay?" Zeke asks.

"Probably never again."

He gives me a sad smile while releasing the rifle butt from the machine vice.

"Looks like I'm having a little bonfire tonight. Perhaps I'll toast marshmallows in celebration knowing the bastards won't be coming for me like some kind of backwoods crime syndicate. I'm just a rogue farmer for Christ's sake."

"I thought you were a welder?" I ask confused.

"Ah, I can see how you might. No, I grow and sell marijuana for a living. Asheville is, well, different. Those who couldn't bear to give up on the fantasy of a communal utopia dreamed up in the sixties gravitated toward the Bay Area, and to a smaller degree, Asheville. It's the kind of place where any gender can walk around topless, people smoke pot openly, and no one notices or cares. I grew up here and have no reason to leave."

"You have one more thing to worry on. The shotgun's bloody stock left an outline on the carpet in the hatch compartment. We're going to have to cut that out. We'll burn the carpet on the fire too."

Zeke retrieves a box cutter from his bench and begins slicing out the carpet remnant. The fabric makes a ripping noise as he and Nate free it from the underlying adhesive.

"Oh shit," Zeke says. "The blood has soaked through."

Nate and I glare at each other with concern.

Zeke makes his way to the shelf under his workbench. He pulls out a power tool with a metal body that resembles a drill with a short neck. There is a circular fixture attached to it with metal wires sticking out.

"This is an angle grinder with a wire brush," Zeke says. "I can use it to strip the glue off the metal, as well as metal off of metal. It should scape away any bloody residue."

Zeke puts on a respirator and pulls down his welding hood. He flips the dark lens up, revealing a clear one beneath it. This allows me to see a distorted image of Zeke's green eyes. He plugs the grinder into an orange extension cord and leans into the cargo space of the old Volvo. The stiff wire ends on the disc will remove the adhesive and smooth down any surface metal that may have been exposed to Arthur Mace's blood.

As Zeke works away, Nate and I hold our ears for what seems longer than it is. All the while, the smell of burning carpet adhesive rises from the rear of the car and is ejected by the exhaust fan installed into the roof of the workshop. Once finished, Zeke points to Nate and says, "Get the Shop-Vac next to the workbench. It's your shift now."

Nate does as told, and wheels over what looks like a metal drum with a hose attached. He vacuums meticulously for more than half an hour, eyeballing for any legally admissible errant speck. All the while, Zeke begins gathering wood for the firepit off to the side of the back deck. It looks as though the pit had once been a tractor-trailer tire rim, but has been transformed into a metal flower with petals fashioned from plate steel spreading out from the center.

A few minutes after Nate shuts off the vacuum, Zeke comes back carrying two spray bottles. One is white, the other, brown.

"Nate, vacuum up the slag from the gun barrels," Zeke asks politely.

As Nate moves to scrounge his new evidence hunting ground, Zeke puts the white bottle, and a set of dish gloves in my hands, followed by a roll of thick blue shop paper towels.

"Bleach?" I question.

"It gets out any remaining visible stains. There probably aren't any, but this is a due diligence kind of affair."

I clean the cargo compartment of the Volvo thoroughly with the bleach, making several passes. Nate finishes vacuuming up slag around the same time I can't stand the bleach smell any longer.

"Are we done?" I ask Zeke.

"Nope. Bleach only gets rid of the visible stains. DNA has to be oxidized. For that, we use hydrogen peroxide. It has to sit and work, then wipe it up and repeat the process several times. It's an industrial concentration of thirty percent. The stuff on drug store shelves is only about three percent. It'll oxidize what remains of the blood cells, which is essentially what fire does. In a sense, you're chemically burning away the DNA evidence. You'll need to wait a few minutes for all the bleach to dry before applying it."

Zeke hands Nate his own set of gloves, then respirators and safety goggles for us both before stating, "it's dangerous stuff. Do not get it on your skin."

While we do that, Zeke dumps the contents of the Shop-Vac into the fire pit, then flushes the hose of the machine by sucking up hydrogen peroxide. He opens the vacuum and carefully wipes down the interior with a hydrogen peroxide-soaked rag.

By the time we finish, night has fallen. We gather up whatever remains into the fire pit, along with split logs. Using lighter fluid, Zeke creates flames with a dramatic woosh that makes me think momentarily of Maddie Bellew's house.

We each sit in a mismatching assortment of folding lawn chairs.

Still in his welding attire, Zeke pulls a small metal tube from his pocket. He unscrews the top to reveal a single joint. Deftly, Zeke returns the cap back to the empty cylinder. Out of the same pocket, he produces a black torch lighter. Zeke lights the joint with all the care one gives a fine cigar. He takes three nice long draws off it before silently motioning by holding it in my direction, all the while still holding the smoke from the last hit.

"No, thank you."

"That's cool," Zeke responds while exhaling smoke. "No pressure. It's not for everyone."

Zeke is a man of steady calm. It's like he knows something the rest of us don't, but can't articulate it. His mind is written in a cryptic, yet-to-be-spoken language, but he does his best to translate for us.

We sit quietly staring into the fire, aware of each other's presence but feeling no need to for flimsy chitchat. That kind of horseshit small talk is for the human cattle hemmed into cubicles. Once you've murdered someone to save another's life, or corroborated in destroying evidence of said murder, there's nothing remaining but real talk. Only after the carpet has melted away, and the fire has begun to crumble to embers, does Zeke up and ask, "What in the hell happened to you, Hannah?"

"Everything."

For the first time, I tell the story of Tiffany, my imprisonment with Charles, and how I came to find Al and Milly. We spoke and kept the fire going until dim light breaks over the Black Mountains.

As they listen, the warm mountain air is filled with the resonance of my singular voice, uninterrupted. I had Al and Milly, but they were parental by nature. Most of our conversations were back and forth, not protracted listening. This is divulgence to peers without the pressure of time constraints or looming abuse. It makes me think of my last night with Tiffany at the lake, waiting for the Perseids. That seems so far from me now, as to have occurred in another geological epoch. We each folded up our chairs and place them inside the garage.

Zeke turns to Nate and asks, "Do you still want to do business? What happened today, I did for karma. Don't think you owe me for it. Either way, the Mace brothers would have found their way to my door eventually."

"It is going to take the rest of my cash to cover Herschel's hospital bill, so I am going to have to decline momentarily," Nate says.

"How much did you buy from Tommy? Zeke inquired.

"Two pounds of blueberry. I have found it to be a good investment, but the turnover is slower. Herschel wants to buy three pounds of outdoor-grown skunk from you."

"How much is a pound of skunk?" I question.

Zeke says, "Two thousand per pound."

"So, six thousand dollars?"

Zeke nods his head yes. He looks at Nate and says,

"I have a bit more than three pounds left over from last fall. I'll save it for you. You need it more than anyone else."

I put my left hand into my pants pocket, retrieve a wad of hundreds, and begin counting out six thousand dollars.

"Are you sure you want to do that?" Nate interjects.

"Very. Milly always told me that everything happens for a reason. I don't believe that. However, if I've ever seen providence, this is it. My agnosticism will have to make an exception in this case."

Nate replies, "Never say anything like that in front of Herschel. He'll be an emotional martyr, claiming he had to sacrifice a finger just so we could all meet."

"Nate's right, Herschel can be an asshole like that," Zeke says. He stands there for a second before continuing, "I'll go get what you need," then wanders off.

"Where the hell do you hide this stuff?" I press Nate.

"In the kayak cargo holds. There are two on each, one in the aft and the other in the stern. Did you actually think Herschel kayaked? I love him as my brother, but he struggles physically with miniature golf. Hiding it out in the open like that is so brazen, no one would even think to look. Police officers are always looking under things, instead of up. We also make sure to obey traffic laws, but not enough to be suspiciously doing so. Our rule is to travel five miles an hour above the speed limit when on the highway.

Zeke pops back out the door carrying a black trash bag. We follow him to the garage. Behind closed doors, he opens the bag to reveal three extra-large vacuum-sealed bags, each filled with what looks like tiny Christmas trees.

Loaded up, we roll out into the dawn and get back to the hospital around sun-up. Herschel is still sleeping when we get to his room. We enter quietly. Nate finds his way to a recliner in the corner. He kicks it back to an almost horizontal position. I begin toward a hard waiting room chair sitting on the other side of the room.

"What are you doing?" Nate sternly announces. "We can both fit in this thing."

I'm not sure how I feel about that, and it must show on my face.

"What are you worried about? I'm a gay man and you're a lesbian. It'll be like sleeping beside your sister."

In a moment of Charles-like literalism, I say, "But I don't have a sister."

Nate replies, "Well, you do now."

27

We are roused by a nurse at eleven in the morning saying, while glancing at a clipboard, "It looks like the doctor is going to let you go home today."

I lie there listening to the nurse give Hershel follow-up care instructions he is unlikely to follow. As she leaves, I sit up, which unpeels my face from Nate's arm.

Herschel looks at us and mouths, "what the fuck happened?"

"We will discuss that later," Nate replies.

Nate and I head to the parking deck to retrieve the car while Hershel receives his complimentary wheelchair ride to the front door. Nate drives, I hop in the front, which leaves the backseat for Herschel. He slides into the backseat butt first, clutching a heavily bandaged left hand against his body. The nurse gently shuts the door behind him as he lies across the backseat with his head resting behind the driver's seat. He lets out a groan as his body comes to rest on the old vinyl.

"You totally fucking killed them, like, for real," Hershel says with a state of disbelief.

"There was no choice," I respond.

"No, just, thank you, is all. I mean, what else do you say to the person who saved your life?"

I'm taken aback by a genuine display of emotion by someone who seemed a real wise-ass only hours before.

Looking directly at Herschel I say, "The Mace brothers deserved what they got. So few monsters ever get their tickets punched. I don't feel guilty. I would kill them over and over for all eternity, if for no other reason than that they deserved it.

"Like Sisyphus," Nate interjects.

"Who?" Herschel responds.

"He was a Greek God who fancied himself smarter than Zeus, only to find out he wasn't. Sisyphus was punished by having to push a boulder uphill for all eternity, only to have it roll back each time."

"Yeah, but I'd rather shoot someone than push a goddamn rock," I say.

Both nod their heads in agreement.

As we drive, I explain the reality of who I am to Hershel, the way I had to Nate and Zeke last night.

After, the rest of the ride is relatively quiet. We head to the only place we can, Little Washington, Hershel's family home.

We arrive downtown right before dusk. Nate pulls the Volvo into the short paved driveway of a tall, two-story Victorian house off of Market Street. It nestles tightly among similar homes. The house has white trim and shares the same canary yellow as the car, which I assume isn't coincidental. There appear to be two porches: the main sitting porch downstairs and a small sleeping porch out of a bedroom doorway upstairs.

The silhouette of a tiny figure waits at the front door. Of course, this is Herschel's mother. As the car comes to a stop, Herschel becomes sheepish, clutching his hand, seeming to fear admonishment.

Nate says to me, "I need you to stay put for a few minutes, this is going to be a bit uncomfortable."

Through the window I can hear the muffled, terse tone of a mother for several minutes, followed by silence, then crying. This goes on for about fifteen minutes.

After the commotion calms, Nate motions for me from the porch steps. I open the car door slowly, apprehensive that this mother's rage could render the lightning of God himself.

Approaching this sickly figure, I begin to sense her love.

"Naomi?" she says.

"Yes, Ma'am."

"What a pleasure."

She steps down the stairs and embraces me with no semblance or warning.

"I hear you had a really bad couple of days."

"Yes, Ma'am," I reply, not knowing what else can be said.

After a prolonged, huggy silence, I say "It could have been worse."

There's a lot of truth to that statement. I delivered her ninety-nine point nine-nine percent of her son, one hundred percent of her adopted son, and myself as one more burden. It could have been an empty driveway instead, and an endless missing person case.

"Darlin', come in," Diane says with utmost sincerity.

Diane is barely five feet tall, emaciated from chemo, with light brown hair and eyes. She has a small nose. Her skin looks sickly and pale. She wears a pair of greenish plaid pajamas, a blue sweatshirt that appears to have once had a logo that long ago faded, a pink knitted hat, and a pair of brown slip-on shoes. She seems surprisingly girlish and youthful in character, despite being quite ill.

The door opens to a staircase on the right and to the left, a wide-open kitchen with a dining area separated by a bar covered with white tiles. The kitchen floor is covered in similar but larger white tiles, which give way to a wooden floor an equally open living room. There's a matching floral print couch and chair-and-a-half combo, and a ratty old recliner. The door under the staircase is cracked wide enough that I can see it's a half-bath.

On Diane's table, dinner waits for us: ham, butter beans, collards, black-eyed peas, cornbread, and tea so sweet it hurts my teeth. My hunger is obvious. I try to restrain myself, but I haven't eaten in more than a day. We didn't think to.

There are no bullshit niceties at Diane's table. She doesn't make small talk about the weather or other such nerve soothing utterances. No blessings are said. There is silence, eating, and contentedness with still being alive, for whatever it's worth.

About the time my plate is empty, Diane says "I'm glad you killed those sorry sons-of-bitches. Don't you ever feel bad or guilty on it. You did what the rest of us hope we'll have the bravery to do if the time comes."

"I don't feel guilty about it."

"You don't know just how strong you really are, yet. You're getting a damn good idea though," Diane says, pointing the tines of her fork in my direction. Collards flap with every word. "We can talk about that another day. After dinner, the boys have work to do, but what you need more than anything is sleep."

I am given a fresh toothbrush and an old pair of gray, lint-ridden sweats, which I assume belonged to Herschel's dad. The shirt hangs loose and I have to tie the waistband string extra tight. I make sure to transfer Hannah's Social Security card and folded birth certificate from my jeans pocket to my sweats. I'll keep them on me until I have an ID. They're the most valuable thing I own.

I head upstairs to take a shower. The top floor has a full bath and three bedrooms. After my shower, I curl up on the couch in the living room and fall into a long-needed slumber.

The next morning, I'm awakened by the sound of Diane having a coughing fit from the kitchen. I go to her and arrive just as it subsides.

"Side effects of the chemo," she says in a raspy voice.

"Did you sleep at all?"

"No, sugar. When you're close to possibly dying, sleeping before an eternity of it seems counterintuitive. Fuck cancer, I'm living to see my grandbabies."

I smile at her frankness. I haven't been around another woman, save Maddie Bellew, since Milly died of her own cancer. Milly couldn't fight it with medical treatment, nor would she have. She believed the Lord had his plan and resigned herself to it. She longed to be with Hannah.

"The boys haven't been in bed for more than an hour. They probably won't be up and coherent until this afternoon."

"What were they doing?"

"Making dime bags."

"And that would be?"

"Little bags of marijuana. I don't know why they call them dime bags. They're not ten-cent or ten dollars. Each bag is a sixteenth of an ounce. The blueberry bags go for twenty-five dollars and the skunk twenty. What you guys brought home last night is worth a bit shy of thirty-thousand dollars. The boys will pay you back with interest in a few weeks.

"Keep it. I'd rather buy in. I have money to invest. I've committed far worse crimes than selling dried-up flowers. I'd be willing to invest a third of all costs for the same percentage in earnings."

Diane can tell I'm serious. She doesn't even attempt to discourage me or make a counteroffer.

"That would be fine. Now, this is a three-way endeavor. One-third for Herschel and myself, one-third for Nate, and the remaining third for you."

"What else am I doing?" I say flippantly.

With a serious tone, Diane interjects, "however, I expect you to take your high school equivalency exam and apply to college."

I look at her with shock.

"Dealing isn't a career path and you're way too smart not to do something worthwhile. It can be a great financial springboard, but it's a casino. One day, you'll have to leave the table, by choice or by handcuffs. You need to lay plans to have something better to walk into after you walk away. I don't believe in much of anything, but I think karma owes you a fortune."

"I've seen cancer before. It didn't look like this. It was far worse."

"Money. It's funny what wheelbarrows of that shit can buy. I'm not well, but I'm still here. The chemo and radiation are devastating physically, but this helps."

Diane pulls a thin joint out of her robe and lights it.

"I don't have any hair left."

She lifts the pink wrap she has around her head to reveal a bald scalp so pale I can see her veins through it.

"I feel downright ghoulish; like a reanimated corpse occupying time I was never intended to be given. The doctor said my hair would come back when the chemo is over. They're hoping I'll go into full remission eventually. Hospitals are cash vacuums, they never ask where it comes from, but they would easily turn me away if I couldn't pay. Instead, I get 'Please sign here' as the billing department casually takes wads of cash worth five figures as though

I'm buying a pack of gum. I began to wonder why it even mattered where the cash came from if no one else is hurt by my actions? I was always taught to do an honest day's work, but the cash spends just the same. I'm determined, if I make it through this shit, we're going to deal ourselves out of ever having to obey anyone else again. Why not? I'm tired of following laws that don't make a goddamn bit of sense, just to find myself miserable for being a 'good girl.' If I hadn't been a little naughty, I'd already been dead."

I nod in agreement."

"Would you mind shaving off all my hair?" I ask.

Diane looks at me dumbfounded and says, "Buy why, honey? You've got pretty, long blond hair. Do you know how many women want what you have? Don't feel like you have to take some kind of solidarity stand with me. I'm grown and can be the only bald bitch in town. It doesn't bother me."

"No, that's not why. I don't feel feminine and never liked having long hair, but until now, it hasn't been my choice to make. I figure, why not overcorrect? I've been through so much in the past few days. I want something striking to remind myself of where and when I am each time I look in the mirror for now. I want to see a physical manifestation of the power I have over my own body. I am finally free."

"George, my husband, had a beard trimmer. I'll have to dig around for it."

Diane casually puts the joint down. It is still burning in the white porcelain ashtray on the kitchen table. She wanders off to her bedroom. I sit there, staring into the faded red ash. I have a flashback of the Sillman's house on fire. My thoughts become pictures and feelings. There is a physical void where their house once was, now surrounded by ash. There would be an eventual reclamation of the property by the wild world that still laps at every door. I do feel bad for abandoning Milly's bantam silkies. They've likely been eaten by hawks and coyotes by now.

I must have blanked out a bit and headed inward. I am noticeably startled when Diane walks back in with two blue towels and a beard trimmer whose cord-end drags across the darkly stained wood floor. I let out an audible gasp and jerk my stare from the ashtray up to look in Diane's direction.

"Jesus, I'm not that scary, am I?" she asks in jest.

"No," I say, whipping one stray tear from my right cheek.

Diane pulls one of the chairs away from the kitchen table. I sit down and she drapes one down over my chest and one over my back, giving me a protective layer against falling hair.

"Are you sure you want to do this?" she asks one last time.

"Yes, very fucking sure."

28

The trimmer makes my whole head vibrate. I begin to sense cold air against parts of my scalp. Within minutes, I'm encircled by an explosion of blond hair. Diane shakes the towels off onto the floor.

"The broom and dustpan are in the small closet," she says, pointing to a broom closet just outside the kitchen, in the hallway. "I'm getting tired and need to have a seat."

I sweep the hair into one lumpy pile so large it fills up the dustpan three times. Diane continues smoking at the kitchen table. I sit down across from her again. She says, "you need some clothes."

Diane has already washed the pants and shirt I was wearing when the boys picked me up along Highway Nineteen. I get dressed and accompany Diane to the J.C. Penney's in Greenville. We take her sand-colored Toyota Camry. It's about a twenty-minute drive.

Walking into a department store after being in isolation for four years is a bit overwhelming. The lights seem extremely bright and it's surprisingly loud to a person who is used to hearing nothing but the elements speak. At the cabin, there were few passing cars, no television, and only two other people to converse with. What strikes me the most is all the branding. I just want clothes, but everything is deemed more or less special based on whose name is emblazoned on the item. I buy everything but underwear in the young men's department. I essentially buy identical uniforms: three pairs of jeans, a collection of black, grey, or dark green t-shirts, and a black pair of men's boots. It's summer. I won't need cold weather clothes for several months.

In the car, I get to hear a sampling of Diane's musical taste. It's mostly rock from the nineteen-sixties and seventies. I had forgotten how much I love the sound of a distorted electric guitar.

As I carry my three J.C. Penney bags through the front door, I am greeted by the sight of Herschel and Nate, who have just awakened. It's one in the afternoon. Nate has just begun a fresh pot of coffee. He is wearing a pink ladies' bathrobe, which I imagine he commandeered from Diane. Herschel is in a full set of Star Wars pajamas that certainly only belong to him.

As I place my bags on the bar, Nate asks, "Would anyone like French Toast?"

"Really?" I question.

"Yes. Why not?"

"Okay, sure I'd love some," I reply.

"Mark me down as a 'hell yes,'" Herschel boasts.

"I'll second the 'hell yes,'" comes from Diane.

We are each treated to a thick stack of French toast, made out of Merita white bread and served on paper plates. I couldn't be happier at this moment, considering my circumstances.

"You both worked hard last night," Diane says to the boys. "What do y'all have planned for the afternoon?"

Nate replies, "I thought we could take a walk through the marsh off Chocowinity Bay to pull in my crab traps and maybe cast a few minnows?"

A long groan comes from Herschel. "I fucking hate mosquitos, man."

"The feeling is not mutual. They love you," Nate says with a light-hearted retort and a rare smile. "You don't need to mope around the house all day mourning your lost pinkie. You won't even have to touch fish because of the wound."

"Nate is right. You can't just sit around here all day watching movies. Go get some fresh air. Just wear bug spray." Diane says.

"Fine!" Herschel begrudgingly responds.

"Will you come, Naomi?" Nate inquires of me.

"I haven't seen a large body of water for years. So, yes please."

We exit downtown by taking a bridge over the Pamlico river to a tiny peninsula that separates Chocowinity Bay from the larger river. The road down the peninsula is called Whichard's Beach, though there's not much beach from what I can see. We turn right down a dirt road, which is basically a long driveway into the woods. To the left of the water's edge is a small clearing used as a makeshift parking area.

As we exit the Volvo, I ask, "Are we allowed to be here?"

"After the things we've seen you do, to ask if we're allowed to be here is ironic," Herschel says.

Nate chimes in, "that was certainly an unexpected query, but I believe to be considered irony, it would have to be funny somehow. When you have seen the action that contradicts the presumed spirit of the commenter up close, it is perceived a bit differently. I suppose irony itself is always relative to the parties at the receiving end of the communication."

"Right on," Herschel comments snarkily.

I laugh a bit under my breath at Hershel's flippant response. Nate looks faintly irritated.

Herschel replies to Nate, "look at that smartass. I just proved your hypothesis."

Herschel and I stand there watching Nate remove his socks and shoes.

"Are you heading out there?" I ask Nate.

"Yes, that crazy motherfucker is going," Herschel informs me.

The reason I asked is Nate's better dressed than either of us. I'm wearing jeans and a t-shirt. Herschel is wearing khaki cargo shorts and a three-button pullover shirt with a worn, wavy collar. Nate, however, has on brand new pastel pink shorts and a nicely pressed white dress shirt whose sleeves are stylishly rolled up his forearms just below the elbows. Off Nate's feet come canvas shoes, with no socks. I suppose that means he's being casual?

After getting to about knee-deep, Nate begins to pull on a rope, which is attached to a rectangular metal cage, covered in dead reeds and general muck. He begins tossing small crabs out by hand with precision. That's like sticking your bare hand into a cage full of furious animated scissors. There is no fear in this boy. He hauls the trap to shore teeming with about twenty good-sized blue crabs. He empties them into a five-gallon bucket. Nate throws a few bits of chicken entrails into the bait hold of the trap, walks out, and tosses it back in roughly the same spot.

For his next trick, Nate takes another bucket from the trunk containing a cast net, a collapsible fishing pole, a cooler with ice, and finally a tackle box. The three of us ferry the items to the shore. Nate pulls the net out of the bucket and fills it with water. Leaving it onshore, he wades out a few feet and begins casting the net with immaculate precision. This leaves circles of misty water to hang momentarily like halos around the net as it falls home. At first, it was a bit rough going, but he has enough minnows to fill the bucket after about two dozen tries.

Nate ties what's called a 'Carolina rig,' which is a way to use a slip weight to keep the line in place while allowing the minnow to swim freely in the vertical water column. As Nate hooks the minnows above the eyes, Herschel turns away. He can't stand the cruelty of the whole thing.

Eventually, I roll up my jeans and join him. We fish until early evening. Upon returning home, we eat boiled crab with Old Bay and fried catfish. It has been a good day.

The next week goes on in a similar manner. We spend time outside, hike Goose Creek State Park, fish, or just do nothing at all. Life seems unnervingly normal. A SWAT team hasn't put a battering ram through Diane's front door. Herschel uses America Online to search for and read news from around the world. There is nothing about the Mace brothers' deaths. There's a blurb about a prominent church leader who died tragically in an accidental gas explosion. Vernon has likely received the gifts I left behind in the fireproof safe. I want him to know I'm alive. Everyone else at Solid Rock believes I died in the cave back in nineteen-ninety-four. But, I want to be Vernon's ghostly secret, always obliged to apparate at any time into perpetuity. Though, I desire nothing more than to forget him and move forward.

My respite is short-lived, as the curse of normal life looms: a schedule, expectations, work, school, money, and the basic travails of the ordinary.

We are well into August now, and the boys will be headed back to campus in less than two weeks. Then they will have classes to attend, weed to sell, homework to complete, and papers to finish. I need somewhere to be, which means I need to have someone to be. Eventually, I'll have to become accustomed to being called Hannah.

No one walks around with their birth certificate and Social Security card. Hannah needs an official North Carolina driver's license. For that, I also need proof of residency. Diane uses a photocopied generic form to draw up an official sublet of one of her bedrooms. She has it notarized, and simple as that, I have proof of residency. Staying with Diane isn't a good long-term plan, though. I feel as though I have been separated from my generation for so long, I won't know what to make of them when I return to society. I will need sherpas to guide me back to modern life. Because of this, I decide it's best to head back to Raleigh with the boys and rent a month-to-month efficiency hotel room while I figure it all out. My most immediate problem is that I've never driven.

Sunday morning, the boys take me to the empty parking lot of Washington's municipal library. Nate drives. After parking, I climb into the driver's seat. Nate takes over the passenger's side. Herschel is supposedly in the back seat, but his head is directly between Nate's and mine the entire time.

"Alright, Naomi, you're not stupid, so I'm going to assume you know how a car works," Herschel says.

"Yep, the gas is on the right, the brakes are on the left, and the wheel turns it. Which button makes it fly?" I say sarcastically.

"It'll be available on a future-model Volvo decades from now," Herschel quips back.

I belt out a laugh that culminates in one of the few unforced smiles I've experienced since being separated from Tiffany. Without hesitation, I put my foot on the brake pedal and shift the car into drive. Then, slowly, I creep forward, nervously braking at first. I eventually smooth out my pace. By afternoon, I am illegally driving the Volvo through downtown and back to Herschel's house.

I mull over the DMV manual most of the evening before going to sleep.

First thing in the morning, the three of us are at the DMV. I get deductions for my three-point turn, but I pass the driver's test easily. What amazes me is how little regard is given to the authenticity of my identity. They happily take the birth certificate and social security card, then issue me a brand-new driver's license, still warm from the laminator.

It's Monday. The boys will be heading up to Raleigh for move-in next Saturday. The most important question I have to ask myself this week is, 'What kind of car do I want?'

29

It's January of two-thousand four. My life for the past six years has been fabulously mundane, considering. Yes, I'm a drug dealer. But it's not so unlike other businesses. We sell a scarce product, much like oil. A lot of our time is preoccupied with revenue, planning, and the politics of it all. Our only competition is law enforcement. But imagine running a successful company your competitors weren't even aware of. If you remain in the shadows, they cannot compete.

Many wish for an adventurous life. What they really want are the stories. While you're in it, there are no guarantees. Most who have lived such lives will not be around to tell of it in old age. That's the price and the gamble.

When the summer of nineteen-ninety-seven came to a close, I returned to Raleigh with Nate and Herschel. I helped them move their stuff into their second-floor dorm in Tucker Hall, then rented a hotel room near campus. I was tempted to stash my wad of cash in the room but thought better of it and decided to keep it stuffed in my pockets in the interim. At least I would have a chance to fight off someone who would want to rob me.

After two weeks, I settled on renting a small efficiency in a beige eleven-story building named Westgrove Tower, which was situated less than two miles from campus. Room seven-o-four had a small kitchenette to the left as you walk through the heavy wooden door. There was a bathroom directly across from the kitchenette, with a full tub. The main room contained a double bed and desk. I had to pay first and last month's rent as well as a small deposit. At five hundred dollars a month, it wasn't a bad deal considering the location and it came fully furnished.

Westgrove Tower had a large unassigned parking lot that led down a short road directly to a small bus stop immediately on the right corner. For most of my needs, I was able to walk to the KMart in the adjacent parking lot. The vantage point from my room, seventy feet off the ground, gave me a detailed view of its grubby-looking roof and the green chain-link fence that separated the properties.

Inevitably, I needed a car. I choose a nineteen-eighty-five black Jeep CJ-7. I bought it from some bearded dude named Harrold through Craigslist. It suited me. I could have spent less, but I wanted something capable, yet ubiquitous. And I enjoyed riding around with the ragtop off. It wasn't particularly fast or pretty, but the damn thing can go anywhere.

I bought a safe the size of a dorm refrigerator. The boys and I used a furniture dolly to wheel it into the building at three in the morning. The cheap bastards who ran the place only had a security camera in the office where the cash was. We installed the safe on the left-hand side of the efficiency's double-sized closet. I pulled up the carpet from around where the safe would go so I could bolt it to the floor. Nate and Herschel took it to Zeke on the back of a trailer so that he could drill four holes in the bottom. Large masonry lag screws were threaded through those holes, then driven into the concrete floor to make it immovable. We had to drill the pilot holes very slowly. I figured when I moved out, I'd reinstall the carpet over the holes.

The boys sold our product out of their dorm room, but we kept the majority of the weed and cash stored away in the safe. I continued to finance the bulk purchases at a higher rate because I refused to go anywhere near Solid Rock. Members made regular shopping trips to Asheville. I couldn't afford to have someone recognize me. It was unlikely, but considering how my life has gone, it seemed like a reasonable amount of paranoia.

I started to let my hair grow out, but not too much. I liked having something to style. But I never forget I'm in the drug trade. I needed to blend, and a woman who purposefully shaves her head isn't exactly incognito in Raleigh.

It was a surprisingly easy academic transition from the Sillman's kitchen table to a University Classroom. They had taught me well. I took the GED with minimal preparation. After that, I enrolled at Wake Technical Community College, just down the road during the Spring semester of nineteen-ninety-eight. In the spring of nineteen-ninety-nine, I was accepted into the college of Biology at North Carolina State. I took on heavy course loads. By the fall of two-thousand, I had caught up with the boys and was a senior. In the spring of two-thousand-one, the three of us graduated together. I was keen on grad school for Marine Biology at The University of North Carolina Wilmington, but put that off for a year to advance the second step in our business model: our own grow house.

The house had to be out of the way. We choose a mid-twentieth-century brick house in North Raleigh off Millbrook Road, amongst the boorish suburbanites. It was a clunker of a house. We tore out the interior under the guise of renovations. The house is a one-story, three bed, one bath unit. Despite the shabbiness, it's a solid structure.

We renovated it so when you open the front door, a well-kept foyer and kitchen are visible. What isn't apparent from the outside is the locked door around the corner. Behind it exists the yellow glow and heat of high-pressure sodium grow bulbs. Since we didn't actually need appliances, we had free rein to use a normal household's worth of energy to grow without setting off any suspicions via extraordinarily high power bills.

Diane had bought the place with our earnings. It would have seemed odd for people our age to buy a house outright. We keep the exterior immaculate and are unobtrusive. Thus, we were ignored.

Within a year, we had cleared over a hundred thousand dollars. After that, I went back to school.

The boys run the business, and I reinvest at a higher rate to offset the labor. They keep more of their money, and Diane gets the best healthcare it can buy. Our goal is to stop when each of us clears one million in revenue. Invested properly, it will be enough to live modestly on for the remainder of our days.

Today Diane received a frantic phone call. It was from her sister, Beverly, Zeke's girlfriend. She had let herself into his house with take-out that evening and found his place in tatters. Whoever it was stole the weed and the cash, and kidnapped Zeke.

All the items on the kitchen counter lay shattered and upside down on the floor, bar one envelope, neatly placed, was intended to be conspicuous. The letter is brief. They demanded the presence of all three of us within forty-eight hours or they will cut Zeke's head off. The author was very specific about the decapitation part. There is a phone number. We decide to have Nate make the call. He is the more articulate of us, and far less likely to lose his cool. He calls on speaker phone so we can hear.

On the other end is a man's voice damaged by years of smoking. Everything he says is filtered through a low pitch grumble.

"It's about goddamn time you called," the voice announces, without waiting for Nate to speak. He continues, "You killed Authur Mace and George Keller. They were our tribal brothers. No one kills a brother without paying a price. You have two ways to pay up, either with your lives or your money. Because if we have to cut this weird fucker's head off, we will hunt you down. And if you put in that kind of effort, we're gonna torture you to death for days as restitution. So here's the deal, you will bring five-hundred thousand dollars in cash, and from now on you and Zeke grow exclusively for us. What you get paid is what you get paid. These terms aren't up for negotiation. Do you understand?"

"Yes, I understand. But we do not keep that kind of cash on hand. We have been laundering it for years through an offshore bank in Vanuatu. The clean money is in our bank account, and small banks don't keep that kind of cash on hand."

"Well, goddamnit boy, how much can you get in cash at a time?"

"We can probably get fifty-thousand."

"You can pay in installments. Bring fifty-thousand tomorrow, and then you can head to the bank every few days to get more. After that, we'll let fucko over here out of hock and get down to our new business model."

He demands the three of us meet him next evening at nine o'clock. The address is in Marshall, just north of Asheville. Directly after finishing dictating the address, the man simply hangs up.

We stare at one another. Our shared panic seems justified. We decide to head back to my studio apartment and lock ourselves in, hoping they will avoid coming for us in a more populated space.

No one sleeps. A specter of silence hangs down upon us. We just lie in place staring at the walls and ceiling, waiting for the sun to come up.

30

Just as dawn breaks, I shut my eyes and enter the space between waking and sleep. That's when I hear the retching from the bathroom. Nate and I reach the bathroom door at the same time.

"I'm so scared. I'm so scared," Herschel says, then keeps mouthing it over and over in a whisper.

I've never seen Herschel break like this. He seems like a little boy. I feel protective of him in the way an older sister might, or even a mother. The two of them are brilliant but so fucking clueless in many ways.

I wonder if this is how generals feel when they send children to war? Herschel doesn't want to go, but there is no choice. Something horrific is going to happen. We don't know what it is, but it is predetermined and cannot be stopped. Because of this reality, I can't console Herschel with the typical, 'It's all going to be okay,' because it's not going to be. All I can do is say, 'I'm so sorry.'

Herschel lies on the floor and sobs. Given pre-knowledge of it, we mourn the end of our own lives in a variety of fashions. Nate and I deal with it internally. I can imagine myself in a state of relief in those final seconds. My young life has been difficult. Put the weight down? Why not?

Herschel's crying tapers off a half-an-hour later. He is solid and stiff in personality, quite the opposite of his typical snark. Herschel is one of those people who can't suppress just one emotion. He has to rid himself of all feeling to function.

"We have to go," Herschel says.

Nate and I nod. I quietly say, "I know."

The look on the woman's face at the bank is priceless when I request to withdraw fifty-thousand dollars. I have to go into a back room where the sum is counted in five hundred one-hundred-dollar bills, which I split up and slip into my two front jeans pockets.

We load ourselves into my Jeep and set forth. Relentless anticipation throughout the long drive makes my stomach burn. I never intended to come this close to Solid Rock ever again.

I drive the final one-third of the trip. We ascend highway forty toward Asheville. We pass through town and continue north to the small enclave of Marshall. Nate begins to navigate with a map he printed out on my PC. The driveway we are looking for doesn't have a mailbox or identifying markers. We miss it the first time and I make a U-turn. The time is eight-forty-five. We only have fifteen minutes.

The driveway is a narrow slice into the woods, just wide enough for the Jeep to get through. The patch winds upward for about half a mile into the dense forest. As we reach the top, it levels out. In a small clearing, we see an old weathered wooden barn with a gabled roof. Orange light illuminates the edges of the large front double doors as well as the human-sized door on the barn's right side. I hear the guitar solo of a heavy metal song, and the rumble of a small generator. We pause momentarily after the Jeep comes to a stop.

"Just know I think of you two as brothers, and I love you," I say before we exit the vehicle.

"Same here," Herschel says.

Nate just nods.

There is smoke billowing out of a stack coming through the roof. The odor of burning wood cuts through the cold air.

"Don't slam the door," I say to Nate and Herschel. "You don't want to spook these guys.

We walk toward the ruckus of the barn, about fifty yards away. It's me on the left, Herschel in the middle, and Nate furthest right. We walk about a dozen paces or so when I hear the click of a large revolver behind my left ear.

"Hands up and turn around slowly," says the large man with the weapon.

We do as instructed. I turn to see the glint of a stainless-steel revolver inches from my nose. The figure behind it wears camo. His face is covered with a black balaclava. He is taller than me, about six-foot-three. I stare straight ahead and catch a glimpse of a second man. He's of average size. He's wearing a similar outfit. He has a long gun in his hands.

"All of you'ins put your hands on your heads," says the taller man as he stuffs the revolver into his waistband.

All the while, the other man keeps his gun pointed at us.

"I'm going to pat you down but if you do anything besides stand there like a tree, we will kill you."

He then proceeds to search us for weapons or recording devices. The cash in my pockets is confiscated. The tall man is too good at this. It's almost like he has a law enforcement background.

He pulls the revolver out of his waistband and instructs us to turn around and walk to the barn while holding our hands on our heads.

As we approach, the music becomes all-encompassing. The heavy metal guitar solo shrieking toward us cuts out after the tall man bangs on the side door. It opens, but the person doing the opening stays behind the door so we can't see them. We file in one at a time. I'm first in line.

Inside, the dirt-floor barn had been turned into a kind of clubhouse. In the back, two men drink at a simple bar that looks like it was bought before an actual bar was to be torn down, then plopped in the dirt without much thought. To its right, along the same back wall, stands an old jukebox responsible for the phonic chaos that just preceded. Above are small white Christmas tree lights, strung crisscross across the rafters in no conceivable order. There are two pool tables. Both are leveled by flat blocks of concrete. The pool table to the left is occupied by three men: two players, and a lone spectator. In the dead center is a double-barrel wood-burning stove made from old drums. Between the wood stove and us sits an octagonal, green-felted card table. Behind it stands a small man in his early fifties. He's thin, about five-foot-five, clean-shaven, with salt-and-pepper hair, and hazel eyes. He could almost be described as pretty. Like all of the men, he wears blue jeans and a plain white t-shirt covered by a black leather jacket. Each man wears a necklace featuring an upside-down, silver double-sided hammer. Their black jackets have the same symbolism as a huge back patch. The patches are white with the word 'Odin's' above the upside-down hammer, and 'Oath' below.

As he speaks, I recognize his voice from the telephone.

"My name is Marx Klein. I'm the leader of Odin's Oath. We are a brotherhood bound by our pledge to each other, the white race, and the All-Father, Odin. Our oath is an unbreakable bond. What is done to one brother is done to all. When a brother is happy, we are happy for him. When a brother is sad, we are sad for him. When a brother is murdered, we kill for him."

Marx lifts his finger and points in my direction. "Hannah, you murdered Arthur and George Mace. That warrants your death. And the two of you," he says, pointing the same finger in Nate and Herschel's direction, "are the ones she killed for. You boys can't take care of yourselves? You need to rely on a girl?

We are, all three, quiet.

"While you earned a death sentence, I hate to kill useful white folk, so what you're getting today is a prayer for judgement. That sentence will be commuted indefinitely if certain stipulations are met. It will require the financial recompense we discussed and you will work for me now. That's not a position you can leave voluntarily. Doing so will void your commutation. In other words, as of this moment, you belong to me."

Marx pauses for a moment and peers at something behind us.

"Now, I believe we have some business to attend to, and when I do business, I always like to have collateral in my pocket. Take a look behind you."

Behind the door we had just entered, Zeke sits in his boxers, duct-taped to a wooden chair. His face is turned toward the wall. On his upper back, there is a black bullseye drawn crudely with a marker. As my eyes focus, I realize I am looking at dozens of darts sticking out of his back, and multitudes of puncture wounds in varying degrees of bleeding, clotting, or scabbing over.

"The police didn't find George and Arthur, we did. They were given a proper ceremony and buried out back of our clubhouse. For years, we weren't sure what happened. That was, until a rumor started going around that Tommy was the last person who had seen them alive. It's his own fault. He slipped up and told that shit to a girl he'd just started dating. When the rumor reached our ears, we grabbed up Tommy. He cracked immediately, giving up your boy Zeke over there. Unlike Tommy, this bastard's tough. It took a hell of a beating, cuts, burns and the amputation of the middle, fourth, and pinky toe of his right foot before he gave you up. And even then, I think it's only because we threatened Beverly. Zeke thinks a lot of you three, just not quite as much as he does her. So, your two choices are one, become dead or two, serve Odin's Oath. However, there is something worth so much to me, I'd be willing to let go of your latter obligation if you achieve it. You'll still owe me your territory, money, and grow house, but you'll be free of us. I could just force you to do this, but I don't think you'd try as hard unless there's a real reward. Hannah, you're in a master's program of Marine Biology, aren't you?

"Yeah."

"You don't happen to have any diving experience, do you?"

"A little. I only have an open water diving certification."

"Well, that's more than I do," Marx replies laughing. "To be honest, we've placed a small bet on it. If you accept, I'm figuring you for dead. After that fact, Nate and Herschel still belong to me. I'm in the majority on the bet."

"Let me tell you a story," Marx says. "During the nineteen-eighties, this pharmacist named Bernard Wetzel ran a lucrative business in illegal prescription medication. He owned a nice spread out on Lake James. His lake house even had a small aquatic garage for a floatplane, which he used to transport illicit products. His house wasn't far from the Catawba dam, which has a long, deep strip of water where he would land the craft. In the summer of nineteen-eighty-nine, Bernard and his plane crashed in the water ahead of that dam. He was transporting cases of some of the last known LEMMON 714 Quaaludes on the planet. The plane went down in over ninety feet of water. Neither he nor the plane were ever recovered. Legend is, Bernard carried his cargo in two blue airtight storage cases, originally used for Naval gyroscopic navigational equipment. If they've done what they were designed to, those pills are sitting dry and safe at the bottom of the lake. They might be a bit weak, but yuppie customers in big cities love the novelty and are willing to pay for the bragging rights."

"It's January," I reply.

"That's the thing, if you were to do it in the summer, every assshole who vacations there would be curious once they saw you pull something up. At night during the warmer months, you'll encounter a significant number of fishermen on boats trying to hook the next record catfish. If you can slip out there at night, right now, in the full grip of winter, you'll have the place to yourselves. If you retrieve the two cases and bring them back to me, all will be forgiven. They should be somewhat rusted shut, so we'll know if you open 'em and try and Jew us outta what's rightfully ours."

"I'll die of hypothermia."

"Wouldn't you rather die trying to win your freedom than being assured an existence that isn't worth living?"

"How can I trust that you'll hold up your end of the bargain?"

"You can't. But, when you fail, I'll kill Zeke and keep the boys for myself. They won't live long lives in our care. Each will only eat dog food, be beaten daily, and do hard manual labor until they die. You have exactly one week. If you're not back here by next Saturday at nine o'clock, he dies. Then we will hunt you down. Do you understand those terms, Hannah?"

"Yeah," I respond with subtle anger.

"Good, now get the fuck out of here before I change my mind."

31

We limp our hearts back home, arriving in Raleigh at daybreak. There's very little in the way of conversation on the way home, though my internal dialogue is ceaseless. Instead of plotting an escape, I'm putting together a list of everything I'll need to put my hands on those two cases. The only things I already have in my personal inventory are a mask, snorkel, and fins. I check the *News and Observer*'s classifieds for boats. Of course, this being North Carolina, there are more than enough offerings, even in winter. I settle on a sixteen-foot Carolina Skiff with a ninety-horse four-stroke Honda outboard. It's sitting on a well-cared-for trailer with new tires. We had the option of purchasing a larger boat at the same price, but it had a carbureted two-stroke outboard. Carburetors are infamous for being hard starting in cold weather. We can't risk such unreliability.

I arrange to meet the owner on Monday afternoon. It's a nice rig. It even has a small aftermarket swim ladder on the back, just in case I arrive back to the surface alive. I don't haggle over the price. We don't have that kind of time.

I pull our new boat back to Diane's house in Little Washington, where we will stage our venture.

Diane takes the news as best she can, then gets really stoned.

I need a dry suit. Such a suit will do exactly as it says, keep the diver dry with seals around the wrists, ankles, and neck. Underneath, the diver is able to dress in a dry, insulative layer. I pay the shop where I earned my certificate to have one overnighted. I rent the rest of the gear from them: a BCD, weights, four full tanks of oxygen, and extremely powerful dive lights. The system allows me to use two tanks at a time, so I might double my time at the bottom. The only drawback is size. If I have to get in and out of the airplane ninety feet below, bulky tanks will be a hindrance.

To retrieve the cases, I rig up one-hundred-fifty feet of dive-line with a galvanized chain, along with a heavy gauge carabiner. The units should have handles If I'm to believe my research. Military surplus stores sell similar cases online. Most people in the civilian market use them to keep supplies dry in the bed of a pickup. If the handles are missing, I'll have to wrap the line around the cases from all four sides and hope it holds.

I arrange to rent out the dive school's pool Wednesday and Thursday for an exorbitant amount of money. I need to train. We figure on making our attempt Friday. We'll head down during the day and get going right as it turns dark. For now, I need to train. I spend hours listening to the sound of bubbles exiting my regulator as I practice maneuvering in the cumbersome gear. I want to get a good feel for the drysuit, but I quickly become overheated. At least I know it fits, despite how difficult it is to get in and out of.

Thursday night, we prepare the boat in Diane's driveway. The gas tank is full, the outboard oil was recently changed by the previous owner, the trailer bearings are lubed, and the tires have the correct amount of air. Before loading the gear, I run the engine, using a water hose adapter to make sure it won't overheat.

We set out at mid-afternoon Friday. We decide to use the boat ramp at the mouth of the Linville River since it is, by far, the most remote. We arrive at nine o'clock. Because it's winter, the days are short. It's been dark for several hours already, and the water has formed a thin layer of ice. As the boat and trailer are backed down the ramp into the water, it creates multitudes of tiny crackling sounds. After freeing the boat from the trailer, I moor it to the dock. Even though it's a four-stroke engine, I run the outboard for ten minutes to ensure it won't cut out.

With our gear strewn about the floor of the Carolina Skiff, we putter our way toward the dam. I should have secured the tanks, but there really isn't a reasonable way to do it. The boys hold them in place while I point the stern toward the alleged location of the wreck. Our breath leaves a trail behind us in the night. We try to ignore the cold, but when it's twenty degrees and windy, that's not easy. Each of us is dressed in multiple layers. I fear what may happen if those layers become soaked with frigid water. The moon is half-full, which makes it dark enough for cover. There is just enough ambient light to function.

After arriving at the long stretch of water in front of the dam, we begin scanning for sunken structures with our fish finder. We weave our way up and down perpendicular to the dam, like a farmer plowing their field. Eventually, on one pass, we begin to pick up larger and larger objects.

"There's a debris trail ninety feet below us," I say.

The most sizable debris comes at the end, which must be the plane.

"Shit, that was the last of it," I remark, pointing at the backlit fish finder.

"Turn around," Nate says.

After doing so, I see the same outline again.

"That's the plane.", I reply the Nate.

"How can you be sure?", Herschel asks.

"I can't. But what else leaves a trail like that other than the wreckage of a man-made object as it loses bits and pieces? It must have skidded sideways, dipped a wing into the water, and flipped end over end instead of just sinking. The fact that the body was never recovered is curious. Wetzel must have come in on a night like this one for it to go unnoticed. Since we couldn't dig up anything online, it's likely there was no flight plan or FAA report. It could just be a rumor, but it's our only chance to save Zeke and get free of these Nazi-fucks."

Turning to Nate, I say, "I'm going to turn back around and I want you to drop anchor when I tell you."

"Okay."

Nate begins making his way to the bow. He opens the anchor box and lifts out a two-foot-long, galvanized fluke anchor. It has a chain attached followed by a whole box worth of line. I have Nate drop it about thirty seconds after crossing over the largest object in the debris trail. I rightfully assume the boat will drift back toward the dam. The anchor snags ahold of something and we come to a stop right where the debris trail begins to show up on the fish finder.

"The current should push me toward the crash as I descend."

Before getting in the water, I check over my gear. Everything is in order. I instruct Nate to feed me the line and pull up whatever is attached to it when I yank hard three times. I enter the water by falling backward over the gunwale of the boat. I make sure to hold my mask in place. Thin bits of ice crinkle past my ears as I enter the biting, opaque, abyss.

Despite being in a dry suit, my face is numb in seconds. My body feels colder than I expected. As I sink, all I can see is Nate's headlamp as he looks over the side. It fades, taking on the appearance of a single faint star in a black, lonely sky. I shine my dive light down. It manifests as a concentrated beam as it bounces off of tiny particles afloat in the brown water.

The bottom of the lake is covered in wooded debris and tree stumps that, despite being dead, are still rooted in the ground. There are remnants of the dry land that existed before the valley was flooded by the dam. I begin blindly sifting my hands in the muddy bottom as I swim inches above it. I continue this task until I'm almost halfway through my oxygen. I only have a few more minutes before I have to slowly ascend the ninety-foot column of water so that I don't get the bends.

Then my hands hit rusty, brown metal. It's the front of the floatplane laying upside down. I approach the side and yank the fragile door open. The first thing I find is Wetzel's horribly decomposed corpse. His glasses are still on his face. Without hesitating, I reach in, grab what is left of the body, and pull it out of the airplane. It slumps right outside the door. I am just able to fit inside. One case is behind each front seat. I pull them both to the front of the plane and stack them atop one another. Their handles both face my direction. I weave the line through them both and clip the carabiner to the rope, forming a loop. As I back out, the bottom edge of my left tank won't slide past the opening. I wiggle and bang into metal several more times to no avail. I am on a razor's edge with my oxygen supply. I hear the metal groaning and fear the plane may have started to shift. The sound of metal ripping resounds above my head. The entire bottom of the plane is gone, exposing the water column above me. I back out of the cockpit and turn around to have a look at the plane. The bottom section of the upside-down craft has been peeled open like a can. I am startled by the view of fur rippling in the water. It's Mara. She pauses for a moment and stares directly into my eyes. She then drifts back out of sight into the brown void. I pull the cases from the wreckage. They're heavier than I imagined. I tug hard three times on the line and they disappear above my head as the boys pull up the line. As I ascend, taking breaks for equalization, I begin to contemplate whether what I saw could be explained by oxygen deprivation. I make it back to the surface with only a few minutes of oxygen left.

As I surface, I hear Herschel say, "Shit, there you are. We were worried you might have passed out."

"I regret to inform you Herschel, but I'm very much alive."

I remove both flippers while holding onto the boat, then toss them in one at a time. I climb cumbersomely up the small ladder mounted to the back of the boat. With the full weight of my gear on me again, I feel like I'm lugging a boulder on my back. I remove my BCD with the tanks attached and lower them gently to the floor of the vessel, nearest the transom. I'll change out of my drysuit when we get the boat back on the trailer. There is no way to get warmer than I am until then.

Herschel says, "These fuckers are too heavy to just have pills in them. And there's no sloshing when I move them, so It's not water from a leak."

"Yeah, I thought that myself. I just hope it's not Bernard Wetzel's rock collection."

Nate pilots the boat back to the Linville River boat ramp at the same excruciatingly lethargic pace. When we get to the pier, Nates hops out of the boat and starts up my Jeep. I take over the helm.

Herschel stays aboard with me. I maneuver back into the lake, away from the ramp. Nate backs the empty trailer down the ramp until it is partially submerged. I pilot it onto the trailer. We secure the boat to the trailer with no complications. Nate pulls the boat into the gravel parking lot with Herschel and myself still aboard. Nate exits the Jeep and comes to the port side of the boat. Herschel jumps out next to him, stumbles, and falls on his butt.

"I'm fine," he says.

I catch Nate rolling his eyes.

I hand each of the boys a case and they load them into the back of the Jeep. I pull off my drysuit and stow it away in one of the boat's storage compartments. Now exposed to the elements, I hop out barefoot onto the frigid, sharp gravel, then briskly walk to the front passenger's side of the Jeep, where the heat is running as hard as possible. Herschel gets into the back on Nate's side.

"What now?" Nate inquires.

"Head back east. We're not due until tomorrow, and the further away I am, the more comfortable I feel.

Our retreat takes us to Winston-Salem which is about a two-hour drive. We come to rest in the rear of a Wal-mart parking lot. The idea is to get a few hours of sleep. Herschel snores but Nate and I just keep watch for the sun.

32

We sit quietly staring across the Wal-mart parking lot waiting for the sun to show up. Once the first light hits, I break the silence by saying, "We're going to have to leave the boat here. We can't take it up the road to the Odin's Oath clubhouse. And what if we need to get away quickly?"

"I agree," Nate responds plainly.

"Let's get this the fuck over with, those cases make me nervous," Herschel says.

Herschel heads into Wal-mart to purchase a set of tire chocks and a hitch lock. We stay in the Jeep. We don't dare leave the cases unattended.

I back the boat into one of the furthest parking spaces, chock it, raise the hitch off the ball, and lock up the receiver on the boat trailer with the new lock Herschel purchased.

The boat being stolen or impounded will be inconsequential if we die, but I can get most of our money back out of it if we happen to come out of this alive. Or, maybe Nate and I will keep it for fishing?

I call Marx on a burner phone to let him know we'll be at their clubhouse around noon. He is as unpleasant as usual but cheers up when I tell him we had the cases. I fuel up before getting back on the highway, and we make sure to fill ourselves with gas station coffee and doughnuts. I feel the most alert, so I volunteer to drive. We make sure to take a pee break before hitting the steep climb of Highway Forty from Old Fort to Black Mountain. Zooming up a thousand feet of elevation at fifty-five miles an hour is not the time to figure out you need to go.

The path to Odin's Oath's clubhouse is somewhat less foreboding in the daytime, but the sight of the barn still gives me chills.

It's the same routine as before. The aforementioned men sticks guns in our backs and searches us. Nate and I carry one case each toward the barn while Herschel walks in front of us.

The door opens to reveal Marx Klein exactly where he was before, behind the card table. But this time we find ourselves surrounded by several more men, probably fifteen or so. Each wears an upside-down, double-headed hammer pendant around their neck. All are clad in black leather jackets sporting the same hammer and title, 'Odin's Oath,' on the back.

This time, Zeke is nowhere in sight. Marx stands as Nate and I both lay the cases on the card table, which results in a thud much louder than they expected.

"This better not be full of fucking mud," Marx says.

"Where's Zeke?" I ask sharply.

"Look up."

Above, on the edge of the rafters, stands Zeke, roughly twenty feet above the ground. Zeke's hands are cuffed behind his back. There is a noose around his neck. The other end is tied to a support beam over the center of the barn. Behind Zeke stands one of Marx's half-wits, ready to push him off.

"Are we in a western now, Marx?", I inquire.

"Nah, that's just insurance against any bullshit you might want to pull."

"There's no bullshit. I brought you what you wanted."

"Perhaps. We will see momentarily."

"No, I brought you what you asked for. I'm not responsible for what's inside, Bernard Wetzel is." Pointing at the case, I say, "Look, we didn't open them. Do you know what I had to do to get those? I could have died. I got tangled up in an upside-down airplane ninety feet down, at the bottom of a frigid, dark lake. Yet, here I am holding up my word. I expect the same."

"Why would your death matter to me?" he inquires.

I lean over the table toward Marx, while raising my voice and painting my left index finger at him, "Well, perhaps because you're looking at the four best indoor pot farmers on either side of the state. You have to fund Odin's Oath somehow. I got you what you asked for, but that doesn't mean we still can't do business after this is over. We'll just be on equal terms. Are you really going to throw that away just to find yourself slinging shitty brick weed? That might sell in the trailer parks, but you're not going to be able to compete in larger cities where it counts. Right now, you're probably buying from drug cartels, your direct competition. That makes you their middlemen. You can't beat our quality or wholesale prices. So, if you're happy jerking yourselves off up here to pictures of some one-eyed fairytale man, instead of making metric shit-tons of cash, go ahead and kill us!"

Of course, I would never do business willingly with these sorry motherfuckers, no matter how much money is involved. But those who lack scruples assume everyone else does as well.

"Alright, alright,", Marx says as he holds his hand up as a

signal he'd like me to stop. "I don't even know if these cases are legit, so why don't we get to that before I begin to make reckless judgments, Okay?"

"Fair enough, let's open them."

Looking at the boys, I can tell they're floored by my manner with Marx. But nearly drowning in tea-colored, freezing water can affect one's mood. Nate keeps his stoic facade, but Herschel's mouth hangs wide open.

I look up and make eye contact with Zeke. He looks back into my eyes momentarily without moving. Marx opens both hatches on the first case but is unable to pop it open. The same occurrs with the second. Frustrated, Marx sends one of his men to fetch a crowbar.

"Well, you weren't lying. You really didn't open them," Marx comments while we wait.

Now armed with a crowbar, Marx opens the first case in seconds. The lid lifts toward me. It blocks my view so I can't see what's inside. A look of shock comes over him. Marx shut the first case and quickly cracks the lids on the second. He drops the second lid shut in the same manner. His eyes are even wider now.

"Execute Zeke!" Marx shouts.

The brothers of Odin's Oath drunkenly cheer at the proclamation. Every member but Marx shuffles their way toward the center of the barn to catch a better view of the show and to hurl final insults at the man soon to swing above them.

Then there is silence. My ears feel like they are under pressure. As they pop, I begin to hear ringing, and I have the sensation of floating. I can't make sense of my surroundings. There is no up or down. It seems like a translucent bubble has enveloped whatever existence I am in. I assume myself dead. Perhaps I was shot in the back of my head by Marx as I turned toward Zeke?

The edges of the bubble begin to glow a translucent blue, behind the darkness. Gradually, the void of infinite blackness fills in with the awareness of a place. It's the field where I had a vision of the chimpanzees and Tiffany years before. It isn't a real space, but a construct of my mind. Yet, I can feel the warm air and the ground beneath my feet. I wonder if this is my own personal heaven. I haven't earned it.

Mara walks out of the forest. The troop of chimps, which charged before, exit the wood line and wait. Calmly, Mara approaches me. When we come face to face, she holds out her right hand. I instinctively know she wants me to extend my left hand to hers the way children play patty-cake. Our palms touch and I feel searing heat enter my scar. The warmth fills my body. My eyes are on fire with the righteous flames of hell, meant to cut down those who trespass against the weak. The sensation is what I felt when I lost control on Arthur Mace and stabbed him in the face repeatedly with the shattered shotgun stock, but amplified. I can feel the static electricity in the atmosphere with my left hand and the heat of the Earth's liquid outer core. In the back of my mind, I sense a separate, almost parasitic, consciousness. It feeds my baser instincts and an understanding of what I have just been gifted.

Mara turns and walks back into the woods. Everything fades, and the sphere is surrounded by darkness once more. As the surroundings clear, I find myself standing, looking toward Zeke. It's the same tableau as before, but now everyone is frozen. Then, in the rafters behind the man who was instructed to push Zeke from the platform walks Mara, unaffected by the time disruption. She reaches over the top of the man's head and places her oversized middle and ring fingers into his mouth. Her forearm rests atop his head.

I begin to hear sound again. Linear time catches up to me. Only now I'm experiencing it at a much slower rate. My new consciousness plants the thought that I should look to the right. There I see Marx with his 1911 pistol drawn at my head. "No!" I scream in my mind. Then I hear what is my voice in the distance screaming it aloud.

I turn my left hand toward Marx's gun and place it over the muzzle. I reach my right hand out into the air and begin to pull an electric charge from the atmosphere. I force the static charge through me. It exits the scar on my left hand with a bright white arc. Our rate of time syncs together just as Marx pulls the trigger, but the muzzle is already welded closed by the heat. Marx releases the pistol as it violently ruptures. He drops the fragmented gun. I place my left hand over Marx's face and charge it with the same bright arc, severely burning him. The intensity of the arc turns Marx's eyes white, blinding him. He falls to the dirt screaming while covering his face.

At the same moment, Mara snatches back the hangman's head, decapitating him from the mouth up; leaving his jaw attached to his neck. She drops his limp body and head off the rafter. It lands at the feet of the brothers of Odin's Oath below. Aghast at what had just transpired, the whole of them reach for their sidearms. Before any can fire, Mara wraps herself around Zeke, placing her back toward the men below. Round after round deafeningly goes off. Each that hits Mara's body disappears inside of her, causing a puff of dust to exit each entrance wound. As the men reload, the firing slows.

Marx's screams turn the men's attention towards us. As barrels begin to shift in our direction, my secondary consciousness tells my right hand to reach down toward the Earth, and my left toward them. With my right hand, I begin to draw the fine silt and dust particles toward my palm. This creates a small vortex of spinning matter from the ground toward my hand. I draw the tornado of dirt into my palm, up my right arm, and into my body. I force it to accelerate through my left arm, and out of my scarred left hand. It's like an enormous shotgun blast that sprays billions of minute granules. The men are all struck with an equal multitude of pin-sized through and through shots. A giant cloud of brown dust and bloody mist exits behind them as the dirt particles go on to pierce the rear of the barn. The back wall begins to disintegrate as though it were rotted wood. Each man falls limp to the floor. The dirt around them is soaked with their blood. The air smells of copper. A cold wind whips through the barn from where the furthest wall once stood. The outside is eerily quiet. The only thing left to hear is Marx wailing in agony behind us.

"Jesus fucking Christ, Naomi! Mara is real?!" Herschel shouts as we turn around toward Marx. Nate says nothing, but I can hear the anger transmitting between his every synapse. I couldn't have predicted it, but Nate charges Marx and begins to stomp on his head. He gets a few in before I pull him away. I turn him around so he can no longer see Marx.

I hug Nate and say, "That's not for you. You don't want it. I promise."

I can feel the warm tears as they flow from his cheek to my shirt.

"Turn away if you need to."

I let Nate go and approach Marx. He lies on his back wheezing in the dirt. I place my right boot on Marx's neck, reach down and rip his shirt open with my left hand. With my right hand, I pull the heat of the Earth's outer core into my body. I charge the pointer of my left hand with an intense white-hot glow. Reaching down, I use my illuminated finger to make an incision in Marx's chest from his neck to his navel. As he wails in horror, I slice away ribs until his still-beating heart is exposed. I sink the same white-hot index finger into Marx's heart. After piercing halfway, I cool my finger and feel his last few heartbeats from within. It flutters rapidly for a moment, then quickly slowed to a full stop. I remove my hand from his dead chest and stand. As I pull my foot away from Marx's neck, I see a burn in the shape of my hand across his face.

"Well, fuck him anyway," Herschel says in amazed relief. "How did you do that?"

"Mara gave it to me. I really don't understand. It's like I can feel every particle of the Earth around me."

Zeke slinks down the staircase toward us while Mara remains in the rafters. She reaches her right hand out toward me and pulls a bright orb from my chest. We watch as it returns to Mara, who pulls it into her hand. Once the orb exits my body, I can no longer feel the energy of the Earth or atmosphere.

"It's gone," I say.

"All things are temporary," Nate replies.

Mara evaporates. In her absence, the bullets she absorbed protecting Zeke rain down to the floor where she stood.

In each case were two-and-a-half million dollars, twenty-five one-kilo bars of gold, and one kilo of diamonds. There were no pills. It must have been some kind of payoff. Me, the boys, Zeke, and Diane split it evenly and exited the illicit cannabis trade permanently.

33

I am no longer afraid. I have felt the pleasant touch of love as Naomi and worn the bitterness of Mara as a second skin. Today, I am Lazarus as I lay in wait for prey who believe me dead.

It's just past six in the evening, Saturday, March thirteenth, two-thousand-four, roughly three months since the incident at the Odin's Oath clubhouse.

I'm standing outside of my newly acquired burgundy, nineteen-ninety-nine Ford Econoline panel van. I made sure to get the model without windows in the cargo area.

I pull left onto a gravel turn-around near the top of Seven Mile Ridge Road. I can peer over the edge of the ravine out of the driver's side and look down at the entire valley as the sun recedes behind the Black Mountains. I make sure to pop the hood and turn on the hazard lights to indicate my vehicle has broken down to anyone descending the twisty mountain road in my direction. I know exactly who it will be.

I've been tracking Sheriff Morton's Jeep Cherokee patrol unit for a month. Alton lives in town, not more than a quarter-mile from the lot that held Maddie Bellew's now-demolished bungalow. Alton wasn't difficult to find. He's the only person in town with a new Jeep Cherokee patrol unit in their driveway.

Three days after locating his house, I paid a visit in the wee hours of the morning. I got my hands on a fleet management tracking unit. It's a GPS receiver the size of a small book, commonly used on delivery vehicles. It needs to be hardwired to the Jeep's battery, though. I parked my van down the street from the Sheriff's house. It took about five minutes to make it through the darkened side yards into his driveway. I had a pair of wire stripper-crimpers, zip-ties, and wire butts in my front right pocket. Under my left arm was the book-sized black box that makes up most of the GPS unit. On one side, the box has two wires for twelve-volt power and on the other, a lead wire that connects to a magnetic antenna about the size of a fifty-cent piece.

I lie down behind the Jeep and wiggle underneath, then patch into the wiring harness for the trailer connector to provide power. I zip-tied the black box on the underside of the bumper and ran the small magnetic transmitter under the passenger-side rear wheel well. I zip-tied the wiring down as I worked my way back. I made sure to pick up the striped wiring insulation and severed zip-tie tags, and made my way up and out.

The GPS pings the patrol Jeep's location every few minutes and records its latitude and longitude, which can then be superimposed onto a digital map. I let the GPS run for a month. The data was mostly from Sheriff Morton's home to his office, then back. He ate most meals at a local diner. The one anomaly came each Saturday evening when he made a trip way up to a remote location, high up on Seven Mile Ridge. On the third week, it finally clicked. Alton is out doing something he doesn't want anyone from Solid Rock to see. Of course, that also means none of them will be around to see what happens to Sheriff Morton, either.

At around seven I hear the roar of large tires barreling down the mountain road above me. I take my place in this act by positioning myself as though I'm looking cluelessly at my engine block with a pen flashlight, alone, on the side of an abandoned mountain road, at night.

I turn to see the patrol Jeep's headlamps. Sheriff Morton slows and pulls over into the gravel in front of me, coming to rest so that the noses of both vehicles are roughly two yards apart.

He steps out with a presumed swagger.

"What's wrong there, young lady?"

"Something's wrong with my van. Can you help me?" I say in a feigned, ditzy manner.

"I can call up a buddy of mine and have it towed down to his shop. He only charges three dollars per mile. That's about a twenty-mile trip, so it'll only run you roughly sixty dollars."

"I don't have that much cash, sir."

"What's your name, darlin'?"

"Crystal," I say.

"That's a pretty name, for a pretty young woman. Well, I might could take care of the tow and the repairs if you'ins do me a favor."

"Oh, could you? I reply, clasping my hands as though I am excited. "That would be a huge help. What do you need?"

"To get my dick wet, darlin'," Alton says with a coy grin.

"No, I don't think so."

"Well, let me put it this way, either you do it willingly, or I'm just gonna have my way with you'ins anyhow," he says sternly while pulling the nightstick off his belt. "What are you going to do? Call the police? I could just easily beat you, and throw you in a cell so my deputies can have a go after me. Or, you can just do what I say without a struggle, keep your freedom, and get something in return. Your call."

"Please, please don't make me. Don't hurt me," I say, lip quivering. I get on my knees as though I'm begging and begin to cry. "If you don't hurt me, I will. What do you want?"

Still clutching the nightstick, Sheriff Morton says, "Well, I'm figgurin', cause you already on you'ins knees you can stay there. Come on now, why don't you'ins take my pants down for me."

I reach up, unbuckle the Sheriff's belt, unbutton and unzip his pants, then pull them down to his knees. He pops out, fully erect. I suppose the sick power trip is a turn-on for him. I reach my right hand up toward Sheriff Morton's genitals, as I slyly pull the service pistol from his holster with my left hand. Violently, I wrap my right hand around the top of Sheriff Morton's scrotum and squeeze downward, simultaneously standing before he can react through the shock and pain. I push the muzzle of the Sheriff's pistol under his chin.

"Mara! Come get it!" I shout.

A deafening, sustained roar erupts from thin air several yards away as Mara materializes, already in full gallop toward us. Sheriff Morton's expression is one of open-mouth awe.

I release my grip and slide to the right as Mara hits him full force in the chest. I point the pistol at his head as he lies sprawled out on his back. Sheriff Morton's eyes gaze up after a moment to catch his breath from the impact to see Mara at his feet and me to the side looking down the sights of his own gun.

"Now, I need something from you, Alton. Get-in-the-fucking-van," I say, enunciating each word very slowly to demonstrate how serious I am.

"Pat him down." Mara runs her huge hands all over the Sheriff. She pulls a snub nose thirty-eight off an ankle holster.

"Chuck it in the ravine."

Mara rears back and flings the revolver with a force greater than any big-league pitcher.

"Cuff him, Mara."

Mara removes a set of handcuffs from Sheriff Morton's downed belt and tightly restrains his hands behind his back.

"Move forward, Alton," I say.

Sheriff Morton meanders like a prisoner in foot shackles, except his are made of downed trousers. Upon reaching the rear of the van, Mara opens the righthand-side rear door and throws the Sheriff, face down, into the interior. I step in. Mara slams the door behind us and remains outside to stand guard. Sheriff Morton is alone and cold, with his pants down and a gun to his head. He is flaccid now.

I put my feet between his legs as he lies nose to the metal floor. His trousers being down allows me to lock my boots to the inside of where Sheriff Morton's pants meet his ankles, immobilizing his legs.

"What exactly are you doing up here, Alton?" I ask.

"Who are you with. What family?

"Family?" I ask

"Which moonshine clan are you with?" Alton responds.

"Is that what you do every Saturday? Moonshine? Really?"

"Yeah. I gets our protection monies from the Price brothers for allowin' thems to run a still. Solid Rock and the Sheriff's Department sanctions the corn liquor. It's okay, it all goes back to the church. See, it might look bad, but it's all goin' to pay for God's work. That's all."

Al's wise, emphatic words flash into my mind. "If a man can own someone's greatest vice as well as their salvation from it, he can own that person."

"I don't give a shit about moonshine, Alton. I care about dead children. Where is the body of Daisy Chambers?"

"Who the fuck is Daisy Chambers?"

"She was the little girl Patty Proffit shot in the back in December of nineteen-ninety-four. Where is her body? I saw Patty Proffit kill Daisy with my own eyes. You and Vernon Proffit are tight. I witnessed Vernon load her body into his car, never to be recovered. I know the Sheriff's department of Yancey County is a de facto private police force for Solid Rock. You once chased me through the tunnel system below the Proffit's house. You covered up the murder of Hannah Sillman. For years afterward, you held her parents, Al and Milly, prisoners with fear, and eventually burned down everything they owned after Vernon shot Al."

"Who'ins the hell are you?!" Sheriff Morton screams.

"I'm the little girl who refused to die."

34

"You're a weak coward, Alton, but you don't have to be dead. Tell me what I need to hear, or I will have my companion toss you into the ravine the way she did your revolver. Where is the body of Daisy Chambers?"

"You're talking about the girl Patty shot in the back?"

"It's interesting you had to qualify your response with the location of the gunshot wound. For fuck's sake, how many were there?"

"Six, no, I mean seven, if you'ins count Daisy. Most don't die."

"Most of whom, Alton?"

"Them girls who was to be with the prophet. They are to have his baby, but Pastor Proffit has been sterile from the measles since he was a boy."

"You just said he's sterile."

"God must decide who is to carry the child. He's only to sire one offspring through a miracle. Pastor Proffit is meant to conceive the one who will bring about the end of all things. Armageddon."

"You're telling me, Vernon is attempting to bring forth the anti-Christ?"

"Yes. Without him, there can be no end to this wicked world."

I pull a National Geographic Pisgah Forest wilderness map out of my pocket, unfold it and place it next to Sheriff Morton's face. "Point out to me, with your nose, where Daisy is buried."

Sheriff Morton stares at it for a moment.

"That girl is buried in an unmarked grave, here, in Hickory Hill Cemetery."

"Just like Charles," I say.

"I remember you now. They had you'ins around the same time as that boy. Your name starts with an 'N'."

"Naomi."

His face shifts to a grimace upon hearing my name.

"You'ins two killed Brent."

"He was alive when we left. Perhaps he'd still be alive if he weren't a child rapist? Had you considered that?"

"No," Sheriff Morton says dejectedly.

"Why aren't all the bodies in the cemetery? I've seen his sepulcher in the caverns, through the flooded cave, across from the golf course. Why are some there and others in unmarked graves?"

"The prophecy states that the girl must be a virgin and within one year of her first period. She only gets one chance for conception. Once she is chosen, she must receive the communion of Pastor Proffit's ejaculate. The girls who struggled had to die for the crime of rejecting God himself. Either way, once the communion is inside the girl, her body becomes holy regardless, so it has to be honored. Those who die before the communion burn in hell. Pastor Proffit was real mad with Patty about sendin' that poor girl to hell."

"And you believe this stupid shit?"

"Yes. It's the only way to my reward in heaven."

"I just sent sixteen men to Vahallah. I can oblige you your trip to heaven."

I reach down and remove the keys from Sheriff Morton's belt, then open the van door.

"Mara, toss him far into the ravine, but make sure to remove his cuffs first."

Mara reaches into the van, grabs the cuffs restraining Sheriff Morton, and shears them away from his body, immediately severing both of his hands to a symphony of screams as both hands strike the ceiling of the van and then the floor with a double-thud. Sheriff Morton flails the stubs at the ends of his arms as they spray a sanguine painting in blood and terror across the interior of the van. Mara grasps the downed pants of the Sheriff and uses them to drag him outside. Still holding on to the pants, she proceeds to swing his entire body in circles. Once Mara is satisfied with the momentum, she releases him to fly into the darkness of the ravine. The screams cease with several deep thuds in the distance; presumably, his body bouncing off rocks before coming to a rest.

Mara evaporates back into the wind.

I crawl under the Sheriff's Jeep and clip away each zip-tie holding in the GPS components, then chuck the unit and stray ties into the bloodied van interior. I retrieve a four-foot-long piece of rebar I picked up off the ground at Zeke's on a whim the day before. When I first looked at it, I couldn't help but think of Patty's bamboo cane. I figured, why not upgrade? I take it along and begin driving the Sheriff's patrol Jeep down the mountain toward Solid Rock.

I park it directly in front of the garage at Vernon's house, pop the rear door of the Jeep, and turn on the blue lights without the siren. Rebar in hand, I dash off into the wood line across the dirt road and bide my time. Within a few minutes, the Proffits's bedroom light illuminates.

Out walks Vernon in nothing but his tighty-whities, limping slightly from the gunshot wound I gave him, with an eyepatch over his right eye where the shrapnel from a flashlight took his vision those years ago. Looking upon him now, I am almost disappointed. I honestly expected a more formidable opponent after years of dreading and remembering him from the aspect of a helpless little girl.

Vernon begins examining the Patrol Jeep while calling out for Sheriff Morton. As he makes his way around to the open rear of the Jeep, I begin to advance quietly. As he sticks his head into the cargo area, I make my move. Running up on his blinded right side, I raise the rebar above my head and bring it down across Vernon's right clavicle. There is an audible snap as he crumples to his knees. I follow with a rebar strike to his temple, knocking him unconscious. I lift his body into the back of the Jeep, roll him in, and shut the door. He won't be going anywhere.

Just then, at the door to the garage, I see Patty level her Garand at me. It's the same rifle she used to murder Daisy. Quickly, I'm back in the bubble, surrounded by slight blue illumination in the peripheries, like before in the barn. I see a white light strike me in the chest, then a surge of awareness about the Earth, and the energy it contains. This time, there is no secondary consciousness. I command it.

As I flashback into real-time, I instantly know what to do. I reach my left hand down and pull up a large flat cleave of granite from the ground. It bursts forth with a rumble, taking on the appearance of a large, jagged tombstone, higher than I am tall. Then I hear the ricochet of Patty's bullet as it strikes the granite surface directly opposite of me.

"Grab her, Mara!" I shout.

Mara materializes behind Patty and immobilizes her by wrapping her arms round Patty's chest. This causes Patty's rifle to drop to the ground.

I walk out from behind my granite shield, holding up my scarred left hand for Patty to see. Her face goes ashen with fear.

"Patty, you once subjected me to a witch's confession. You said those who don't drown are burned. What about the witches who escape?"

I reach down to the Earth and begin to pull up a shaft of molten lava from the Earth's outer core, roughly a yard in diameter. As it reaches the surface, Patty's feet begin to smoke and light on fire. Her screams are extinguished instantly, as her body drops swiftly into the scorching void. I pull my hand away, and the Earth's surface cools, which leaves a circular, flat, molten rock nestled in a black circle of grass.

I drive the patrol Jeep, with Vernon unconscious in the cargo area, back to my van. With Vernon inside the van, I cuff his hands above him using a loop in the rear passenger side corner. Zeke welded it into place for this very purpose.

After picking up Sheriff Morton's hands, I walk over to the patrol Jeep, open the driver's door and wrap them around the steering wheel at ten and two.

Reaching toward the ground with my right hand, I pull moisture from aquifers below and pure oxygen from the atmosphere. I force them into the molecular structure of the Jeep's steel frame, causing it to crumble and disintegrate from accelerated rust. As the springs holding up the Jeep fail, the body collapses to the ground. Air hisses from the tires when the steel wheels lose their shape. The condensation creates a miniature cloud inside the Jeep's cabin. I reverse the process and pull every particulate of water from the

Jeep's structure. The cloud in the interior pours out of my left hand, and falls heavily to the ground, creating a mist that silently begins to spill over the edge of the ravine. Without a trace of moisture, the inside surfaces begin to deteriorate from dry rot, sending cracks in the shape of interlinking spiderwebs across everything. Sheriff Morton's hands swiftly mummify in place. The patrol Jeep takes on the appearance of a vehicle that has sat unmoved in the same spot for more than half a century.

I begin back to the van when Mara materializes in front of me, reaches her hand out, and pulls an orb of white light from my chest. My new awareness and abilities disappear once more.

35

As I drive east on Interstate Forty, I watch Vernon's head flop side to side through a mirror Zeke mounted on the dash for me. The Van itself didn't come with a rearview mirror because there are no windows in the back doors to see out of. The right side of his face is severely bruised with the imprint of the rebar's diagonal line pattern from the blow I dealt him. I made sure, though, to pick up Vernon's glasses and put them back on his face. I want him to see. At some point, he lost control of his bladder, causing the van's interior to reak of urine.

After four hours, Vernon begins to moan as he stirs back to consciousness.

"Do you remember the day we met, Vernon?"

There is a metallic clink that comes to a dead stop when Vernon tries to pull his hands down from above his head only to realize they are restrained.

"I was fourteen. The year was nineteen-ninety-four, and I was madly in love. Her name was Tiffany. But I was only allowed to love in a preordained manner, written down by ignorant men thousands of years before. To your cult, my mind, my love, and my body are not my own. They belong to men like you. But you cannot force love. It exists in an organic state none can comprehend. You incarcerated me, beat me, had me mutilated, and raped me. Your deacon murdered my friend, Charles. Then you took away the only father I ever had, Al."

"I, in turn, took your right eye, mangled your left leg, stole your money, and incinerated Maddie. You know my name, and you know what I am. My existence is the manifestation of the furnace which brings forth the weeping and gnashing of teeth to those unfit to exist amongst the lambs. I speak the ancient language of vengeance for the innocents who no longer have a voice, strength, or life. Now, do you know who I am?"

"Naomi," the man says breathily.

"That's right, but I wouldn't let my name pass through your lips again, or she'll rip your head straight off."

"Who?"

"Her,", I say as Mara flashes into existence, sitting diagonally across from Vernon. Her exterior, fuzzy with electricity, vanishes as quickly as it appears."

"Dear Jesus!" Vernon says as he shuffles his feet, pushing himself back into the corner in an impotent attempt to distance himself from the creature.

"That's not Jesus, Vernon. Her name is Mara and she just ripped both of Alton's hands off and threw him in the ravine."

"Just have a look," I say while turning on the cargo lights to illuminate the double arterial spray lacing the van's interior.

Vernon falls silent as the lights extinguish once more.

I continue. "We're headed to Narrow Path Baptist Church in my hometown of Rocky Mount. Did you know Brad Kershaw is the pastor now? He's the man who raped Charles, causing him to end up in your hands. Old Pastor Howell died of a heart attack last year. It's unfortunate, really. I would have loved to catch up with him at some point."

"After Brad's marriage ended suddenly, he was shuffled around between several churches before being offered the position at Narrow Path. It was a move up from the tiny congregations he'd pastored for the past few years. Lucky him. I suppose his last name finally paid off. Since Brad is broke and single, he's been sleeping in a Sunday School room turned efficiency apartment for visiting pastors. We'll be arriving there shortly."

Quiet falls over the van once again as my mind's eye projects a series of futures that could have been across Highway Sixty-Four East somewhere between Raleigh and Rocky Mount.

I take an exit on the far east side of Rocky Mount, just inside of Edgecombe County. Upon leaving the highway, the roads dissolve into a series of dark, lonely tracks of blacktop crisscrossing pine forests. We come to a modestly sized church, whose chapel faces the country road proudly displaying stained glass. The lighted sign up front says 'Narrow Path Baptist Church.' I turn the van into their gravel parking lot and continue around the rear of the building. I reverse the van as close as possible to the back door, which leads to the administrative wing.

"Mara, would you mind?" I ask while extending my right hand, which is holding a black bag. Mara flashes into existence. She grabs the bag, lunges forward, and grasps Vernon by the neck with her right hand while slipping the bag over his head with her left.

"I'll get the door," I say to Mara. I don a pair of black leather gloves, pick up a gray bookbag that has been riding in the front passenger floorboard and sling it over my back. After opening both van doors, I hop down to the ground, then up four brick steps to the double backdoors of the sanctuary building. On the right-hand side door is a handwritten note which states, "On a date, do not disturb."

The doors open up to a pitch-black hallway. I turn back and uncuff Vernon's hands from the restraint hook over his head. Free now, Mara picks up Vernon and throws him face-first into the brick steps, whereon I again cuff Vernon's hands behind his back. Upon entering the building, I reach to my left and flick on three switches, igniting the lights throughout the entire administrative wing. The hall we've entered leads straight through to the center door at the rear of the chapel.

"The keys you hear belong to Brad Kershaw," I say. "Getting them didn't require much work. He used his church e-mail to sign up for dating sites and singles chat rooms. It took me less than an hour to find him posing as a sixteen-year-old boy in one such room. In less than two minutes, he was sending me pornographic pictures of himself. Once I was certain it was him, all I had to do was ask for a date, posing as a thirteen-year-old boy who supposedly would have his sister drop him off. He even had the nerve to invite me to meet him at his apartment in the church's family life center. That was yesterday afternoon. He left a sign on the door, stating he was on a date, and not to disturb him. They are so desperate for Brad to marry that the church elders are willing to let him have free rein of the facility to entertain and fornicate as long as it is with young white women. But, as we both know, Brad only lusts after little boys. He got a chance to meet Mara instead.

I lead Vernon down a dimly lit hallway by the handcuff's chain. I pause at the rear entrance of the chapel, which is accessible through the administrative wing, to flip on three more light switches. I then push Vernon through the doors, into a fully illuminated chapel.

The inside of the chapel is constructed of lightly stained pine, from the peak of the two-story vaulted ceiling down to the shoe molding that meets the light-blue, high-traffic carpet. A dark oak altar lies directly in front of the stage. The aisle between the pews on either side leads to it from the rear entrance of the chapel. The podium is at the center of the stage, close to the edge, right above the altar. Behind where the pastor would preach sit choir risers, each of the three curving rows taller than the next. A baptismal pool sits, higher still, behind the choir risers, under a stained-glass window depicting a white Jesus praying while a beam of light shines down upon him. A piece of thick, clear polycarbonate makes it possible to see into the water itself. On either side of the baptismal pool are changing rooms. Next to the changing room door on the right is a piano. An organ sits next to the corresponding door on the left.

I force Vernon up the stairs and onto the stage.

"Kneel to pray, pastor," I say.

Vernon hears the distinct sound of chains clinking and a putrid smell that feels like a retching punch to the throat.

"I was able to make a few upgrades to the church before we came to call on you," I say, and attach leg irons to each of Vernon's ankles. I pull an auto knife out of my pocket and click a button to release a single-sided blade. I cut away Vernon's urine-stained tighty-whities at each hip. They fall unceremoniously to the floor. I grab the chain of the ankle irons and give them a good yank. They snap to a stop.

"The chains are welded to a piece of plate steel and bolted to the floor, so if you attempt to run, you'll fall flat on your face," I whisper into his left ear.

I walk around Vernon's pale, naked body and stop in front of him.

When I whip the bag from Vernon's face, he gets his first proper look at me in nine years. When we last met, six-and-a-half years ago, I was only a voice. And since then, a ghost.

I remove my left glove and place the palm of my scarred hand in Vernon's face.

"It's really me."

Having shown little emotion before, Vernon shudders slightly. He knows that hand means death.

Looking up, Vernon sees Brad Kershaw nude, tied to an upside-down cross, suspended fifteen feet over the baptismal pool from a thick manilla rope extending to the ceiling through a pulley. The end of the rope is tied to a large cleat, secured to the stage floor with heavy bolts, directly in front of where Vernon is kneeling.

Duct tape is wrapped around Brad's head, lacing through his mouth, but leaving his eyes and nose exposed so he can see and breathe.

Vernon cries uncontrollably. Through his gasps, Vernon says, "I'm not the monster you think I am. God guides me. I only live the path he has laid before me. The choice isn't mine."

"You're really sticking to that horseshit? Are you willing to take that position to the death?"

"Yes, the Lord is my master, not you."

"I'm not your master, I'm the Arbiter, and they're your jury," I say as I point toward the five corpses.

"Where's your friend," Vernon asks, finally noticing Mara is no longer present.

"She's only about when I need her. Mara doesn't force me onto a path, she makes sure it isn't interrupted. Mara is the manifestation of some kind of cosmic will. She's not a being with sentience, but a tool, used by whatever rules apply to this reality, to balance a profoundly out-of-sync human equation. She's a shield. Since the day we met, I've been impervious to death. She helps me maintain direction when things get out of hand, or if I ask for help on my path. Once this is over, I don't think I'll see her again, which is fine. Mortality suits me. Without an end, there is no demand, and nothing is accomplished. Time squeezes you into an ever-decreasing allotment. I wish I could have found the direction to my path earlier. Doing so would have saved two lives.

36

"I reckon you're wondering about your five jurors. We made a trip up to Yancey county on Thursday. You'd be surprised what a roadwork sign can make people ignore. They focus on getting around you, not at you. All it took was a seven-millimeter-thick wetsuit and willpower. I wrapped each body in thick plastic, then sealed the seams to abate the smell. Safely stowed away in the van, I prepared for my date with Brad Kershaw on Friday night. It didn't go well for him. He's been hanging upside down for more than twenty-four hours, looking at what remains of these five girls and pondering his own fate. The rope holding Brad inverted on the cross isn't the only ligature. Look closer."

Vernon scans toward the pulley, then down. Only when he passes the blue hue of the baptismal pool's, thick, clear polycarbonate viewing panel, does he spy a slight line of dark marshy-green. It continues down the stage and onto the carpet in his direction. Vernon's gaze ends between his legs where he sees a small loop tied into the thin green string.

"That's a slipknot tied into a piece one-hundred-pound braided fishing line. The green color camouflages it in dark water. Each of the microscopic strands is made of extremely strong, slick, synthetic materials. Their robust properties make it so cutting the line requires a special type of titanium scissors."

I kneel in front of Vernon, just out of range of any possible headbutt. I pick up the loop of the braided fishing line from in front of him. Carefully, I reach up and lasso the slipknot around Vernon's retreating testicles with enough tension to keep it in place.

"The green braided line is running through the side of the pulley body suspending Brad above the baptismal pool. It's been well greased and should slide with ease. On the other end, it's looped around Brad's testicles in the same manner. The predicament is, there's not enough fishing line. This shit is responsible for pulling the skin off many a fishers' fingers, leaving only the bone exposed."

"Do you gather what's next? If the rope holding Brad up is released, you both get castrated, then Brad drowns. However, if you confess your crimes on tape, I'll unshackle you to make a run for it, naked, through the night."

I pull a miniature academic tape recorder from her bag, flip it end over end in the air, and ask, "What do you say, Vern?"

Vernon nods his head in silent agreement.

"For practical reasons, I won't be on the recording. I'll hit stop when I need to ask a question and record again when you answer. If you even acknowledge my presence while I'm recording, I'll pull out my knife and cut the rope."

"Their bodies are in order from left to right, based on the level of decomposition. I'm sure you're noticing absences. I left Daisy, Charles, and Hannah in their graves. When I'm finished unraveling your cult, I'm going to make sure Daisy and Charles receive proper burials. Milly, Hannah, and Al rest where they should. Soon, they will get proper tombstones. I've already begun proceedings to have their property transferred to me under my legal name, Hannah Sillman."

"One day, I'll rebuild their cabin and visit when I can. Then, when I'm a very, very old woman, I'll retire there. It will be a home filled with laughter. Outside, there will be silkie bantams. And inside, I will crochet in the style of Milly each night as I rest in my own recliner, happy in the knowledge that I have given the world as much justice as I could in the time I had."

"You're not Hannah," Vernon replies.

"Aren't I? It says so on my driver's license. Al gifted me her identity for my eighteenth birthday."

Naomi continues, "I'm going to hit record. I want you to state your full name and that this is your confession."

Naomi turns on the tape recorder.

"I'm Vernon Proffit and this is my confession. The girl furthest to the left was Sheriff Morton's Daughter, Audry. Audry Morton was twelve when I, ugh, she died."

Naomi takes out her knife and shows it to Vernon.

"I killed her. I killed Audry Morton in the fall of nineteen-eighty-nine. I began watching Audry a few weeks before it happened. Her development had become noticeable. I began focusing a lot of my time in the pulpit staring directly at her as I preached. I used to get hard and have to use the podium to hide it. I approached Sheriff Morton about this. He was a true believer, and overjoyed that I had selected his daughter as a potential vessel."

"At first, this idea didn't sit right with Patty. She told Alton that I was sterile. Al informed her: Mary was a virgin, yet gave birth to Christ. Somehow, to him, my sterility was similar. He believed so fervently, even I couldn't have convinced him otherwise."

"When she undressed for me, I bent her over my bed and forced it in. Audry screamed and lunged forward, leaving me laying on top of her. I wrapped my right arm around her throat and squeezed until the screaming stopped. By the time I finished, Audry was already dead."

"The next girl was Katherine Evans. This was nineteen-ninety-one. She was the daughter of Susan Evans, Solid Rock's sixth-grade teacher. She was widowed three years before when her husband died suddenly of an aneurysm. Katy, as I called her, came to me. She was fourteen. By this time, the prophecy had really taken hold and congregants were wantonly bringing me their daughters. Some, like Katy, came to me on their own. She showed up at the chapel about half an hour after the end of my Sunday sermon. We were alone when I began to fuck her in the front pew. Katy said I was crushing her, and that she couldn't breathe. I put my hand over her mouth to shut her up so I could concentrate. Evidently, my hand also covered her nose which slowly suffocated her."

"In nineteen-ninety-two, it was Samantha Peters. Maddie informed me little Sam had gotten her first monthly. She was nine. I knew that she was the youngest I would ever get a chance at. In most Abrahamic religions, menses is the cutoff between girlhood and womanhood. I couldn't dip below that and maintain my image. God has rules, and it would be logical that a prophet would as well. Without rules, there would be no spiritual struggle. She was tiny, though, still a stick-thin child. When she began to struggle, I squeezed her neck with both hands, crushing her windpipe."

I turn off the recorder.

"From the looks of the decomposition, you didn't kill another girl again for a long time. Besides killing Al, you stayed away from girls for some time. Why?"

"Being blinded in one eye and shot in the leg took a toll on my health, and yeah, I was spooked. That's why I moved on Al.

He knew what I was and wanted me dead. When Milly died, Al became unstable. If he was brazen enough to exhume a body from my crypt, he might have gone to an outside police department, even if he thought it meant the rest of his life behind bars for child pornography. Al knew he wasn't guilty, and so did his God. Having me put away would have been worth it to him. Then, there you were: a ghost who became a ghost yet again when I couldn't find your bones in the ash. If you were able to hide under my nose for years, what else could you do?"

"I also became very busy. After nine eleven, the masses suddenly began to find faith again. Church, and church-school enrollment, went way up across the country. I was overwhelmed and lacked time for my hobby."

"Who is the fourth girl?" I ask and click the tape recorder back on.

"Next is Eve Collins. She became a ward of her maternal grandmother in two-thousand, when her mother overdosed. The next year, Eve's grandmother had a heart attack and died in her sleep. Eve lived with Patty and me for about a year, earning her keep by doing chores. Having her in the house was exhilarating. I knew at any moment she could become fair game. Patty would be sure to tell me of her first monthly. That didn't happen until the Spring of two-thousand-two. When Patty came out of the bathroom to tell me Eve had begun her period, I took her directly to her bedroom. When she resisted, I held her down by her throat and continued."

"You have to understand," Vernon says, "I didn't kill most of the girls I was with, the ones who did what they were told never saw my violent side."

Turning off the recorder, I tell him, "It's all violence, regardless.

There is no such thing as consensual sex with children." I pause for a second. "Why didn't you kill me?"

"I don't kill for sexual reasons. I kill for the sin of rejection. It's the humiliation I can't stand. I find it unbearable to think a girl might tell others so they can have a laugh at my expense. If I didn't act, doubt could grow in my followers. You have to understand, power itself is imaginary. Authority is just being the loudest voice in a pool of people who already agree. Once they're looking, it's all about image, because the message has already been heard. When it comes to image, a small tarnish is like a virus. It replicates, infecting the rest. Introducing a new belief to an already fervent group requires one thing: critical mass. Once members agree about a new idea, the rest rush in looking for acceptance. I convinced them I was infallible."

"I didn't kill you because you aren't capable of rejecting me."

"Excuse me?"

"You're a lesbian. Anything you say is going to be dead on arrival to my congregation. Their agreeance on who the enemy is binds them. I didn't kill you because there was no need or want. You and Charles were filling a function successfully. The house and camp were being kept clean. I just felt the need to punish you. I doubt that's the answer you've been seeking, but it's the truth."

"What about the last girl?" I turn on the tape recorder.

"The last girl is Rachel Emerson. She was a fourteen-year-old drifter. We picked her up hitchhiking to Asheville. She had run away from home in Maine and thumbed her way down highway ninety-five. We told her she could stay in one of the bedrooms. After she showered off, I cornered her in Charles's old room. She didn't put up much of a struggle. Obviously, she had been raped several times before. Her expression became blank and her body limp.

After I got off of her, Eve reached over to her jeans and produced a knife. She took a couple of swipes at me before I retreated to my bedroom and recovered a pistol. I shot her in the stomach. She howled and writhed for hours while I watched her die."

I turn off the tape recorder.

37

"While I can't record your confession for the murders of Hannah, Daisy, or Charles, I still need to hear them. Begin."

"By nineteen-eighty-six, I had raped several girls from the congregation but had yet to kill. That changed with Hannah. After Sunday service, I trapped Hannah in the women's bathroom. I was able to finish the act, but when I went to stand afterward, she punched me right in the jaw. I lost my cool. In a rage, I removed the porcelain lid from the back of the toilet tank and bashed the back of her head in. Morton and I buried her shortly after. I realized there would be more bodies, and I wanted a better place to keep my trophies. I devised a plan for a secret crypt hidden in plain sight right off the road. Each time I pass the cavern's entrance in my car, I'm overcome with waves of pleasure that culminate in an erection. It took six men a year to hollow out the spaces for their bodies with nothing but hammers and chisels because air-powered equipment couldn't be transported underwater into the crypt. There was a small hole leading to an aquifer in the floor. The men chiseled it out to a larger size so they could toss the leftover rubble down the hole. It would have been too much work to transport it out of the cave and away. After completion, Sheriff Morton dug Hannah up and delivered her body to the crypt."

"I raped Daisy Chambers and Patty murdered her in nineteen-ninety-four. She used to attend church with her paternal Grandmother, Marilyn Chambers. Daisy was willing for a little while when I first made my move on her, but when it began to hurt, she resisted. Daisy ran out the door. Patty never really liked Daisy, so she took it upon herself to shoot her in the back so that the girl's soul could burn in hell. I was furious, but there was nothing that could be done. Patty stepped out of the bounds, but she would have been too difficult to replace. Congregations like preachers with wives. They seem stable."

"Charles Laboda was murdered in my home, but not by me. Charles was sixteen in nineteen-ninety-five. He was sent to my school as a sort of last-ditch effort at making him straight. His parents thought maybe we could beat a bit of man into him. It didn't work. His function was as a personal servant. It was convenient, so I kept him around. He was killed by Brent Shoals, one of the men in my inner circle, during an escape attempt. Brent sliced open Charles's thigh, causing him to bleed out. Brent was shot and took a fall during the struggle with Charles. Eventually, Brent succumbed to his wounds."

"Thank you for your frankness, Vern."

"Will you please let me go now?"

"You're a psychopath, Vern. I can only assume you were born this way. I, on the other hand, was made the way I am by your actions. I like to refer to it as selective sociopathy. I feel empathy for almost every other human. But when it comes to those who truly deserve it, I feel nothing but glee to see them in pain. I'm not talking about the person who cuts me off in traffic. I'm talking about monsters who rape and murder innocents. People like yourself. Earlier, I was lying about letting you go, but I'm still going to give you chance not to become a eunuch. Mara, would you grab the rope, please."

Mara materializes and, without effort, unties the manilla rope still suspending Brad Kershaw above the baptismal pool. Doing so causes the rope to move his body up and down. Awakened by the movement, Brad becomes aware of what is about to happen. The upside-down cross sways as he struggles.

"I got the cross out of their storage building. It's used for the Easter passion play Narrow Path puts on every year. Mara is going to walk behind you and place the rope in your hands. It's your job to hold Brad up. He's a fit young man, who weighs at least two hundred pounds. To give you a bit of help, I've made sure there is a knot tied at the end of the rope to provide you with an easier grip."

Mara slides the rope into Vernon's hands. When she releases it, the knot begins forcing itself into Vernon's thumbs and forefinger knuckles. As Vernon begins to lean forward, he grunts and takes short, labored breaths. Within half a minute, he's facedown and holds up as high as his arms will allow. The braided fishing line wrapped around his scrotum burrows itself into Vernon's shoulder as gravity begins to take the upper hand. After about a minute, he begins to hyperventilate. Each breath is followed by a whimper. Vernon's shaky hands begin to sweat. The knot starts to travel through his palms, clicking past each finger like a gear until it reaches his pinkies.

The rope makes a whoosh as gravity frees it from Vernon's hands. Synchronous screams echo through the chapel. Brad plummets headfirst into the baptismal pool. The foot of the cross leans forward onto the polycarbonate, leaving Brad's feet hanging over the edge, toward the pews. His scrotum lands on the surface of the water right after. It floats, leaving behind a small blood trail as the lump of flesh rides little ripples on the water's surface. Brad's feet jerk and kick as he struggles for air.

The braided line simultaneously shears off Vernon's scrotum, snatching it out from under him, leaving the wrinkly pouch resting against the left side of his face.

Exquisite screams spackle the walls of Narrow Path's chapel. They elevate as Vernon turns his gaze left and realizes the warmth against his left cheek is a flap of disembodied scrotal skin.

As Vernon writhes on the floor, I walk up to his left side and roll him over with my boot. The chains wrapped around Vernon's ankles immobilize him further as they twist. I place the same boot on Vernon's heaving chest and say, "I'm going to help you." Vernon turns away from his testicles and begins retching up hot yellow bile. I remove my leather gloves and places them on top of the podium. I pull a pair of latex gloves from my pocket and don them with the appropriate ceremonial snap. I use a gloved hand to reach into my other front pocket and retrieve a green plastic pouch. Pulling along the open tab reveals neatly stacked gauze, folded like in a zigzag pattern and roughly two inches by two inches. "This is a hemostatic gauze," I say. "It will pack your wound and stop you from bleeding to death."

Vernon replies by spitting bile into my face. I don't turn my head in disgust; I punch Vernon hard enough in the nose to elicit an audible crack. Blood pours from his nostrils. I reach my right thumb and forefinger out and grab Vern's nose, twisting it back and forth. After his gasping shrieks subside, I tell him, "Your nasal bones are completely disarticulated from your face. Keep it up and I'll cut your nose off. Or, you can do what you're told and save yourself from a slow, cold death."

Vernon nods his head in agreement and allows me to get to work. Moans and jiggling legs follow each time I poke another layer of hemostatic gauze into the wound. The blood flow from Vernon's groin slows.

I leave Vernon lying on his back. His penis has shriveled to a fleshy crayon tip, as though it's attempting to hide from potential danger. Out of the bookbag comes two objects encased in bubble wrap. I reach down, feeling for the jean clip of my pocket knife. With a clear snap, the black-handled auto knife extends its singled-edged, matte stainless steel blade. A single slice to the bubble wrap around each object reveals two Mason pint jars filled with a yellow-tinged liquid. I place each on opposite sides of the altar. I pull two index cards and a pen out of the front pouch of the bag. I place both on the altar and begin scribbling. On the first card, "Brad Kershaw—", on the second, "Vernon Proffit—".

"I suppose neither of you is an M or a V?" I pause before writing 'Chomo' on both cards.

I remove the lids from both jars and place them back on the altar. The smell of formaldehyde begins to fill the front of the chapel. I hop back up the stairs, making my way toward the baptismal pool. I reach over with my right hand and scoop up the disembodied scrotum of the drowning Brad Kershaw. Working my way back down, I snatch up Vernon's scrotum, which still rests a few inches from his sweaty, pale body. With two handfuls, I return to the altar and drop both into their respective jars. After sealing the lids, I placed the corresponding index cards atop them.

Stillness has overcome Brad's legs.

"You're all categorized now, so I reckon it's time to go. It'll be daybreak in a few hours, and I wouldn't want you to miss the sunrise."

Mara appears in the periphery of Vernon's remaining left eye. The dark shadow of her body looms over him as she unlocks the leg irons. Mara then swings Vernon over her right shoulder. He remains silent, in a state of acceptance. I am the last living one out of the chapel. I retrieve my gloves from the podium and leave the scene of incalculable horror behind. Brad is tied to an upside-down cross and drowned in the baptismal pool. On the choir risers, a jury of corpses sits in judgment. On the altar, two jars rest as an offering for the sins of two wicked men. Between them, a microcassette tape lies in wait, ready to tell the truth.

As I follow behind Mara, I turn off every light I had turned on. I use Brad's key to lock up behind us, then rip the 'do not disturb' sign from the door.

Mara already has Vernon restrained and tucked away in his corner of the van. He is in a trance of sorts. I enter the van, shut the doors behind me and walk, crouching, through the cargo area, then take a seat at the wheel. I take off the latex gloves, tuck them into my bookbag, then toss the bag into the footwell of the empty passenger seat.

It's going to be one hell of a Sunday service tomorrow.

38

We travel in silence for another two hours, south down highways ninety-five and forty.

"We're here."

We back down a long driveway. I put the van into park and turn around to look at Vernon. The rear doors open one at a time. Standing on either side of the van's rear entrance are two figures, strangers to Vernon. On Vernon's left is a fit, blond man. On his right is a pudgy man with brownish-red hair and nine-fingers. The blond man undoes Vernon's handcuffs. They both grab one of his arms and jerk his naked, castrated body onto the concrete below. The blond man again cuffs Vernon's hands behind his back while he still lies facedown. Picking him up, they begin dragging him away from the van. Vern can feel the skin on the tops of his feet being scraped away as they're drawn across the rough surface. He glimpses a two-story house to his left and water ahead. A pier comes into view, lit by silver moonlight. Floating next to it is a large, white boat. At the base of the pier, a figure waits. It's a wiry, pale woman with freckled skin and curly red hair down to her shoulders.

The two men lift Vernon to his knees to face the young woman.

He's nude, beaten, his legs bleeding, and the wound from his amputated testicles is still seeping fluid. He looks up to make eye contact with the redheaded woman. She slaps him so hard it causes her to wince at the pain it brings to her hand. Vern hears my long boot-fall behind him. He hears the sound of my feet cease, smells cigarette smoke.

"I thought we talked about you quitting?" the redhead says

"I said after, okay?", I tell her.

"Sure, okay," the redhead sarcastically whispers.

"Vernon, I see you've met Tiffany. The gentleman on your left is Nate, and to your right, we have young Herschel. Fellas, be so kind as to show our guest to his quarters."

The boys drag Vern parallel to the boat and throw him onto the deck behind the pilot's seat. They follow, opening a cabin door below the helm. Nate and Herschel sling Vernon down the two steps into the hold. On the left are a booth, a kitchen area to the right, and a door directly ahead which leads to a small wet bath. They prop Vernon up in the booth seat furthest from the door. Nate leaves first. As Herschel follows, he pauses at the door, looks at Vern, and says, "Sic semper tyrannis, bitch."

"The keys are already in the ignition," I tell the boys as we meet on the deck of the vessel. The boat sways slightly, as each of the two men steps off, and back onto the pier. Vernon sees me come through the cabin door and shut it behind me. I walk forward and sit directly across from him, on the bench closest to the door. The table sits between us, like we're customers in a restaurant booth.

"The two of them are delivering my van to a friend who will chop it up and make it into beautiful artwork he will sell in his brand new shop located in downtown Asheville."

As the boat's dual engines fire up, and they begin idling away from the dock, I ask, "Do you know where you are?"

"No," Vernon gasps.

"We're on the sound-side of Wrightsville Beach. We'll slip past the south side of the island, then accelerate into the open sea. That was my house, and this is my personal dive boat. The redhead piloting us is the woman I love, who was ripped from me those many years ago."

"Three months ago, Mara and I gave sixteen Nazis the only thing Nazis deserve: death. This act jettisoned all of my fear. I hired a private investigator to track Tiffany down. After I was sent off to Solid Rock, Tiffany's mother enrolled her in a program run by an organization called Exodus International. It's a farce of a program that purports to convert queer people to straight. It can't. All it does is poison the minds of its victims with self-loathing. The members who complete the program are referred to as 'ex-gay.' For some time, they convinced Tiffany that she, too, had been converted and saved by Christ's love. Instead of love, she found misery. They arranged a marriage between herself and a young man who was also supposedly ex-gay. Two weeks before their first anniversary, he took his own life."

"Tiffany sank into a deep depression, quit her job, and eventually began crashing on couch after couch until there were no more, and she resorted to sleeping on the street. To dull her pain, she started using. Debts she owed to dealers found her forced into sex slavery and drifting aimlessly toward an early death."

"It only took two weeks for the investigator to track her down. She was bouncing between a series of houses in Charlotte filled with poor souls numbing their pain together. When I found Tiffany in one of these houses, she was crumpled up in a corner with a needle in her arm, clutching a copy of *The Bell Jar*, a pen, and a notebook. I picked her up over my shoulder and brought her home."

In a haze, she asked me, "Am I dead? I dreamed of you. Did you kill him?"

"For weeks we battled her withdrawals by using cannabis and psilocybin mushrooms. Tiffany is now eating well and has put weight back on, though she still wakes up screaming. When she does, I hold her tight and convince her that I am real."

After traveling out to sea for two hours, the engines quiet down, and the boat slows to an and idle.

"Last stop, Vernon." I grab him by the hair, drag him to the floor, then push him out the galley door. The sun shines brightly through the clear blue sky. A repugnant odor fills our noses. Vernon dry heaves as I drag him toward the starboard of the vessel. I turn him toward a gruesome scene.

It's a raft of putrid black and white flesh, larger than the boat. There are gray rotting organs afloat in the water and an oily sheen on the ocean surface near the appalling mass.

"That's a dead humpback whale, or what's left of one. This big guy died during migration, probably of old age. I affixed a GPS tracking tag on the thickest part of his belly. This is your new home. Do you see those dark shadows under it? Those are great white sharks. They're attracted to the leaching scent of blubber from miles away. Lucky for you, white sharks don't like the flavor of human meat. No, if you go in, they'll only taste you. More than likely, after you die, your bits will drift to the ocean floor to be consumed by a multitude of small fish. Your digested body will become detritus snow, which will go on to feed plankton, and thus the circle of life moves on."

Tiffany steers the starboard side closer to the carcass as I push

Vernon Proffit forward. I tip him over the rail, causing him to flip forward and land on his back upon the floating muck.

I look Vernon in the eyes one last time. "Now you will become fear."

Just as Tiffany begins to idle the boat away, Mara appears on the deck by my side. Then, Mara begins to levitate above the boat. Tiffany and I both look up at her as the wind scatters Mara into dust, leaving behind a brief fine silty cloud that takes the shape of Charles. He turns and smiles at me, then is broadcast like fine seeds into the wind. The remaining plume falls away revealing the sphere of light. I raises her left hand, summoning it. The orb is drawn toward me, then enters my chest, filling me with the same awareness of the Earth and its energy as before.

As the gust of wind that dispersed Charles passes my ear, I hear him whisper, "Know you were my best friend, and I will always love you."

For Vernon Proffit, there is nothing but silence and inevitability.

Epilogue

More than one hundred pieces of paper transcribed with calligraphy line the walls of my bedroom. Each holds poetry written for me by my beloved. The calendar posted over my desk has a giant red circle around today's date, Thursday, August twelfth, two-thousand-four. Encompassed by that red circle are the words 'Perseid Meteor Shower!' It peaks tonight.

Inside my desk is a marriage certificate from the state of Massachusetts, stating that Hannah Sillman and Tiffany Bullock are legally married.

As I sit and reflect, Tiffany peeks her head into the bedroom.

"It's time."

We board our boat and head out to sea, where it is still dark enough to view the Milky Way. After dropping anchor, we lie back on the deck, hold hands, and watch as the Perseids slice across the sky.

Printed in the USA
CPSIA information can be obtained
at www.ICGtesting.com
JSHW081715090823
46226JS00002B/164

9 781953 971418